RODION KORABLEV

THE OTHER SIDE

BOOK 1

MAGIC DOME BOOKS

The Other Side
Book #1
Copyright © Rodion Korablev 2025
Cover Art © Alexander Rudenko 2025
Cover designer: Vladimir Manyukhin
English translation copyright © Hugh Frederick Nugent 2025
Published by Magic Dome Books, 2025
ISBN: 978-80-7702-270-5

TABLE OF CONTENTS:

CHAPTER 1

THE TRADER

THE TRADER WAS HIDING on the far side of the Moon.

A long time ago, an armada of spaceships set out for this sector of the Galaxy in search of intelligent life. They were not interested in material resources or new territories. In the galaxy, there was a Law that could not be circumvented and even the powerful masters of the armada would not dare to enslave young worlds.

But there was one exception.

The Law did not prohibit making deals and demanding their fulfilment at any cost. So, when the desired resource appeared on Earth, the time for Trade came.

*   *   *

A closed meeting at Tolmach base

"...the second group consisted of three hundred and fifty people," a slightly overweight man was droning on monotonously. "The expedition lasted a month, forty-three percent returned out of—"

"Viktor, please! Stop!" one of the listeners wearing an expensive suit couldn't stand it anymore. "We know these figures perfectly well without you. Stop torturing us. Just tell us in your own words how the landing went, otherwise you'll send us all to sleep."

The speaker gloomily scanned the audience. There were thirty of them all sat at a round, well-polished table in the small hall.

They happened to be very influential people and every one of them had come here to listen to him.

Victor grinned to himself. He didn't need to kid himself. These bureaucrats were hardly interested in the report. They had gathered to see the portal in person and to get the latest news hot off the press.

Someone coughed impatiently.

Victor pulled himself together and continued in a more confident tone,

"Ok! I'll summarize quickly. The second expedition to the Other Side was more successful than the first. That's because we used equipment developed while working with the Tamedian representative, whom you know under the code name "The Trader". We tested weapons and protective gear, but most importantly, we extracted pollen and sent it to the Merchant…"

"And what was the result?" someone called out impatiently.

"It was a perfect fit for him!" announced Victor triumphantly.

"So what? We expected that," the man in the suit muttered. "What do you plan to do next?"

"That's up to you. The expedition has completed its mission. I think we should start training civilians now…"

"Civilians? What the hell do we need them for? Isn't the army enough?" interjected a senior general.

"The army won't cope on its own. To collect pollen, we need to teleport at least twenty million people to the Other Side. Otherwise, we won't be able to buy the first package of technology for a long time. And that's the government's primary goal!"

"And how are you going to get civilians to work?" the general persisted. "According to you, less than half of the soldiers returned from the second expedition and, on the first one, no one came back at all. Civilians won't want to risk their own skin so much!"

Victor grinned.

"We have something to offer them. It's not in the report, but the Other Side can give people inexplicable powers."

"What kind of powers?"

"I'll tell you…"

CHAPTER 2

ALEX

ALEX KNEW EXACTLY THE MOMENT which changed his life forever. It all went back to a vivid childhood memory. He and a group of classmates went on an overnight trip to a nature reserve.

There was a clear sense of freedom as the children all sat around the campfire. At midnight, all his friends went to their tents but Alex stayed behind, fascinated by the flickering flame of the campfire. He stared at the flames for a long time, warmed his hands and listened to the twigs crackling until the wood burned out and turned into embers. Teenage worries and anxieties faded into the background and he felt calm and peaceful.

After a while, Alex looked up. The starry sky was unusually bright and it seemed as if the myriads of stars were calling to him. He distinctly felt the infinity of space. It seemed clear to him that he was part of the Universe, and the Universe was a part of him. The effect of this thought on such a young mind caused Alex to momentarily stop breathing.

*   *   *

Alex didn't remember how long this experience lasted. Maybe a few minutes, maybe a few seconds. He didn't feel the passage of time or the chorus of thoughts in his head — only a feeling of extension, freshness and flying. Later he learned that many people have this experience in their youth when looking at a starry sky but, normally, they quickly forget about it.

The next day Alex didn't say anything to anyone. He became more thoughtful and silent than usual. It seemed to him that he had touched something very important, something that would change his life. And as it turned out, he had. The memories from that night did not fade away. Nor did they dissolve in his memory. On the contrary, they remained the most significant impression of his youth and determined his future path.

Alex decided that he wanted to study space. He made a plan in which he detailed what he should do. What knowledge and skills to acquire and what university to go to. At school, while his peers were playing video games or having fun, he studied and did an internship for high school students in a research center. After graduation, he went to a good university, gained some useful connections and after a few years, finally got an assignment — a laboratory assistant at a space station near Jupiter.

* * *

The station was huge and could accommodate four thousand people. As it was mostly the established specialists who worked there, Alex had had to make a lot of effort to get a posting.

However, events rarely unfold the way a person wants them to and, at this point, events in Alex's life took a sharp turn. At the pre-flight medical commission, which should have been purely a formality, the doctors gave him their verdict — Kotler's disease. A very rare and new disease. As they explained to him, one of the recently discovered food preservatives was causing thalamic dysfunction. The thalamus is the organ responsible for sleep. Simply put, someone with the disease would sleep less and less, to the point where sleep was impossible and, eventually, they would die of exhaustion. The preservative was, of course, banned but that only happened several years after it was first used.

A cure was never found, either because it really was a complicated disease or because of the small number of victims with which to work with — only about a thousand people. Expert doctors did not want to engage in the study of such a rare disease — it did not promise them fame, nor a potential rise in their careers. Also, at that time, mankind was actively exploring space and leading scientists preferred to engage in more promising areas.

As a result, the victims were left to deal with their problems on their own. Ordinary sleeping pills did not work so they were prescribed stronger drugs for immersion in medically induced sleep, but the drugs were addictive and destroyed people's minds. The end results were just the same. Artificial sleep helped for a while, but it did not stop the development of the terrible disease.

Alex remembered the words of an elderly doctor from the Brain Research Institute, one of the few major specialists dedicated to the problem. There were rumors that his wife had passed away from Kotler's disease.

"Young man. I know the situation is critical, but if you give up, the disease will eat you up! Gloom and depression will only bring death closer," the doctor sighed. "You've got to hold on while we search for a cure. You can't give up!"

"What do you advise, Doc?"

"If you really are finding it hard, you can use medicated sleep, but it causes irreversible consequences. So it should be used only if absolutely necessary."

"Tell me honestly, is there any progress in the research? Even a hint?" Alex had become friends with this doctor over the past two years and was sure he would be given an honest answer.

"Well, we need extensive research and we just

don't have the funds for it. All that we can do is slow the progression of the disease. But I will keep working. There are options we haven't tried yet and we're pursuing them now. Just hang in there until we find a solution. I believe we will."

Alex wasn't going to give up. It wasn't in his nature. For years he had longed to become a space explorer and he didn't want to give up on his dream. If he submitted his life to the disease, it would be a defeat. Yes, disaster had struck, but he was still alive!

For now, the trip to Jupiter would have to wait but Alex's qualifications and connections helped him get a job as a probe operator in the asteroid belt between Mars and Jupiter. The laboratory where he worked just so happened to be back at his university. Alex found the job tedious. It was boring to follow an automated machine with a gigantic response time but at least, through a virtual observation system, he could be where he always wanted to be — in Space.

Alex explained to everyone that he had to stay on Earth to build up experience before being allowed to fly into space. Also, there was his Ph.D. to think about...

He didn't want to tell everyone about his problems. He was generally reluctant to open up to people and he didn't like to complain. Nobody except members of the medical committee and his doctor knew the truth.

It was true that something had to be done about the disease. There was no immediate solution but Alex rejected the medication method straight away. Yes, it gave relief, but it destroyed his will and ability to think clearly. But he really had no idea what to do and, at first, he just tolerated it. But his sleep time was decreasing more and more and, at this rate, he would reach point zero, where he wouldn't be able to sleep at all, in ten or twelve years. But it was unlikely he would last that long. More likely he would just die of exhaustion.

Alex believed his doctor and really hoped for a breakthrough but he realized that his chances were slim. So he decided to become an expert in the field of sleep to find out how to overcome the consequences of its deficiency. He went through many different methods. The most promising direction seemed to be the techniques of attention management and meditation. They had been well studied by experts over the years. Of course, in the modern world everything had become automated but the old practices remained. Such techniques were frequently used in some Eastern teachings in psychology and a number of martial arts. They helped people focus and, at the same time, relieve internal stress.

The main thing for Alex was efficiency, which he measured with the help of a personal chip. These chips were implanted into everyone during childhood. They acted as a personal computer and a means of identification. In some cases, the chip could even serve as a personal doctor. The device could monitor hundreds of indicators so any patient would know exactly their condition and could assess the effectiveness of attention management techniques.

However, the chip did not track brain activity, so Alex turned to his doctor. Being a major scientist, his doctor had little confidence in meditation but agreed to help and provided equipment for the research.

Such voluntary help was encouraged by much of society but the old doctor didn't care about that. He just didn't want to deny Alex such a small thing. It would mean taking away the last hope from a man condemned to an agonizing death. The doctor didn't want that on his conscience and, besides, he didn't see much harm in someone trying to meditate...

*   *   *

"Well, how are the results, Doc?" Alex removed the sensors and got up from the chair where he had just spent two hours not moving.

"Let's see. Hm... Brain activity is decreasing but attention levels are stable. You're doing better than a month ago," the doctor flicked off the hologram and looked at the next graph. "Theta rhythms are increasing. That's not bad either. Not bad at all! How are you feeling?"

"I feel better and more awake like I've had a bit of sleep but then I've been woken up at a bad moment. I'm glad about that, though. At least it's something. I think I'll keep doing the exercises."

"Remind me what it's called again?"

"The Way of Emptiness. I found a reference to it in an old guidebook on Eastern practices. It's actually very similar to the technique of volumetric de-concentration for air traffic controllers, only deeper."

"It doesn't matter what it's called. The main thing is that it helps."

"You've changed your mind," Alex laughed. "You didn't believe in it before when I came and told you about it."

"Yes, I have," admitted the doctor. "I've seen a lot of people clutching at straws to save themselves. And, normally, they only make things worse for themselves. But the equipment shows that your brain really is resting and recovering with all this meditation."

"Maybe you should learn the way of emptiness too."

"I'm too old for that," the doctor smiled.

"What do you mean!? You'll probably live longer than me."

"Don't joke like that. Black humor — only for doctors. You must believe in success."

"All right, you got it!"

*   *   *

Over the next three years Alex's sleep dropped to five hours a day. This might seem like enough to some but few people have experienced chronic fatigue for long periods of time. Regular sleep deficiency, if not compensated for, leads to mental changes in even the most resilient person.

Alex studied and trained the technique of volumetric de-concentration for four to six hours a day. It was called volumetric because it required the distribution of attention over an area of space. In the original source the description sounded like this: "The Way of Emptiness — by training his attention, the warrior becomes one with the space and the world around him. His mind is calm and unshakable, he is motionless, but he sees everything and is ready for action at any moment. No one can get close to him unnoticed". The text implied that after several years of training a man could sense the actions of an opponent with his eyes closed.

At first these exercises were just meditation to stop the disease but, after a while, Alex experienced a renewed feeling of infinite space, as he had once done as a child. And the more he was in a state of volumetric de-concentration, the more vivid this feeling became and the feeling of chronic fatigue fell away.

After two years, his sleep decreased to three and a half hours. Alex spent most of his free time on mastering the technique. His sense of space improved considerably. Sometimes, after a long meditation, he could feel objects around him but, most importantly, he managed to stay in a more or less functional state and continue working, although he could have easily received an allowance — the diagnosis would have allowed him that.

Alex tried several times to find other practitioners. But he just couldn't find anyone. Neither in Russia nor in China, the birthplace of the method. He only found out that there used to be a small school founded by a former Buddhist monk who went by the name Donid. It was he who created the Way of Emptiness. Donid later left the community, set his sights on "knowing emptiness," retreated into the mountains and has not been seen since. After the disappearance of the founder, the community languished and fell apart and only the description survived, thanks to the work of enthusiastic Chinese historians who carefully preserve these traditions.

Towards the end of his sixth year, Alex focused entirely on the technique and unlocking its potential. Not even Donid's closest students had trained so intensely and now, it wasn't even about surviving. Standing on the threshold of death, he felt how his entire system of values was changing. Everything unnecessary was gone but the main thing remained: communication with his relatives through the virtual — his parents and two younger sisters who lived on the other side of the country.

His small role in space exploration had definitely taken a back seat in his life but Alex definitely had a new, main focus — mastering his abilities and unlocking the potential inherent in every human being.

Alex felt that he was gradually drifting away from society. He wasn't interested in the news, didn't spend time online and neglected entertainment. He didn't worry about career and money, moreover, he didn't follow the personal rating of a citizen. If it weren't for his passion for space, he would have lived as a complete hermit. Remote work at the university and communication in virtual with colleagues, family and his doctor — that was all his contact with the outside world.

Another three years flew by. His sleep dropped to two hours. Human strength is in adapting to any condition, but Alex felt that he was balancing over a precipice. There were only a few other people living in the world with the same diagnosis and most had already been put into a coma.

Work had to be abandoned and the number of meditations increased. Alex didn't want to leave unfinished business so he talked to his parents. The conversation was a hard one, but necessary. He felt that he had now cut the last of his ties. Ahead of him was only the unknown.

For six months he had been approaching point zero. His inner tension increased with every day. Sometimes, in moments of remission, Alex realized that he was going in circles, that he did not give up only because he was used to fighting and could not remember how to live otherwise.

But every day he saw less and less sense in the struggle. It was already an unfair fight and he'd gone further than many others. But every time the thought of giving up came to him, Alex threw it aside. This became such a habit that it was the only thing keeping his mind clear. There were no more fears or worries about the future, only defi-

ance and... unimaginable fatigue. But persever-
ance had become so ingrained in his soul that it
had become part of his outlook and a way of existence.

These days, the only support was a trance during meditations. But after three months Alex felt
that he had reached his limit. Everyone has their
limit but usually people don't know it because they
stop much earlier and reach it only in extreme situations. And when they reach it, many people talk
about how you can go beyond. But beyond is a de-
ceptive word. What a person can do is always
within his capabilities, it's just that it's rare that a
person can use all their strengths together: body,
mind and consciousness. A mother lifts a car to
save her child, a soldier sees a bullet flying at him
when his perception is accelerated to the limit —
all this is within the limits of human capabilities
and usually such a mode is activated at the expense of vital resources.

Alex had reached his limit and that meant that
he had exhausted all his resources to the end.

At night, during his exercises, he saw — not
felt but saw! — that this was his last day of self-
preservation and, beyond that, he could see only
regression and death. On the threshold of death
Alex felt calm and did not regret anything. He
knew that he had done all he could and, to some
extent, had even defeated the disease and this
gave him strength and pride.

The fateful hour came when he could see his
consciousness begin to fall away. He viewed all of

this like a spectator — it was only his highly developed attention that allowed him to follow the process. At the last moment, when his mind was almost gone, all he wanted was to experience the immensity of the universe once again. However, it was too late and, just a second later, all his thoughts and desires had disappeared.

Afterwards, events took their own course. None of this worried Alex anymore but he was part of a society in which order and accountability were elevated to an absolute. As his body slowly fell to the side, the implanted chip sent a signal to the emergency services and to the doctor as his supervising officer. The medics arrived twenty minutes later. The diagnosis was known so the standard protocol was followed. The patient was taken to the hospital and placed in a room with other coma patients. There wasn't enough funding for a full-fledged study of the disease but there was money to keep the patients alive.

Alex was asleep so he didn't know that a week after he was taken away, the Earthlings discovered they weren't alone in the universe.

*　*　*

Several years passed.

CHAPTER 3

THE AWAKENING

Information from the "New Encyclopedia of Earth" — cosmological ideas of the Tamedians:

Prior to contact with the Tamedian civilization, Earth science believed in the hypothesis of the thermal death of the universe due to entropy. Simply put, when all energy sources become exhausted, life in the universe will cease to exist. But that was before we knew about the existence of the Other Side.

It turns out that every planet, inhabited by intelligent inhabitants, has a parallel world — the Other Side.

The Other Side of mankind is a manifestation of human culture, a reflection of the subjective world of our civilization. It is there that the energy gener-

ated by people is accumulated.

We still do not understand where the Other Side is and whether it is "virtual" or "material", but we can say one thing for sure — it exists and you can go there!

The Other Side was born when humans were separated from nature. Once the first man realized himself as something separate from Mother Nature and began to invent words and concepts, human culture emerged and with it the Other Side.

We know now that reason did not just appear. Intelligence is a prerequisite for the existence of the universe. Humans and other intelligent beings generate energy which is gathered by the Other Side. Thanks to this energy, the Universe grows and expands. This is how intelligent life exists.

Philosophers, of course, dispute this theory and religious figures reject it altogether. However, many scientists have already sided with the Tamedians. Either way, we will only know the truth once the Other Side has been investigated thoroughly...

*   *   *

From a discussion at the forum "We the Earthlings":

Serge: Everyone knows we made a deal with the Tamedians. A lot has been written about it, but the details haven't been published yet. I don't know why we have to rely on rumors and speculation! Let the government finally reveal the contents of this treaty with the Tamedians! Those who agree, please sign this petition...

Earthling 3567: Serge, don't be stupid! It's been known for a long time that we'll be mining resources on the Other Side together. Scientists have already been there with the army, they even wrote about it at this forum and gave us links. How didn't you notice that?! At least read the attached post above. Better yet, think about how to get points for rejuvenation. You'll need a rating of at least a hundred, if not more.

Serge: Don't worry about me, I've got a rating a hundred and forty!

Pretty girl: Wow! How'd you get that high?

Serge: I've been working as a schoolteacher for over thirty years, I don't break any rules, I help my students and I'm always actively involved in public life... that's how.

Earthling 3567: Yeah... I would have saved up too, if I had a job. Sadly — I live on benefits! And you don't get points for that. But still, I hope the government just gets on with everything. I can't wait!

Serge: Maybe you should volunteer. That's one way to get your rating up quickly.

Earthling 3567: I live in the European Con-federation, we have volunteers like... well, there are a hundred people for each place. Everyone needs a rating. I'm still boosting my education in-dex, for that I get some points, but not much.

Pretty girl: Rating is gold dust! You have to fight for every point, if not you'll relax and become a freak. My ex-boyfriend got so down. And apart from food and housing in an anthill, he can't get anything else, not to mention rejuvenation...

*   *   *

The awakening was a slow one. The coma turned into a deep sleep which stretched on for a long time as a kaleidoscope of vague sensations. But everything ends and the vague images dissolved like morning fog under the sunshine. Alex woke up and the first thing he felt was peace and inner silence. The tension that had been accumulating all these years was gone.

Strangely enough, next came the sense of space around him, followed by hearing, sight and touch.

Several hours flew by unnoticed. Alex lay in a pleasant half-dream and felt people appearing and disappearing around him. He could hear distant voices:

"He's the only one... the others didn't survive."

"Lucky guy, he pulled through. It's a miracle!"

"His doctor will be happy. We'll let him know as soon as we can ..."

Alex fully came to his senses the next day and his doctor briefly came to see him. He congratulated his patient and asked a few standard questions about his well-being. After that he gave an order to rest and left.

The next day he came back and they turned to the main topic:

"Doc, I heard in passing that I'm the only survivor. What happened to the others?" — asked Alex in a whisper — his vocal cords still weren't working well.

"The coma hasn't stopped the progression of the disease, it's only slowed it down. The condition of the others worsened and, in the end, they just passed away in their sleep... Not the worst death, if you think about it," the doctor was silent for a while.

"So how come I woke up... and why do I feel so good?"

The doctor smiled but his eyes remained serious.

"There's good news and bad news. Bad news first, your feeling good is temporary. We've controlled the symptoms but we haven't got rid of the disease. The good news is, there is a cure, but you might not like it... I'll tell you everything from the top down."

The doctor sat down in the armchair next to the hospital bed and began to tell all about the latest events in the world: about the contact with the Tamedians, the Other Side and the technology that humanity had received...

The conversation dragged on but Alex did not interrupt. He only listened in amazement and at the end he asked:

"So, what, we're working with the aliens now! Just like that, they're transferring us their knowledge?"

"Almost... In fact, we haven't really learnt that much and all the technology is only meant to be used on Earth. No spaceships or interstellar travel. However, the most important thing we got is a system of rejuvenation. It's based on a method of cell control. We've already developed new drugs based on it, one of which I tried on you. It was a risky move, but it worked!"

The doctor went on talking about new directions of medicine with a passion, peculiar to any specialist who got to his favorite subject but Alex saw that he was holding something back. It can't have been easy to get permission for that kind of experiment. He wasn't a fool and he knew how society worked.

"Do we know about any other civilizations besides the Tamedians?" he was fascinated by the idea of contact with other races.

"There's not much information. We've never even seen a Tamedian in person. We know even less about the other races, only that they exist. The Tamedians are sort of our handlers now."

"Too bad," Alex said disappointedly.

"Don't worry! If everything goes as it should, you'll find out everything yourself... First hand," the doctor looked at his patient with a smile.

"So you said that interstellar flights won't be happening for us!"

"Nope! But if you get better, you'll live to see your aliens," laughed the doctor.

Alex winced:

"It's too early to talk about that. Doc, you said there's bad news and that I might not like the treatment."

"Yes, that's complicated..."

The doctor told him that once the excitement about the first contact with aliens had calmed down, it turned out that the government had made an agreement with the Trader to extract an energy powder, commonly known as pollen.

According to the doctor, the pollen contained a special kind of energy that living beings could use directly without any adaptations, but he didn't know the details. It was also known that the pollen was needed to create new types of materials and medicines, including for the process of rejuvenation.

The agreement required the humans to pay the Trader a specific amount of pollen in exchange for technology they'd already received, but the details were kept secret.

According to rumors, first the military was sent to the Other Side, then the first volunteers and a year later a mass development program was launched. At the same time, authorities carefully monitored publications on the Internet. All negative information was removed, however, sometimes news of losses and difficulties got through the filter.

As a reward for pollen extraction, a significant increase in the citizen's rating was promised and many people were drawn to that because in Alex's world money meant very little. Technological advances and the automation of industries had relieved people of the need to worry about their daily bread. If a person from the past came to this modern society, he would be amazed at the number of idlers who didn't have to work to survive. However, this would be a misconception — it simply did not take many people to produce the necessary goods and services.

When this new way of life first appeared, officials faced the problem of how to manage the population. In order to manage everyone, they needed a currency that the people could use to pay for work that would, in turn, benefit society. The citizen's rating became such a currency. It was made up of various indicators, primarily depending on the index of social importance. Education, efficiency, social activity and many other smaller factors were also taken into account.

The higher an individual's rating, the higher his or her position in society. A citizen with a high rating receives a set of benefits that are not available to a person with a low rating, even if the latter has enough money.

In general, the role of money was greatly reduced. It was mainly used for access to entertainment. But in any case, citizens with high ratings had an advantage. The time of money was coming to an end.

The rating also influenced key areas of life. For example, if you scored below thirty, you couldn't get permission to have a child — it was a way of combating overpopulation and selecting the right people. The government cultivated conformity and law-abiding citizens because only a citizen who did not break the law could get a high rating.

But the most coveted reward was rejuvenation. The average life span of an ordinary person at the time of the appearance of the Trader was one hundred and twenty and, even then, people retained clarity of mind and good physical condition and only began to deteriorate right at the end of life.

A single course of rejuvenation allowed for fifty years of life extension but only citizens with a rating of one hundred and eighty points or more had access to it.

As a result of this new rating system people could be managed much better than they ever had before. Breaking the law led to an automatic downgrade. In some regional states, even simple criticism of the government resulted in points being deducted.

But most citizens sought to improve their scores themselves. Not out of fear, but because the rating system was a clear and understandable goal in life and a universal way to earn recognition from others.

Historically, the rating system first appeared in large states and then spread to smaller ones. In the middle of the twenty-first century several conflicts broke out known as World War III or the "plague war." The main weapons were biological and the main soldiers were doctors and scientists. It is not known exactly who started the war but the consequences were clear — the population of the Earth was reduced to five billion people and it was a long time before the numbers were restored.

This seriously changed the balance of power and people's priorities. A world government emerged which began to control the activities of regional forces and monitor the balance of interests. Thanks to the emergence of this new force, a single rating was approved for all which led to the globalization of humanity on a greater scale than ever seen before. On the one hand, it ensured a lasting peace, but on the other hand, it reduced man's ability to control his own destiny. Life became satiated and predictable and, at the same time, boring and monotonous. People from different countries lived identically, unique differences were gradually erased and with them the creative potential that went with it.

The fate of rebels and dissenters was simply a low rating and life in the "anthills" with a minimum number of benefits. Enough to survive, but no more than that. However, despite selections and forecasts, over time, such people became more and more numerous. As a result, a free alternative was created for them — the world of virtual games. The games were an outlet for both marginalized people and citizens with high ratings. In the virtual world you could behave as you liked: break the rules, be disorderly, insult people and, generally, just do whatever you liked. It was one of the few opportunities to release social tension.

The ways to significantly increase a rating could be counted on one's fingers. Either socially significant work, community service or dangerous business. For a long time, space research remained the most reliable way of raising the index, especially at the beginning of the exploration of the Solar System but, as time went on, more and more highly qualified specialists were needed. Alex only got his posting because of ability — he had published several unique papers on the topic — methods for analyzing the age of asteroids — and had the highest score in his graduating class.

The other ways to dramatically increase one's ranking were available to a select few. Try winning the Olympics, becoming a famous actor or making a scientific discovery! How many people can do that? Most people improved their rankings very slowly over a lifetime, so the government's proposed program to explore the Other Side was an attractive opportunity for many to improve their lives, despite the risk. And who looks at risk when "eternal life" looms ahead, even as a promise.

It was not only those from the social ghetto who went to the Other Side, but also adventurers — a boring and saturated life seemed meaningless to them. Other volunteers included rebels, marginalized people and the simply curious.

There were also avid gamers who thought that the Other Side was a big game created purely for their pleasure. And indeed, the rules of that world — the interface, the levels, the monsters — resembled the virtual world they had lived in for years. The explanation that this was not a game world but a reflection of humanity was of little interest to them. Professional jargon even sprang up between them: pollen miner — "prospector", explorer —

"stalker", and gamers — simply "players".

On Earth, everyone's rating was tracked by a personal chip, but on the Other Side no technology worked. That's why points were awarded for pollen collected — the prospectors gave it to their quartermasters back at the base camps and they sent reports back to Earth. What did that give them? Any prospector could easily raise his rating to sixty or seventy points. In other cases, some managed to gain a hundred points and there were even stories of those who'd managed to raise their rating to one hundred and fifty points. But to get beyond that you had to take risks and work hard.

As pollen production grew, so did the requirements for the amount collected. To get to the necessary target one needed luck and a good set of skills. But even with all that you had to hunt monsters for years and life on the Other Side was dangerous and unpredictable...

Alex didn't feel tired after hearing all this information. He was excited by the prospect of travelling to the world-within-a-world.

"So what exactly is "The Other Side," Doc?"

"Nobody really understands it, though many people are trying to," the doctor said cheerfully. "Perhaps it's a materialized subjective reality of mankind ..."

"Subjective reality!? But you're a scientist! There's gotta be a normal explanation for this." Alex didn't recognize his old friend. He'd always considered him such a clever man and here he was with such a roundabout answer.

"Well, sooner or later we'll understand it. Right now, we just don't know anything about the Other Side. We don't know its size or its structure. The prospectors have just occupied a small area and are simply extracting pollen. Just think that the research has only just begun. The government knows more but, of course, that information's not public. Besides, it's not the Other Side you need to worry about, you need to worry about getting on that program. That's what you need to think about! Don't be fooled by your good health. Your condition will get worse and the next time I won't be able to help you."

"Why not?"

"To pull you out of the coma, I used a cell modulator. I only used a tiny bit. It's the same drug used for rejuvenation. You've actually had a mini-course of it. The distribution of this drug is regulated at government level. I barely got authorization for it and I had to pull a lot of strings. You have no idea what it cost me. I said I needed it for research on Kotler's disease. Good thing no one checked that you were the only patient. But I don't think I'll be so lucky a second time!"

"Thanks Doc, I won't forget that!" said Alex sincerely. "So why do I need to get on this program?"

"The effect of the Other Side on the miners" bodies is the hottest topic in medicine right now. We don't know much but we've got a lot of evidence that people there are transformed and cured of many diseases that, here on Earth, we just can't treat."

"So this is my chance! How much time do I have?"

"We've managed to control the disease, but I estimate that in six months it will come back again and start to progress, and very quickly. After that you'll have two or three months before you get to point zero."

The doctor was old, very old, and had been through a lot. One hundred and twenty-five years old — a good age even by the new standards! So he spoke to his patient honestly and directly.

"Right. Thanks for the honesty. So what should I do?"

Alex hadn't been afraid for a long time. Years of struggle had changed him. He had touched death, survived it and was no longer afraid of it. But that didn't mean he was going to disregard his new life, on the contrary, he valued it more than ever.

The Doctor explained the procedure of going to the Other Side and advised him to sign a prospector's contract at once.

"Thanks again, Doc!" Alex realized that the doctor had done a lot more for him than many others would have done for their patients. He suspected that the old doctor saw him more as a son than as a friend and he was very glad that he was his patient.

CHAPTER 4

TRAINING CAMP

TWENTY-FIRST CENTURY MEDICINE could not cure Kotler's disease, but it could help a patient after a long coma. A couple of months of rehab was enough to get Alex back to the peak physical condition he was used to, but his mood remained somber. Every minute he knew that the disease was still creeping up on him.

While doing his rehab, he sent off his application to the ministry. Within an hour it was reviewed and approved. One of the advantages of the rating system was the high efficiency of government agencies. Socially important work, including the activities of all officials, significantly increased one's rating, so bureaucrats worked extra hard as they knew there were being monitored. This high level of monitoring was another reason why the rebels were keen to go to the Other Side.

Three days after his rehabilitation, Alex tied up all the loose ends he had left before the coma and then went straight to the prospectors" training camp. Unfortunately, he couldn't see his parents. During the time he was in a coma his civil rating was downgraded and it was impossible to buy a ticket to the other side of the country. The government didn't encourage unscheduled flights and he couldn't wait for permission. So the future prospector talked to his father, mother and sisters through the virtual and promised them that everything would be fine.

*   *   *

At the reception desk he was met by a young-looking girl with a radiant smile and a badge "Oksana". However, it was difficult to guess her age — until the age of fifty all women looked beautiful and after that they didn't change much either.

"Good afternoon, Alexander! We've been expecting you!" The girl exuded such friendliness and warmth that Alex couldn't hold back a smile from her.

"Hello, Oksana. Glad to be here! You can call me Alex if you want."

"Ok! I'll send you the training program, the schedule of classes and instructors" contacts, as well as directions to the house where you'll be living," Oksana beamed at him as she sent the data to his personal chip. "If you have any questions, don't hesitate to contact me!"

"Thank you. I'll go and have a look around the camp..."

* * *

During the years he'd been in a coma, numerous bases had sprouted up like mushrooms all over the world to send prospectors to the Other Side. From the Earth's population of fifteen billion, over a hundred and thirty million people had visited the Other Side, but only about thirty million worked there regularly. That didn't seem like much, but two factors severely limited that number. The first was the high mortality rate. About a quarter of the newcomers were killed in the first year, although one's chances of survival improved after that period. But death was always lurking in the background and the weight of this often took its toll on the desperate prospectors mining for eternal life.

However, the second factor was more serious. The Other Side took everyone back to the Middle Ages and nothing more sophisticated than a steam engine could be used there. It wasn't possible to recreate electricity, chemical reactions took place differently or didn't take place at all. Even gunpowder didn't explode there, so all weapons, down to an old musket, were completely useless. All the amenities, as they were called, were located in the yard. It was certainly a change from everything on Earth where even the people with the lowest rating could count on a room with constant access to the Internet.

The discomfort and deprivation for many people was even worse than the threat of death. Even the most basic commodities, like a warm shower, didn't exist there.

Having finished with the formalities, Alex settled in his room and started to familiarize himself with the training course. The accelerated program took a month and a half, but even that seemed like a long time.

"Two months for recovery, another month and a half for training... That leaves me ten weeks until the disease gets worse again," he mentally calculated. "Damn it! I need to finish this, fast! No messing about here."

*   *   *

The classes were taught by instructors who were level one or two. That was quite an accomplishment. As a rule, if you didn't take too many risks, it took about a year to get that far. After that, many prospectors decided they'd had enough and just became instructors. That way they could live in safety and teach the next generation of hopeful prospectors.

The program included physical exercises, theory classes, rules of survival and weapons training. It was the last part that took so much time and no matter how hard Alex tried he simply could not take shortcuts.

The next few weeks included a lot of cramming. It was also physically demanding. Alex didn't spare himself and pushed himself as far as he could go. He decided that if he couldn't cut the training program, he would take everything from it. However, the most time was spent on reading and memorizing information, because, on the Other Side, he wouldn't be able to rely on his chip for information.

He learnt a lot: descriptions of the creatures on the Other Side (there were so many of them that there was only enough time to study the most common ones); what he could and could not do, how and where to get food; their capabilities as prospectors and much more. The most interesting fact was that time over there was five per cent faster than on Earth.

He also found out that when people cross over to the Other Side, they go to one of three large locations: the Plains, the Foothills or the Coast. The Plains was the most comfortable location, while the Foothills was the harshest place with many strange monsters inhabiting the area. The Coast was known for its beautiful weather and was considered moderately safe, unless, of course, one went into the sea. In the water, a man had no chance of surviving an encounter with the creatures of the deep.

Usually, prospectors did not choose where they would end up. Two people sent from the same preparatory camp could arrive at different locations, but when they returned to Earth they would invariably end up at the same point from which they had left — another of many mysteries! The

Tamedians did not explain this particular phenomenon, saying that each civilization has its own Other Side and how it works is anybody's guess.

All this knowledge of the Other Side, supplied by the Trader, concerned the extraction of pollen and the production of the necessary equipment. First of all — defense and weapons, and secondly — the container where the energy powder went. Without these, there wasn't even the slightest hope of survival on the Other Side.

Alex had familiarized himself with the detailed description of what energy powder was and why it was so important. The pollen contained modulated energy, which had no analogues in the material world. The energy was called modulated because it contained information in the form of vibrations which humans could not replicate.

At the suggestion of one of the researchers, this form of energy was dubbed Entelechy (entelechy is an internal force driving someone or something towards their destiny). The main asset of Entelechy was that the prospectors could adopt and make use of it quickly.

But it wasn't just humans who benefitted. Tiny doses of the pollen changed the properties of almost any material. Tests showed that the modified materials emitted a subtle vibration. The same vibration that distinguishes Entelechy from other forms of energy.

As a result, armor became stronger, weapons became sharper and many of the monsters on the Other Side fell victim to these new modified materials.

Before his training Alex had signed a contract, which stated that he had to return twenty grams of pollen in exchange for the training and equipment he received on the course. This was his debt, which had to be paid before anything. After that, he was free to spend his subsequent income on increasing his rating, buying advanced weapons or any other commodity to better his position.

The government carefully controlled the turnover of the pollen. It was all handed over to the Quartermasters and any improper use was punishable by a fine and a ban from working on the Other Side. But nothing was more strictly enforced than attempts to smuggle pollen to Earth. These simple rules were instilled in the prospectors from the very first day of training.

Alex chose a spear as his weapon which was the most popular choice among newcomers. Training took place in the Virtual and was often supplemented by practicing on a mannequin in spare time.

The spear made of modified steel was to be given to Alex before he was sent out, but he wasn't entitled to protective equipment of the same quality. The newcomers couldn't afford such a luxury. If you wanted some good armor, you had to buy it with some hard-earned pollen.

The monsters were an interesting prospect. Some of them resembled Earth animals, but there were also creatures unlike anything on Earth. For example, the shadow cow, a popular target for prospectors, was around the size of an ordinary cow. But, unlike a cow on Earth, the shadow cow was not made of flesh and blood, but of a dark, homogeneous substance, nicknamed protoplasm. Fortunately, these animals weren't a threat to newcomers.

However, what interested Alex the most was the interface. Each person on the Other Side had a window with parameters activated. Scientists came to an interesting conclusion, they argued that the interface appeared because people on Earth were so used to evaluating themselves in numbers.

The explanation was simple — in our world every adult had a personal chip capable of measuring activity, assigning points and calculating one's rating... so the Other Side, as a reflection of human culture, adapted to the newcomers and their crazy desire to measure their progress in numbers and percentages.

*　*　*

Though illness loomed on the horizon and time was in short supply, the training flew by quickly. Before Alex knew it, the grueling training had come to an end. In a month and a half one could only learn so much, but he had learnt what he needed to. Now it was time to go to the new world.

CHAPTER 5

THE BUFFER ZONE

THE TRANSITION HALL WAS SMALL, but slightly unusual. Most things about it were normal; it had a floor, ceiling and four walls. But one of the walls was a bit different, as if it was not from here, but from another planet. There was nothing earthly about it at all. Its surface looked like a moving oily substance vibrating at a high frequency. If anyone tried to stare at its shimmering colors for a long time, they became dizzy very quickly.

This fourth wall was called "the door" and led to the Other Side.

A technician in goggles and a white coat pointed to it and said:

"Listen carefully, mate! You hold your breath and go through the portal. On the other side is the Buffer Zone. It'll be a bit dark, but don't be afraid!

There's nothing dangerous there," the technician spoke in a tired but calm voice. You could tell it wasn't the first time he'd said this. "Once you're in there, stretch out your hand and walk straight ahead of you. It doesn't matter which way you go, just take a few steps forward. Got it?

Alex nodded and the technician continued:

"You can breathe in there. As you walk forward, you'll feel a slight resistance. That's the veil of transition. Just keep walking and you'll find yourself on the Other Side. There'll be people to meet you there. So, what else... You might feel a little dizzy or disorientated, but that's normal. Are we clear?"

"Yes!"

In training camp they'd been forced to memorize the rules of the Buffer Zone, so all the future prospectors knew exactly what to do.

"The main thing to remember," the technician persisted, "is that you can't stay there for long. In a few minutes you'll pass out and, after that, no one'll save you! Just don't stand still."

"I know all that. It's been explained to us a hundred times," Alex grumbled." "Never hurts to go over it again," said the technician sternly. "I'm gonna go out now and the green light on the ceiling will come on. As soon as it lights up, go. Don't wait cos the passage only works for ten seconds. If you're late, they'll fine you. They teach you about that, too?"

"Yes."

"Then good luck!"

The technician left. Alex adjusted his rucksack. Each prospector, in addition to personal belongings and equipment, carried an extra load, to be handed over to the commander of the base.

People couldn't run back and forth whenever they wanted. If the journey from Earth was relatively inexpensive, the return trip required valuable pollen, so all prospectors were loaded to the brim when they first arrived. They carried food products, building materials and other essential supplies. Alex had been given energy bars, a welcome cargo for any camp, as the Other Side was not known for its quality supply of food.

Since it was his first outing, he was given a rucksack weighing "only" 130 lbs. He hoped he wouldn't have to run with it. The load must be carried through the buffer zone and any strong, healthy man can cope with that...

The light turned green and the time had come to take a step into the unknown. He approached the portal and stepped through in one swift movement.

The buffer zone, sometimes known as the dark zone, met Alex in the grey hours of twilight. He could only see about a hundred feet, and beyond that everything merged into a fog. Out of the corner of his eye he could make out faint shadows, but they didn't scare him, because everything seemed dead and lifeless, like an old room that nobody had entered for many years.

In spite of the technician's warnings, Alex stopped and looked around curiously. The buffer zone separated the material world from the Other Side, but it looked surprisingly dull. Instead of normal land and grass, there was just lifeless stony soil. There was nothing interesting at all. No one who'd been there had seen any mountains, trees, rivers or, indeed, any sign of nature. But there was breathable air.

Closing his eyes, Alex spread his attention over the space around him, just like when he used to meditate. He wanted to feel this place. Suddenly, he sensed a presence around him. The sensation was faint and unusual, and unlike anything he had ever experienced on Earth. Through all his time meditating he could sense people or animals around him without even opening his eyes, but feeling this presence was a completely new sensation.

Alex looked around but saw nothing. Just emptiness everywhere.

He decided not to waste time and started walking forward, stretching out his hand as the technician had said, but... nothing happened. He was surrounded by the same grey wasteland and gloom, although he'd been told hundreds of times that this is where the veil of transition would be.

Alex waved his hands around — nothing. He walked forward — again, nothing!

He didn't know what to do. The Buffer Zone and the Other Side are realms of the unknown. For several years, scientists had been trying to figure out how the grey wasteland is arranged and why it was always necessary to walk forward. How could a newcomer figure it all out in a couple of minutes?

\- Well, if the mountain won't go to Moham-med..." he muttered, focusing all his attention. He decided to walk in the direction of the presence he had felt earlier.

It changed its position several times, as if it was leading him somewhere, but Alex continued his pursuit. After a few minutes, he started to feel dizzy and it was a struggle to stay focused. Everything around him began to blur. He stumbled and thought it was the end, but then he felt his hand touch something as thin as a spider's web. A veil!

Another step and Alex had reached the Other Side.

CHAPTER 6

THE FIRST ENCOUNTER

Earth
Office at the Institute of Research on the Other Side
Hans Richter

HANS WAS A BUREAUCRAT to the core. In the past, people were often critical of bureaucrats but the term had now lost its negative connotations. In a society where the main value was someone's rating, the position of a government employee was honored and respected.

The performance of government employees, just like everyone else, was calculated by their personal chip. Observations were conducted in real time, the employee's actions and decisions were evaluated and these observations contributed to the overall rating. The modern bureaucrats didn't work out of fear. They worked out of a sense of duty.

Hans was no exception and his work was important. He was responsible for statistics on all the prospectors sent to the Other Side. Who went where, where they came from, and so on. Bureaucracy had been a force before, but the modern, highly organized and efficient new system, almost to the point of absurdity, really did ensure order and accountability. But that was on Earth. On the Other Side there was no automated system. The counting of losses, the arrival and departure of prospectors, pollen collection and other important operations were all done manually.

Depending on the size and frequency of transitions to Earth, the base camps sent regular reports on the prospectors who came to them. The statistics were processed and sent to the department Hans managed.

"Another hundred gone in a month!" said Hans to himself. He'd been working away at these statistics for a long time.

The number of missing people for this month was small. Usually they were much higher. But these people weren't officially dead, they were just missing. Since the start of the exploration of the Other Side, many people had gone missing. At first many thought that they were getting to a distant unknown place, where the danger was so great that they were probably killed by something. But later, when the landing points became known and all the permanent bases had been formed, this theory was abandoned. Another theory was that people were going missing in the buffer zone. But Hans was sure that it was something else. He could see it from studying the analysis of all the incidents. Yes, there were inexperienced newcomers who got lost in the buffer zone, but there were also experienced prospectors and people with high ratings who were going missing as well.

Hans read through the list of missing newcomers. There was an interesting mix this time: a Buddhist monk, a painter and an opera singer. He remembered the singer. He'd been a talented performer and Hans had even been to one of his operas. The other missing people were all experienced prospectors. Even if the newcomers had got lost in the buffer zone you could not assume that experienced travelers would make the same mistake.

"Where did you all go?" said Hans quietly, not taking his eyes off the list.

*   *   *

The Other Side
Alex

The Other Side greeted Alex with a satisfied grumble. He'd barely taken his first few disorientated steps into the new world when he felt a hard kick in his back. It was a good thing they'd forced him to carry that rucksack. He felt the blow even with the 130-lbs cushion.

This wasn't exactly what he'd been promised. He wasn't expecting fireworks, but he wasn't expecting a welcome like this either. Where the hell was this coming from!?

Alex rolled on the unpleasantly hard stone surface and grazed his cheek as he went down.

Having yelled out a few choice words, on Earth they would've immediately lowered his rating for such behavior, he rolled over and saw two ugly creatures the size of teenagers approaching him. Their thick-set bodies looked strong and powerful and they had long arms which reached the floor, compensating for their disproportionately small legs.

Alex realized that he wouldn't be able to get up quickly. Fortunately, he had learnt to draw his weapon from different positions during training. Lying on his backpack, he grasped the spear shaft and jerked it sharply. The locking device came undone and Alex, now armed, turned the blade towards the monsters with trembling hands.

The creatures showed complete indifference towards the weapon, despite its importance in Alex's armory. They advanced towards him sluggishly.

Adrenaline was pumping through Alex's body, he was not prepared for this. The thought flashed through his mind that the monsters must have been shocked by his sudden appearance and he should take advantage of it.

Alex started swinging his spear frantically. Before he knew it he realized he was on his feet, it was amazing how fear could make him act so quickly. His spear waving was not some special technique handed down from Buddhist monks, but the frantic movements of a desperate man. The monsters remained unfazed by this new move and they came at him, faster and faster.

Alex looked around — he was in a large cave filled with a dim, green, fluorescent light.

"I never heard about *this* place," an inappropriate thought flashed through his head as he focused on his enemy.

The creatures were now within striking distance. He lunged. He hit the first monster right where he wanted to. But the point barely penetrated the skin and didn't do much damage at all. The monster seemed to wake up and let out a muffled roar. At that moment, the second one swung its arm. Two-inch claws grew on each of its five hooked fingers.

Time seemed to slow down and Alex clearly saw the dirty claws approaching his side. He tried to move, but didn't have time. His body tensed. Just then he physically felt something appearing between him and the creature's hand. Something invisible.

The monster had connected with a slashing blow, but his arm seemed to hit something and bounced away.

Alex turned and dashed away, barely noticing the weight of his backpack. After about a hundred yards, he stopped. He could make out the walls of the cave ahead and on either side of him. This cave was a trap!

By now the shock had passed, but his body was still on fire from the adrenaline. He turned around sharply and grabbed the spear shaft with both hands.

The unwounded monster was half jumping, half hopping towards him with his companion about a hundred feet behind. Despite their short legs, the undersized monsters could move fast.

"Shit! There's no escaping them!" thought Alex.

He tried to remember what kind of creatures they were. Mankind had accumulated a large database on the inhabitants of the Other Side, but nothing came to mind. He was going to have to think on his feet. Most likely, he was in the Foothills but, clearly, not on the surface. This was bad news. Young prospectors tended not to go into the mountains, monsters of the second and third level lived there which were difficult to handle even for the experienced prospectors.

"What level are they? First or second? Probably, first! Otherwise, I wouldn't have penetrated its skin," he turned over these thoughts in his head.

All newcomers were taught what to do if they encountered a creature whose level was higher. The advice was simple — run! It was in situations like this where most people died. Where a group could easily handle it, especially if there were people there with the right experience, a lone individual would perish.

"They're not that big. I've got a chance!" Alex

thought, looking at the wounded one.

The size of the monsters mattered. The bigger the size, the more effort needed to destroy them. A creature the size of a cat would lose out to a human, even if its level was higher. Knowing this, Alex revived in confidence — he was one and a half times taller and armed. Thanks to modern medicine and a course of mini-rejuvenation, he was also in good shape.

Not waiting for the enemy to reach to him, he dropped his backpack and ran towards them.

The spear was a simple weapon. The long shaft allowed the user to control the situation at medium and long distances. And in case of a single target, with the help of a run-up, a spear was the ideal option. Alex had already practiced such blows in the virtual world.

Running up to the monster, he made a sharp lunge. The creature obviously wasn't trained to fight with an armed opponent and didn't have time to dodge. The blade went into its throat with a sickening sound and the monster immediately collapsed. Instead of a cry or a shriek, there was just a gurgling sound as blood clogged its throat.

"How'd you like that, you bastard!" Alex growled.

He tried to pull out the spear, but it was firmly embedded in the monster's throat. It didn't help that it wouldn't stop waving its arms either.

Alex cast a wary glance at the second monster. It was hesitating, apparently unwilling to follow the fate of its companion, but it didn't stop coming and got closer and closer.

Like most of the creatures on the Other Side, this one was dumb. The prospectors hadn't encountered too much intelligence among the inhabitants of the Other Side. The local creatures were aggressive to humans and would usually attack immediately but, once badly wounded, many would just run away. This one, on the other hand, clearly intended to fight to the end.

While the wounded creature hesitated, Alex tried as hard as he could to free his weapon. Finally, the wound widened and his spear came free.

He warily began to approach the second creature, leaving the first one behind as it struggled to breathe its last few breaths. It was hard to tell what the monster would do next. It was difficult to read its next move by looking at its ugly countenance. Finally, it bared its white teeth and lunged for its prey.

Alex was ready. The blade went straight into the creature's stomach as it jumped right onto Alex's spear. Its legs started thrashing around and sweat ran down its back. After a few seconds the monster fell on its back and croaked as its life ran out.

"So, you freak, not so strong now!" he shouted in triumph.

He felt the adrenaline gradually begin to wear off. Finally, he could have a proper look around.

He was situated in a huge cave with a flat stone floor. Here and there, huge blocks and small boulders lay in a chaotic disorder. Darkness pressed in from all sides and only thanks to the glowing moss on the walls was it possible to see anything at all. The dim, green light gave the cave a touch of gloom and mystery; distant objects were hidden in the semi-darkness. It was a very eerie place. He couldn't even make out a ceiling due to the darkness there.

"So this is it, a prospector's fate! I wonder how many people made it to this place?" Alex thought to himself.

He didn't know where he was and he couldn't remember reading about such a place. But millions of people had been to the Other Side, maybe he just hadn't read the right passage when he was studying. However, he clearly remembered, from reading the instructions on journeys to the Other Side, that there'd been no mention of any caves at all. He was supposed to go to a base camp, not a dungeon!

"If anyone did end up here, they probably just couldn't get out. So God knows how I'm going to get out," Alex pondered.

Many people would have panicked. But Alex quickly calmed himself. Of all people, Alex was best suited to the role of a survivalist. In the last years before his coma, he'd learnt to count on no one but himself.

Even before his illness, he'd been used to being on his own. His whole social circle had consisted of a few friends and rare meet-ups with girlfriends, who quickly became disappointed in a self-absorbed partner, who thought about nothing but his career and preparation for his journey into space.

Kotler's disease had further emphasized his detachment from the rest of the world, leaving him alone with an impending, seemingly unavoidable death. If he hadn't focused on survival then, he wouldn't be standing on this stone floor now, soaked in the blood of these creatures.

Alex looked round once more, trying to figure out where he was and what to do next. Unfortunately, on the Other Side, complex machines didn't work, including all electronic devices that humanity was accustomed to. The main source of information here was memory but, try as he might, Alex couldn't think of anything at all.

Unable to come up with any ideas, Alex decided that it was useless trying so he got to work dealing with the animals he'd just killed.

CHAPTER 7

PLUNDER AND FLIGHT

Earth
Head office at the supply center for the Foothills
Kevin Schneider

KEVIN SCHNEIDER, A TALL, THIN MAN of European appearance, pressed his lips together while looking at the letter in front of him and thought irritably,

"This guy again! What does he want now? How many more times!"

Kevin jumped up and started pacing uneasily around his office, the size and furnishings of which clearly demonstrated the high status of its occupant.

"So what if he's a famous scientist?" He muttered under his breath. "As if we didn't have enough of those! Where's all this stuff gonna come from anyway? The chickens, the feed! And who's going to deliver it all!? Like we don't have enough work to do!"

After a few minutes Kevin calmed down and sat back down. He was an emotional guy, but he was well suited to his job. He was good at getting into the intricacies of a new task while organizing the work of his team in the most efficient way. What he didn't like was dealing with these ridiculous "requests." He looked at the letter again. Requests from the Other Side were made only on paper. The sender of the letter, Stanislav Sergeyev, was one of the most well-known scientists on Earth. He was head of the research base "Amur." On the Other Side, there were mostly base camps which spent their time looking for and gathering pollen, but there were also research bases. Someone had to gather information on this new world.

Kevin didn't deny Sergeev's authority in the scientific community, nor the need for such research bases, he just couldn't stand inventors.

"This is karma. Has to be karma!" he muttered, rocking back and forth in his luxurious leather armchair.

In the early days of his career, Kevin, then a fresh faced youth, had made the biggest mistake of his life. Not just a mistake, but a total disaster! His older colleagues should have shielded him from such a blunder, but they didn't. Without consulting anyone, Kevin announced on the website of the Mars Exploration Department that they needed inventors without specifying exactly what for.

Inventors! Ever since that day, the word had become a nightmare for him.

In the beginning, nothing forebode disaster. The department began to receive letters with rational proposals. Then more proposals kept coming in. By the end of the day, they were pouring in. Kevin didn't even have time to sort through them all.

His experienced colleagues showed Kevin some sympathy, but they didn't go as far as helping him, saying it was his own fault and he should clean it up himself. To make matters worse, his name, position and contact details had been added to the notice. After a while, it was removed, but the letters kept coming. The huge, active population of the Earth did their best to keep Kevin busy with their requests.

After a week he stopped receiving letters, swearing to himself that he would never contact these damned inventors again and that he would act only according to instructions. He would only put out applications through the tried and tested channels, like design institutes or other similar structures. But you can't get rid of inventors so easily. Give them an inch and they'll take a mile. So, they got together and did something unthinkable, they created a website where they discussed how they could help the department in their important mission to explore Mars, with the long-suffering Kevin as a contact person. Visitors to the site posted their thoughts and then got angry when their brilliant ideas weren't looked at. At this point, they even started coming to Kevin in person.

At first, he received a few of them in his office and tried to convince them the department didn't need help and could manage on its own. But they wouldn't take no for an answer. After all, how can you prove to a genius that his ideas are useless? Kevin asked not to let anyone else in, but they were Inventors! They had ways and means of getting to him and he didn't have the same secure office back then. Thanks to these unwanted visitors he just didn't have time to work.

Kevin was moved to another office, but that didn't stop the inventors, rather, it spurred them on and they still managed to find out where their victim was hiding. This all went on for about six months, during which time Kevin learnt all the spy tricks like evading pursuit, changing his place of residence and disguises. But nothing worked. His senior colleagues just found it amusing. In the end, his boss took pity on him and transferred the repentant youngster to a branch on another continent. Kevin then changed his name...

*   *   *

Remembering this experience and managing to calm himself down a little, Kevin read through the letter again. As far as he understood, Sergeyev wanted to conduct some experiments on chickens.

"Good thing it's not cows," he muttered grimly, remembering the ordeal they'd had dealing with another request from a crazy scientist to transfer some pigs to the Other Side.

That really had been a job to remember! They'd had to put the pigs to sleep and carry them in their arms as they weren't so inclined to do what they were told.

However, Kevin had now come to terms with what needed to be done when delivering live cargo and he was ready to step into manager mode. Clicking a button on his desk, he summoned his assistant:

"Annie, get Milos over here and quickly…"

* * *

The Other Side
The Cave
Alex

The first monster lay motionless. In the darkness its blood seemed as black as coal. Its wide, open eyes stared towards the ceiling, as if startled by something he'd seen there.

Alex was sure that it was dead, but he reached out and poked him with his spear to check. The monster didn't move.

"Must be dead," he said to himself. "I'll start with this one."

It normally took less than five minutes to collect the pollen. Pollen was condensed energy and the most valuable resource from the Other Side. Its formation process was similar to the crystallization of salt from an oversaturated solution. Once a creature died, its flesh released energy into the environment. As a result energy in the surrounding area increased and excess pollen was deposited on its corpse and the area around it. If it wasn't collected immediately, it would gradually dissipate and disappear. But not even the most skilled alchemist could rake up this fine powder.

The simplest device used for collection was a metal container made of two compartments. The special alloy of the walls prevented the contents from evaporating. A small thread was stretched in the upper compartment which attracted the silvery dust and served as a crystallization nucleus. Once everything had crystallized on the thread it was simply a matter of shaking off the pollen into the lower large chamber.

From these two creatures, Alex expected to get about 0.1-0.2 grams of pollen. He brought the device up to the first beast and flipped the lid off. He watched curiously as silver dust condensed on the thread. Sophisticated devices didn't work here, so there was no electronic reading on the container.

In theory, all objects on the Other Side contained energy, even rocks and earth, but the quantities were so small that it made no sense to extract from them. There was more energy in peaceful plants (which differed from monster plants), but no one could successfully extract it. The most reliable source remained the monsters. The higher the level and size of the creature, the more pollen could be extracted.

Having finished collecting the pollen, Alex decided to search for a way out of the cave.

He had no idea where to go. Every way he looked seemed to be a dead end. There was a slight clearing with a few huge boulders ahead of him, so he decided to head that way

His rucksack was weighing heavily on his shoulders. It was one thing to walk a few steps in the buffer zone with such a weight, but Kevin wasn't sure about carrying it on a long journey He was amazed that he'd managed to defeat these two monsters considering what he was lugging around on his back.

On the Other Side you could find food and water, but this was an unknown area and Alex didn't know what was edible and what wasn't. It was possible to eat moss or the meat of small animals, but many things could just as well be a terrible poison. To check, you could either count on your skills of correctly identifying food or you could just eat something and hope it was edible. Unfortunately, he hadn't thought to bring the guidebook with him.

Alex threw a glance at the two corpses and decided that he would rather starve than try such a thing right now. Besides, he had plenty of energy bars. It was just his water supply he'd have to watch carefully.

"I'll set up camp, then I'll look around." He muttered, stepping between the boulders.

It was a convenient spot with the rocks hiding him from the rest of the cave. A lone figure like him could easily take cover there if more monsters roaming around.

Alex quickly found a suitable place where two tall boulders stood side by side. An agile man could climb them quickly if he wanted to. It seemed a good place to scramble

However, he didn't settle down. He simply took off his rucksack and moved on lightly. The poor lighting obscured details, so he walked very slowly, stopping and looking around as he went.

*   *   *

An hour later, Alex was running at full speed back to those two boulders. Panting heavily, he was being chased by a distinct rustling sound of some local wildlife he had just stirred to life. Alex was limping slightly, but that didn't stop him. He also didn't need to look back because he knew exactly what was chasing him...

He sprinted across the clearing with the boulders and the cave passage started to widen. In an effort to keep his bearings, Alex stuck firmly to the right of the cave. The other side of the cave seemed to disappear in a green twilight.

Even now, he was trying his best to take everything in. From somewhere far away came the sound of running water. A good sign, as he was in short supply of that. There was a faint noise of wind coming from under the ceiling but, apart from that and the noises accompanying him, the cave was quiet and dark.

Alex ran within an arm's length of the cave wall, not risking going any further away. The wall gave him a sense of security that he could stand and fight back. As he ran, he tried to evoke the feeling of space around him, as he did on Earth, but it was almost impossible to recreate the same feeling.

Suddenly, Alex saw something dash towards his left. He couldn't make it out but something was gearing up to attack.

Thwack! Alex struck out and made connection with his spear. He was acting almost automatically but, luckily, it worked. But when he saw the ominous creature gearing up for a second attack, he realized he would need a lot more than just luck.

Despite being a peaceful man, Alex wasn't a complete novice when it came to handling weapons. All his experience was limited to virtual training at the training camp on Earth and he had spent many an hour practicing quick defense moves on a green mannequin they called "The Green Streak." It was on this green monster-like figure that Alex had honed his skill of reflecting quick blows. He was very grateful for all the training now.

But these quick jabs would only save him from the first few attacks. If the creature continued to attack, he knew it would be hard to keep going. And then, just like with the first creatures, an invisible barrier seemed to form around his body. He hadn't felt it much the first time, but this time he did.

The barrier appeared automatically. As Alex tensed his muscles in anticipation of the blow that was to come, the barrier just appeared a mere inch in front of his right leg.

Alex saw something wisp-like rushing towards his leg, which stopped abruptly once it reached this invisible barrier. However, the barrier disappeared in a moment and the blow caught his trouser leg.

"Fuck's sake! You bastard!"

Although the blow was weak, it did catch his leg and Alex felt a sharp, burning pain. His body jerked clumsily as he struggled to move forward.

Around him several rocks, or rather what he thought were rocks, started moving slowly towards him. They were monsters too! Alex recoiled and tried to move away from them, limping all the way.

The pain in his leg was getting worse, Alex glanced at his trouser leg and saw that the fabric had split like an old rag. He'd thought that the clothing would have offered more protection. Of course, it wasn't the equivalent of armor but its creators had known about the threat of monsters all the same.

"God, how's your luck!" he thought angrily. "How the hell did I end up here and what kind of creatures are these!?"

He went as fast as he could, but every step got more and more painful. He could hear the ominous sounds of pursuit close by. He stole a glance behind, now the creatures no longer looked like rocks and it seemed strange that he hadn't noticed them before. The monsters now looked like giant grey caterpillars.

They weren't fast and Alex started to get away from them as they kept up a slow, dogged pursuit. He slowly managed to put some distance between himself and his pursuers as he dragged himself to the clearing.

He got to his backpack and immediately regretted that hadn't dragged it to the top of one of the boulders. There was no time for that now. His shelter consisted of a large boulder fifteen feet high and another smaller one just to the side.

Using all the strength he had left, Alex lifted himself onto the smaller boulder.

"I hope these guys don't know how to climb," he thought as he watched them slowly approach.

Taking no chances, Alex moved over to the larger boulder. Now, there was nowhere else to run. If these creatures really could climb he would find out very soon.

The top of the boulder was very spacious. There was enough room to walk around, taking several steps in each direction. Clutching his spear, Alex walked to the edge and looked at the caterpillars.

There were eight creatures huddled around the rock. Fortunately, they didn't have enough sense to surround it, they just poked their heads into the rock in frustration that their prey had evaded them. Eventually, they lay down after they realized, they could go no further.

Alex reckoned that the creatures sensed he

had nowhere to run.

"They won't lose interest that easily," he thought, nervously looking down. "They'll just wait till I go down, then they'll have me!"

Somehow, he had to get down. His rucksack was lying on the opposite side from the caterpillars and Alex knew he had to try and get it back.

In half an hour all the caterpillars had curled up and began to look like a scattering of cobble-stones. It was hard to tell them apart from the grey stones scattered around

No matter how hard he tried, Alex couldn't see their eyes or mouths. But somehow, they had managed to attack him. And where had that wisp-like blow come from?

"It must be their tongue or something. I wonder how far it can reach. Hopefully I don't find out the hard way," he muttered uncertainly as he moved away from the edge.

His wound was numb and very red but all the medication he had was in the rucksack. The situation was getting worse by the minute, something had to be done. But first Alex decided to deal with an even more pressing and important issue.

CHAPTER 8

THE INTERFACE

THE FIRST THING TO DEAL WITH was the main mystery of the Other Side — the interface. The strange world, monsters, energy powder and even superpowers, could just about be understood by people on Earth who imagined this magical world that existed parallel to their own. But the interface was another matter. On the one hand, it was something familiar from childhood, a native and even banal concept. On the other hand, it was an unwelcome invasion of their minds. It wasn't a government made chip, but an unknown object that would be forcefully installed with or without your consent. Some people were frightened by it, but you couldn't survive on the Other Side without it, so the frightened ones stayed away, while others people didn't think too much about such trifles.

The interface was discovered by accident when the first explorers tried to activate their personal chip. However, in the place of a holographic screen was a set of mysterious parameters. As they later found out, these new parameters wouldn't appear immediately, but half an hour after the newcomer's first crossing to the Other Side. It was as if the new world needed time to adjust to a particular person.

Surprisingly, the interface was activated by any familiar command. It was as if someone had made sure that people wouldn't be lost in guesswork and would be able to make use of it at once. It was enough for people to say a simple word like "interface" or "status," to make a gesture or even just think about it and the interface would activate immediately.

"Okay, let's get this thing started," said Alex, now remembering all the information from training. "Status!"

A translucent, but readable text appeared before his eyes:

*[**Level:** 0*
***Energy:** 0/35 units.*
***Transformation:** Body: 5.6% / Structure: 5.4% / Brain: 5.3%*
***Signatures: Simple:** Walker (15%)*
***Rare:** Spatial Barrier (2%)*
***Talents:** Touch of Death, Sense of Space]*

Even the font seemed familiar to him, and Alex

remembered all the information he'd memorized during training.

__Level__: The most important figure. It reflects a person's evolution.

Levels were accumulated slowly. Since the discovery of the Other Side, only a few prospectors had managed to rise above the third level and in terms of strength that would outnumber a newcomer many times over.

__Energy__: A supply available to humans.

The Other Side was saturated with it, energy was everywhere — in water, rocks and plants. Prospectors mostly extracted it from the surrounding environment and even coined a special term, "the energy background." The higher the energy background, the more energy that could be collected.

__Transformation__: Transformation shows how close a person is to the next level. The parameter consists of three aspects: body, structure and brain. Only after reaching one hundred per cent in each aspect can the prospector advance to the next level.

__The body:__ This is the first aspect. When the body transforms, tissues and cells change and a person's receptivity to energy increases. They become stronger, fitter and faster. They are also better able to withstand injuries and recover faster.

__Structure:__ This is an energy structure based on the nervous system. The main function of the nervous system is the transmission of nerve impulses. Once transformed, the nervous system begins to transmit not only nerve impulses, but also *energy. Series of reflex points of nervous structures, systematized due to proximity to each other, form energy channels. With each level, the flow of energy increases.*

The brain*: The brain is the aspect responsible for energy management. Transformation doesn't make a person intelligent and doesn't accelerate thinking. With each level, only the control of energy flow increases.*

Every aspect evolves through use. Simply put, whatever a person uses, he would transform faster. The more often he strengthened his body with abilities, the more it changed. The energy structure developed with every discharge of energy. For example, if someone was focusing on activities which required precision and accuracy, the development of the brain accelerated.

Once in the new world, Alex had already begun to transform. Partly due to his killing of the two monsters, but most of the transformation was due to his first crossing to the Other Side and his initiation of the interface. Although he didn't notice it, his body, nervous system and brain were changing thanks to the energy of the new world. At first, the parameters would grow rapidly, but then progress would slow down as time went on

Signatures: *Signatures are energy patterns or matrixes. Scientists didn't know why these phenomena appeared and how a person could best make use of them, but they knew how they worked.*

When the brain gave a command, energy went straight to the matrix and was structured there according to the pre-laid patterns. This was how the activation of skills took place from the simplest to the most complex.

The percentage in brackets showed how a skill was progressing and depended on how often that skill was being used. When one hundred per cent was reached, the skill was either stopped or transformed into a stronger version.

Talent*: Talent was a person's aptitude, their strongest point. Talent was either a natural characteristic or came about as the result of experience.*

Alex moved on to specific parameters and immediately noticed that his energy reserve of thirty-five units was higher than the average for beginners.

Next came the transformation indicators, but that didn't interest him, the next level was still far away. He noted the signature and talent sections as he knew they might come in handy in the near-future.

He also noticed that the appearance of the interface and the names of the items were extracted by the Other Side from the consciousness of each person. The name might be inaccurate, but the main thing was that it was understandable to the user. This close connection between humans and the Other Side was further proof that this new world was a product of human culture.

Most of the prospector's abilities were gained

either deliberately, through concrete actions or through special circumstances. No one believed that a new ability was a gift. The Other Side did not give anything for nothing, but enhanced and transformed a person's already existing aptitude for something. If, for example, a person had an innate or acquired ability to control body energy, then, with the help of qigong techniques, he would be able to control first the internal, then the external energy. In time, he would also learn to throw fireballs. The main thing was to have at least some kind of foundation. Empty fantasies wouldn't help, no matter how much effort you put in.

Some abilities appeared which couldn't be explained at all. Alex had heard about a prospector who'd learnt the skill of levitation. At first, he could just reduce the speed of falling, but in a couple of years he'd learnt to glide and, eventually, was able to fly like an eagle. This skill was a completely new concept and no one had ever been able to explain it.

However, Alex was more interested in survival than in distant prospects. Luckily, he did have one interesting skill, a barrier, which had even managed to save his life twice. Though it didn't fully protect him, he thought, looking at the wound on his leg.

Clearly, the Barrier wasn't called "spatial" for nothing! The name most likely indicated additional properties and he thought he would have to test the skill in different situations to figure out what they were. But the mere fact that it had twice repelled the attack of a higher level enemy was enough for him. He hoped he wouldn't need it too much in the future!

The progress of the barrier had risen quickly to two percent, but Alex wasn't deceived, all skills grow quickly in the beginning. After that, the progress would slow down and would most likely progress at a snail's pace. In the later stages, it would take a truly enormous effort to advance a skill, especially when approaching one hundred per cent.

The second and last ability was the Walker. The analogue of this skill was available to absolutely all prospectors, even the name "Walker" was the most common one. All newcomers knew about it, so the name became common knowledge. Thanks to this, it was put straight into the interface as the Other Side took the word straight from the newcomer's memory when they arrived. It was clear to everyone how to use it and everyone knew its value. Without it, you couldn't return to the material world.

Alex found it strange that this particular skill had a surprisingly high progression rate on his interface, but he put that down to his adventures in the buffer zone.

Well, it's something, but it's not enough to survive... he thought, looking at the curled-up caterpillars below

Before his trip to the Other Side, Alex had carefully planned his first steps and decided then that he would spend the first week in the base camp, honing his skills of attack and self-defense and then he would go hunting for pollen. However, those plans had now gone straight out of the window.

Alex knew he was in serious trouble. It was one thing to train in a camp where he could be helped by more experienced prospectors, but it was another thing entirely to train for real, fighting for one's life surrounded by monsters.

Of course, some skills weren't that difficult to master. Many of them were created quite easily, even casually. For example, sensitive people often got the ability "simple scanner." Observant people were gifted with "detection" and professional athletes were often given "accelerated reaction", "explosive power" or other skills that made them faster or stronger.

A person acquired a skill under two conditions: energy reserve and repetition of actions that initiate the formation of the energy matrix. It was preferable to train in a safe environment with full commitment. Of course, in a combat situation one could discover hidden abilities, but in that situation, death was always a possibility!

Some desperate people even put themselves in such situations in the hope of awakening new powers. Sometimes it worked out and people acquired surprising, new skills. Alex was just grateful that he was still alive!

Shaking his head, he moved to the last point, talents.

There was a pleasant, though somewhat expected, surprise waiting for him there, "The Sense of Space." Deep down he'd expected something like this. He could already tell where the talent belonged and where it had come from. Years of meditation and training in the "Way of Emptiness" hadn't been for nothing. After all, the Other Side intensified everyone's characteristics, so it was no surprise that this one manifested itself here. On Earth Alex had always been able to feel the space around him, so it was no wonder that this new world noticed it.

"Fantastic!" he rejoiced, remembering with gratitude Donid, the creator of the "Way of Emptiness."

Alex had never even met him, but he rightfully considered himself his pupil. Perhaps the best one there'd been.

Having a good talent was his main trump card. Talent is a catalyst for human development. But most people, when they first went to the Other Side, didn't even have a "Talents" section on their interface. And if they did, it usually listed some nonsense like "born fighter" "Hercules" or "acrobat." Of course, most people normally developed quickly and in a couple of years could fight even a small pack of monsters the same level as them, but talents not related to physical development were valued more highly.

People tried everything to discover their talent: self-teaching, psychology, religion, spiritual practices, martial arts — everything worked, but you needed either a developed aptitude for something, or years of training.

Alex believed that his "Spatial Barrier" skill was a consequence of talent. But he was even more excited about what that might lead to. He knew very well that one talent often led to the formation of a whole group of abilities related to it. So, there was a chance that he would add other skills to his already existing "Spatial Barrier."

Another reassuring fact was the rank of abilities. At the moment, people knew four ranks of them.

Simple: This was the most common. Prospectors discovered them without much difficulty. As a rule, such skills were quickly developed.

Ordinary: Available to many but requiring a long time to master.

Rare: Difficult to obtain. Activation required a lot of practice and prolonged application.

Unique: These abilities were almost impossible to learn even in an extreme situation. They occurred only if the prospector had a pre-existing gift.

The last class was the most coveted. The name "unique" implied a person's uniqueness, rather than a "one of a kind" ability.

Ability ranks spoke not so much to the strength of the ability, but to the difficulty of obtaining it. Of course, more often than not, rare and unique abilities were more powerful, but not always. Alex remembered a story about a prospector with the skill "sense of weight". This guy could accurately determine the weight of an object just by looking at it. An interesting but useless skill, except for the fact that he could understand that a stone flying towards him weighed exactly 400 lbs. and not 399.

There were other examples, when a simple ability could become a formidable weapon. The most common case of this was a predisposition to energy manipulation, a predisposition that could be mastered by using various eastern practices. All that was required was time and diligence. On the basis of this predisposition, talents and various abilities of ordinary rank emerged like fireballs and energy bullets. And if a prospector raised a skill up to a hundred per cent, it could change and get a higher rank.

Nevertheless, Alex was happy with the rank of his "Barrier." He knew that such skills often had a higher potential of development. It might not be useful right now, but he hoped that it would be.

He nodded to himself and moved on to his second talent. The "Touch of Death" wasn't a unique ability. Many people got it if they experienced death or came very close to it. This talent reduced the effects of mental attacks, but monsters with this ability were almost unheard of. Furthermore, the prospectors never found out how this talent worked through personal experience, but through the help of interface researchers. The Other Side was always being studied, so researchers worked on a regular basis at all the bases. They compiled lists of skills, kept records of monsters, made maps of the area and they analyzed talents. In other words, they did exactly what people in white coats usually do.

Researchers were hired by the government, but not just anyone was hired. A researcher needed an aptitude for this kind of work and, after a while, they were labelled with the skills "analysis," "understanding of the essence," "identifying" or something similar. As the researchers' skills grew, they were able to extract more and more information about the environment, including the interface. The data was analyzed, classified, and fed into the databases available to the prospectors.

* * *

Having sorted out the interface, Alex looked around. It was safe on the rock, but there were no weapons. There wasn't even a rock lying around to throw at the caterpillars. On the lower half of the rock there was some moss growing which helped to illuminate the surroundings with a greenish light. Thanks to this, he could make out a wall some three hundred yards away. The ceiling just resembled a dark mass hanging above him. It was difficult to make out much else with the little light he had.

He knew it was dangerous to run. Where would he even run to? Back to the place he arrived? He pictured himself lying as a cold corpse, joining the ranks of the missing people and ruled out that option straight away. Maybe he should run forward into the dark and take his chances with the first thing he met? But that sounded even less appealing. No! He had to deal with these monsters and get some new skills. Only then could he explore the cave and look for a way out. But the first thing he had to do was get his supplies back.

Alex gently massaged his leg, stood up and hopped around. The pain wasn't too bad and he could move around on it. Ideally, he wanted to let it rest some more. There was one big plus to the Other Side in this situation. Wounds healed much quicker there than they did on Earth.

Having waited a bit for his strength to return, Alex decided to experiment and jumped onto the lower boulder. He came to the edge with his spear in front of him and looked at the caterpillars. Then he tapped the boulder with the spear handle. The creatures stirred. First one, then the rest of them gradually woke up and started crawling towards him. It didn't take them long to all wake up, but they weren't moving fast after their slumber.

He had about ten seconds before they reached his rucksack. Maybe a bit longer. But going down without any protection would be suicide! He also needed energy for that and the interface showed that he had none left.

[Energy: 0/35 units]

So, he couldn't even use his "spatial barrier" as he had before.

Alex had two options. The easiest was to wait for his reserve to slowly fill up from the surrounding environment. But at level zero, that would take fifteen to twenty-five hours. Fortunately, he had the container containing pollen from the two monsters, which would fill up his energy reserve quicker than anything.

There was very little pollen, but there was enough energy in it to fill his reserve more than once. In fact, there was so much of it there that Alex could fill up his storage at least a hundred times. But the Other Side is not a computer game. Alex was well aware that he couldn't just magic pollen out of thin air.

To extract it, all you had to do was take out a small pinch and wait. After a while, the pollen would disintegrate and the energy background would start to increase. That would reduce the time to fill your reserve by about half an hour, maybe even less if you used more pollen. But it was an inefficient process, as most of the energy just spread around without concentrating on one area.

If he were in the mining camp, he could use special chambers, where the energy is held in by walls made of a special alloy. Another option would be to make a potion, dissolve the pollen in alcohol, which reduces the dissipation rate by half. Most of the energy would still be lost, but it was a slightly more efficient process. He had kept a stash of alcohol in his rucksack for such cases.

Alex took out the container. He removed a knife from his belt and carefully ran the tip of it along one side of the container. Then he brought the knife to his leg and sprinkled a tiny amount of pollen directly onto the wound. He gritted his teeth as he smeared it into the open wound. They'd been taught to use this method in such situations. The researchers had discovered that a heightened energy background not only quickly filled one's energy reserve, but also accelerated the healing of injuries. Pollen was like a dock leaf for open wounds on the Other Side.

There was another way of treating injuries and that was abilities. To distract himself from the pain, Alex remembered a funny story told by his doctor about a prospector from former Europe called Andre. Back on Earth, he had been interested in urine therapy and tried to treat himself and others with it.

Andre became infamous and was laughed at by everyone. Unable to withstand the ridicule he moved away to conquer the new world. There, to his surprise and the horror of those around him, he acquired the ability to heal people with a product of his own making. He became a supplier and user of his own excellent product. Fortunately, its use only required external application! He became famous and, suddenly, his services were in demand. Andre was beside himself with joy and didn't know which way to turn due to all the demand on the Other Side. However, when they tried testing his product on Earth it was found to be completely useless without the help of pollen!

Alex sat on the rock, remembering all these stories of other people. There was a greenish twilight all around him and from somewhere came the murmuring of water. He felt very much at peace, momentarily forgetting that he was in a world that mankind knew almost nothing about.

A mechanical watch dangled on his arm, an unusual gadget for the twenty-seventh century. But with the discovery of the Other Side, the field of mechanics had received a new impetus and many mechanics grasped the chance to create some new inventions which could work in this new world.

The clock showed that five minutes had passed. In that time, his energy level had increased by seven points:

[Energy: 7/35 units]

At this rate, in twenty minutes he could start the second phase. Alex relaxed a little and stared into the darkness again. The tension was slowly subsiding, the silence was soothing and he felt himself falling asleep.

Finally, the energy filled the reserve. The interface confirmed it:

[Energy: 35/35 units]

Now the wound had healed and was almost painless.

"Here we go," thought Alex, but then he stopped himself abruptly. It seemed that the short rest he'd had, hadn't done his thinking any good. But he wasn't surprised about it. He'd never had to run away from monsters before. It wasn't really something they went over at school. He'd been so worked up, he'd forgotten about all the safety measures he'd been thinking about twenty minutes ago.

Surprised at his forgetfulness, he started to think everything through. He couldn't climb down without protection, that much was obvious. The first thing to do was to get answers to simple questions: how the barrier was activated, how much energy was needed and how long it lasted. Could he count on it lasting longer than a few seconds? And how much would it all cost? After all, everything had a price on the Other Side. To activate and use a skill always required energy. Without fully understanding all the properties of this new skill, climbing down off the boulder to retrieve the rucksack was extremely dangerous.

In a camp it would have been much easier for Alex to study this new skill. There you could test everything in safe conditions without having to worry about the risk of death, a luxury which Alex didn't have while sitting in this cave.

He couldn't even remember anything from his studies. He'd read descriptions of more than a thousand skills while in training, but the name "spatial barrier" didn't ring any bells. He couldn't think of anything at all. In that moment, Alex felt like he had spent all those hours cramming in information for absolutely nothing!

"Space barrier! Barrier! Defense! Shield!" his voice echoed through the cave.

Nothing happened. He tried raising his voice slightly but, again, nothing. Alex tried not to despair. He knew that prospectors often found themselves in these situations and he was sure that his skill was something he could master in time. He just needed to know how to activate it

Alex thought back to when the barrier was activated for the first time. It happened when he was fighting the first monsters. One of them had tried to attack and the barrier had just activated. He closed his eyes thinking back over every moment step by step. He remembered the monster's hand with long, sharp claws, slowly approaching his side. In that moment, he'd had time to think that if this thing made connection, it would be bad news. He'd tried his best to move out of the way, but he just couldn't. His body tensed up waiting for the blow and then... the barrier activated. That was it!

The barrier activated when he was under attack, when the body tensed up in anticipation of a blow. It was a reaction to a threat. Now he knew what he had to do. Alex vividly imagined a brick flying at his head and tensed up. There it was! The feeling of something around him protecting his body from harm.

He quickly looked at the interface.

[*Energy: 15/35 units*]

So the barrier used up twenty points. Alex had been hoping for less. He still had to figure out how the barrier behaved after activation.

He stood up and walked around the rock. He could still feel it. That was good news. So, after activation, the barrier continues for some time.

After about twenty minutes, Alex lost the feeling of protection and the barrier disappeared. He stole another quick glance at the interface,

[Energy: 18/35 units]

CHAPTER 9

A NEW SKILL

The Other Side
Base camp Tver
Nikita Sukhanov — Prospector, level 3

"YES! I DID IT!" Nikita was jumping for joy.

After two years of experimenting, he had finally created an enhanced potion.

On Earth, the guy had been a die-hard moonshiner, a common pastime in certain circles. He didn't have a regular job, so he started doing his hobby so he could boost his civilian rating. The government didn't care what a person did. As long as he didn't sit idle, any activity was encouraged. After all, what is a hobby? It's an activity that a citizen chooses himself and if that meant that someone would be doing something, rather than sit about idly and complain about his life, the government was all for it.

There was also a chance that a person would benefit not only himself, but also society by discovering some nuance or improving technology in some way.

However, moonshining didn't promise any huge breakthroughs. Enthusiasts in this field simply brewed alcoholic beverages and sometimes organized open tastings and fairs to exchange their experience with others.

Despite this pastime, Nikita was not an alcoholic. Firstly, that would have negatively affected his rating and, secondly, he didn't need to brew alcohol to get it. He just liked the process experiments and fiddling with devices. He was a romantic and imagined himself as a medieval alchemist.

When people first started going to the Other Side, Nikita was one of the first to sign up, more out of curiosity and thirst for adventure than in pursuit of a higher rating. However, once he started to see the deaths all around him and the reality became clear, he started to wonder if this had really been such a good idea.

He was stopped from returning to Earth by a skill that he'd found in his first week on the Other Side "Varevar." He'd found it almost by accident while he'd been preparing a standardized solution of pollen in alcohol. Thanks to this skill, Nikita could produce a drink that lasted twice as long and restored energy ten per cent faster than others. As researchers later found out, similar abilities were often found in professional chefs and people with a passion for cooking.

Once the authorities found out about Nikita's new skill, they offered him a separate contract, under which he would brew this drink in exchange for an increase in rating and a supply of pollen for personal development. They didn't want a promising employee to get killed while out hunting monsters and they certainly didn't want him to return to Earth.

Nikita gladly agreed and today was the day where he had finally created a new version of his drink that was sixty per cent more effective than the usual solution and lasted three times as long.

* * *

The other side
The Cave
Alex

Alex sat down on a rock and thought over every step. He would only have a few seconds down there. Before descending, he summoned a Barrier around his rear end and legs. That's where the creatures were most likely to hit him.

Having activated his defense, he put his spear to one side, walked to the edge, lowered himself off it feet first and, finally, let himself fall to the ground. Despite all his precautions, Alex had barely landed when he heard a familiar squelching sound coming from behind the rock. The sound was rapidly approaching. He hastily unzipped his jacket and pulled out a coil of rope so well packed that if he decided to unravel it now, he would definitely be eaten for breakfast.

Instead, he pushed the rucksack into the corner, jumped on it, and climbed back up with the rope in his teeth. In that moment, Alex was very thankful he'd been kitted out with some good climbing boots. But despite the boots, he wasn't quite fast enough. Just as his hands gripped the top edge of the boulder, one of the caterpillars struck.

Wack! The barrier repelled the sting, and it gave Alex a bit of a push so he landed even quicker back where he had come from.

He quickly examined himself. Thankfully, there were no new injuries. Then he turned his gaze to the monsters. He had to lure them to the other side of the rock, otherwise he wouldn't be able to get back down. He ran over to the opposite side of the rock and most of the caterpillars followed him. Unfortunately, the two largest creatures stayed near his backpack, but Alex had a plan.

* * *

Half an hour later, once the caterpillars had curled up again, Alex tied the rope to the spear and for twenty minutes tried to use a combination of the spear and the rope to hook onto the rucksack. Eventually, he managed to hook onto the straps and he pulled the rucksack up. The monsters didn't even flinch.

With the rucksack beside him, he breathed a sigh of relief. Now he had food and two large bottles of water to last him for a fortnight. He knew he'd have to conserve the water, but he had plenty of food.

He gladly took a few gulps of water and wondered what to do next. He needed something that would help him deal with the caterpillars and increase his chances of survival if he was going to go any further through this dark tunnel.

He didn't have too many options. He couldn't raise his level right now. That would be too much time, effort and resources. Even if he managed to kill all the caterpillars below several times over, that still wouldn't be enough.

An idea popped into his head. He took a spear with a rope tied to it, walked to the edge and threw it with all his strength at one of the monsters. Bam! The blade made a dull thud as it stuck in the creature's body, but contrary to appearances the caterpillar was a hard nut. The creature slowly turned around and crawled away, but Alex could see that the spear hadn't caused it too much discomfort. Alex pulled hard on the rope and the spear came out easily.

"Great, so they've got armor as well," he thought irritably.

He'd hoped that the monsters would panic and start attacking him while he quietly slaughtered them from above. He threw his spear a few more times to check, but the other caterpillars were no more stupid than the others and they all crawled away to go just out of his range.

"Get outta here!" he raged at them but they remained unmovable.

Alex gloomily looked at them and wondered what his next move should be.

He thought for a moment.

"I can't kill them with a spear and I'll need pollen to return to Earth." He had the Walking skill, but it was useless without a few grams of pollen. That left him with one option, using an attack ability.

There were several options that could be easily obtained, such as "Strong Strike." This one was quite easy to get, all you needed to do was imagine your muscles getting stronger and then strike out. Simple training and nothing more. A couple of hours of saying "my hands are getting warmer… no stronger" and just like that a new ability would form, strengthening the muscles with energy. The effect was temporary, but it was enough for a powerful blow. Many new prospectors, who had no special talents or desire to work for a couple of years to acquire strong skills, used this method. Those who were a bit smarter strengthened the whole body at once. That required a bit more money in the beginning, but the rewards were far greater.

Alex could afford to spend several hours or even days on training, but there was a problem, he couldn't just form as many skills as he wanted. With each new ability, it would be harder and harder to form the next one, especially at level zero. He needed to be selective in the abilities he chose at this stage.

The other difficulty was simply the time needed to develop a new skill. Ideally, he should develop a skill related to an already existing talent. That way they wouldn't conflict with each other and they could develop in a similar way.

So, Alex decided! Within the next two weeks he should form a talent-related skill, master it and defeat the caterpillars or at least scare them away. It was a great plan, only Alex had no idea where to start.

Unable to think of anything useful, he sat down on his backpack in his usual meditation pose, closed his eyes and started spreading his attention to the surrounding area...

That evening, he decided to live according to the time on Earth, which he was able to do thanks to his mechanical watch. But Alex thought that he was doing something wrong. He was counting on his meditation exercises to help him get a new ability on the Other Side. But they didn't.

* * *

The next day, after a good night's sleep, he continued to meditate, disconnecting himself from everything around him. This time, he tried to pay attention and kept himself in a state of heightened concentration, but again there was no result. But he felt like something should happen. He had a talent!

After working like this for several hours, Alex gave up. He was used to being in a life or death situation, but this one was quite different from the last few years of his life.

The caterpillars lay peacefully near the rock like trained guard dogs.

"Maybe the caterpillars are protecting me from other creatures," he thought hopefully, not believing that for a moment. He noticed some bats hovering above him. "God, I need to get outta here!"

Monsters, for the most part, only fought humans. They rarely fought each other. The Other Side's ecosystem was different from Earth's in that sense. The food chain wasn't based on plants and animals, but on energy, which the local inhabitants absorbed directly from the environment.

There was a theory that monsters were parasites which this world would be better off without. But Alex didn't believe that. The Other Side showed enough signs of internal organization and self-orderliness to show there was a clear structure which these monsters were a part of. It was just that people hadn't quite figured it out yet. Alex just didn't believe that the monsters were some otherworldly force beyond the control of this world. No, they were definitely part of this world and they had some kind of purpose!

"Right let's get back to these things, these caterpillars. How can I get some new skills to save me here? — thought Alex aloud.

He went through the activation methods in his

head again. It was true that he hadn't read much on this topic, but he did remember a few things.

The trouble was that almost all the methods concerned physical skills. It wasn't hard to energize some body organ, but how the hell would he channel it into a sense of space? Being in an extreme situation might help, but Alex had already been through that and he wasn't in a rush to try it again.

Another way was to create an energy-rich environment around him. If he managed to do that, he could easily form a new ability. To do this he would either have to kill a monster or just scatter some pollen around.

He decided to go for the third option, even though he was reluctant to use his precious supply in such an inefficient way. But without that he knew the process would go too slowly, and his personal stock was just too small for a new skill.

Having made his decision, Alex pulled out the container and carefully took out a sprinkle of pollen from it. He didn't want to use any alcohol here as he knew he would need all the concentration and attention he could get.

After scattering the pollen around, he sat down in his meditation pose, but this time he positioned himself on the lower boulder about twenty feet away from the closest caterpillar.

Having settled his mind, stripped his body of emotions and completely relaxed, Alex focused all his attention on the monster. He knew he had to discover something, he just wasn't sure what.

He just knew he'd have to work it out for himself.

* * *

For half an hour he pushed, pulled and condensed all his attention on various points of the creature, but it completely ignored everything he did. Alex even started to feel a little resentment, but he didn't want to give up. When the pollen had almost run out he just stared at the monster without thinking about anything. For a moment there was a feeling of desolation inside. He knew from previous experience with the Barrier that this was a sign of energy drain. But he was sure something was happening. He stubbornly kept his attention fixed on the creature and then suddenly he saw written on the interface:

[Cave Crawler: level 1]

Alex immediately guessed what had happened. One of the abilities for receiving information had been activated. It was certainly a useful skill, though not exactly the skill he needed to fight his way out of this mess.

"Well, it's better than nothing," he sighed as he opened his status window:

[Level: 0
Energy: 20/35 units
Transformation: Body: 5.7% / Structure: 5.4% / Brain: 5.3%

Signatures: Simple: *Walker (15%)*
Rare: *Spatial Barrier (13%), Space Scanner (1%).*
Talents: *Touch of Death, Sense of Space]*

There it was! He had gained a new ability, "Space Scanner."

Scanning abilities were not uncommon. Many prospectors had similar skills, only the names and properties differed slightly from one another. In Alex's case he was clearly helped by his original talents in gaining this new skill

While the increased energy background was still in effect, he waited for his reserve to fill up and tested the skill several times. He found out that if he looked at a monster, an inscription with its name and level would appear. But it would only work if he could see them. Direct visibility was a must.

Identification of one creature took away fifteen units of energy so, even with a full energy reserve, he would only be able to identify two creatures at a time.

The maximum distance of the skill was a hundred feet. Alex discovered that when he tried scanning a more distant area, it just wouldn't activate.

The skill was more a basic identifier than a full-fledged volumetric space scanner, but Alex was still satisfied that his meditation had yielded some results. Besides, this skill would gain new capabilities once it was reinforced. That usually occurred at 50, 85, and 100%, so there was a good chance that this ability would prove to be a useful one. As a rule, all skills looked average to start with but the more they were used, the more new properties they gained.

But it was too early to think about that. He hadn't learned anything new. The fact that the enemy was level one, he'd already guessed and the name of the monster wasn't important, because that's always created by the prospector himself after he sees a monster for the first time.

If Alex had seen a description of cave crawlers before under a different name like "cave caterpillars" then that's likely the name he would have seen the first time he looked at the interface. And if he got out of the cave and told others about this new type of monster, other prospectors would probably identify the species as "cave crawlers," just as he did.

CHAPTER 10

CLEVER SPENDING

DISCOVERING THE "SPACE SCANNER" had cost Alex only one tenth of his total supply of pollen. That would have been a great result, if he'd been at one of the base camps. But sitting on a rock, surrounded by eight monsters, it wasn't quite the same. No matter how hard he tried, he wouldn't be able to fight off monsters with a Scanner.

But what choice did he have!? He wasn't going to sit around doing nothing. He'd already been condemned to death once and he'd managed to find a way out of that. Once his energy stores had been replenished, he'd think about how to cheat death a second time.

* * *

Another day passed in the new world. Alex spent thirty per cent of his pollen trying to get a new skill, but, so far, nothing new had happened. Each time he tried to do something with the monsters, the space around him, or any other surrounding objects, nothing seemed to work. He tried not to lose heart. The scanner had worked, and so would the new skill. Just like he'd got the "Space Scanner," he would get another ability.

To bring them closer, Alex tried luring a couple of them with his feet dangling down from the top of the boulder. He didn't even need to use the Barrier for this as he was already convinced that their sting couldn't reach him when he was sat up there.

He'd also had a great idea last night. All this time, he'd been focusing on the monsters but what if he tried something different. He knew he'd struggle to affect the creatures directly, but what if he could affect the energy around them? Alex knew there were energy related skills, it was just a matter of discovering them.

Having considered several options, Alex went for the easy option. He put down a pinch of powder on a rock in front of him. Then he took a small sip of alcohol mixed with dissolved pollen. The alcohol might interfere, but right now he needed all the energy he could get. The pollen on the rock wouldn't last long and Alex knew he would need to concentrate all his efforts.

The pollen immediately began to evaporate. As with the monsters, Alex focused his attention directly on that area of space, trying to stretch it, hit it, or loosen it somehow. He imagined that the space around was like a sea that could be stirred up by his imagination. Nothing happened straight away, but Alex didn't worry. He knew that many abilities didn't appear just like that, so he kept going again and again. He kept going for as long as he could each time.

Alex made two more attempts that day and, by the end of it, he only had thirty percent of his original pollen supply left. Looking sadly at the container, he put it away and kept going without energy powder. His alcohol with pollen mixture was still working. But soon enough, that source ran dry as well. But he didn't stop. Even if his efficiency dropped to almost nothing, he was still practicing. Alex knew that every effort could help and he just had to keep trying. Right now he had all the time in the world, until his food supply ran out.

*　*　*

The next day Alex had a choice. Either he could return to the first method with the caterpillars or he could keep working on the energy in the space around them. He only had enough energy left to keep going with one of those options. For some reason, he liked the second idea better.

"Well, here we go again," he muttered.

Not feeling at all confident, Alex poured out almost the whole contents of the container on to his palm. Then he divided it into two parts. He kept one part for himself and the other half he put down on the rock. Then he started repeating everything he'd done yesterday.

For the first ten minutes, almost nothing happened. He thought he was getting nowhere, but then he started to feel a strange sensation in his stomach. He immediately tried to intensify it.

At first nothing changed, but, eventually, he noticed an emptiness in his chest, which began to fill rapidly. He focused every ounce of attention on this new sensation, trying to memorize and master it. Alex didn't know what it was but he knew he didn't want to let it slip.

Despite his calm outward demeanor, Alex was making a lot of effort. He tried to keep relaxed and let the energy flow freely in his body, whilst keeping all his attention fixed firmly on this new sensation. After ten minutes, Alex felt a change as a barely perceptible vibration travelled through his body.

"Status!" he shouted out in hope.

The interface window opened and Alex, skimming through the now familiar information, quickly made his way to the new item:

[Signatures: Rare: *Pump (1%)]*

There it was, a new ability! He just had to figure out what it did and how it could help him. But he already had a hunch and one look at his energy readings left him in no doubt.

[Energy: 35/35]

His energy was at a hundred percent even though he'd just spent plenty of effort activating the new ability. So, clearly, this skill didn't spend energy, it collected it. It was a very rare skill very much in demand on the Other Side. It dramatically reduced a person's dependence on pollen and hugely raised the chances of any prospector. The main benefit was being able to train more often in a non-combat environment. The few people who did have this ability tended to go far ahead of their colleagues.

Alex hadn't thought that far ahead. His main goal was just to get out of this cave alive. But at least now he wasn't so dependent on saving every ounce of energy he could. He could also activate the Barrier a lot more than he could have before.

Eager to get started with this new skill, Alex activated the Barrier to reduce his energy reserve by twenty units:

[Energy: 15/35]

That's it, he was ready. Distributing his attention to the surrounding space, Alex felt a sea of energy flowing into him from all sides. After three minutes of this sensation, Alex felt strangely full and content.

It only took five minutes to fill up his reserve,

so about one point every eight seconds, Alex thought to himself. Of course, his reserve was still small, but as the level increased, his reserve would grow.

The rest of the day, Alex spent training his three abilities: Barrier, Scanner and Pump. While doing this, he really found out how useful the Pump ability was.

It was an absolute God-send for refilling his energy reserve.

The Barrier's progress had reached thirteen per cent when he started training, but was starting to slow down a bit. Because of that, Pump and Scanner quickly caught up. By the end of the day, the skills had more or less levelled out:

*[**Transformation:** Body: 7.1% / Structure: 7.0% / Brain: 6.0%*
* **Signatures: Simple:** Walker (15%)*
* **Rare:** Space Barrier (30%), Space Scanner (37%), Pump (33%)]*

Alex was ecstatic! He'd only been there a couple of days and he'd already brought all his scores up to a respectable level. He knew he still had a long way to go but he was very happy with the results. He had a lot to thank the "Pump" ability for. He could quickly fill his reserve without taking an inch of pollen. For that reason, such an ability was known to be the envy of all prospectors. People could normally replenish their energy reserve every half hour at best, but the pump would replenish an energy reserve six times over in that time. Knowing all these facts, Alex was really counting on the Pump to be his key to further development.

Alex was also pleased with the progress of his abilities. They had all reached thirty percent. Unfortunately, the Barrier hadn't developed much further than that but Alex had been warned that some skills would be harder to develop than others.

However, he still had the immediate problem of being surrounded by several monsters. And he couldn't fight them. Yes, now he could quickly gain energy, but how could he use it? Defense abilities would only get him so far. Even with everything he now had, he'd probably only last ten seconds if he went down there. In short, Alex had not solved his problems.

CHAPTER 11

THE FOURTH DAY

THE THIRD DAY ON THE OTHER SIDE had been a productive, if exhausting ordeal. If it hadn't been for all his experience meditating, it would have been hard for Alex to stay so focused.

He slept like a log that night and slept right through the morning. He knew it was late thanks to his watch. He couldn't quite remember how many days he'd been there. He thought this was the fourth day but he was finding it hard to keep track. He squinted into the darkness, but there was nothing new to see.

At least Alex didn't have to worry about his energy supply anymore. No more need to gather and save every ounce of energy he could. Fortified by this knowledge, he was eager to get started with it.

Out of curiosity, Alex took out the glowing

moss from the lower part of the rock with his spear and checked it with the Scanner. It didn't show anything. Maybe it only worked on living creatures. He checked the caterpillars again, but he couldn't see any change there either. He wasn't even sure whether he could eat these things or not. On the Other Side, it was possible to find edible plants and monsters. He'd tasted the moss before but it just tasted grassy and bitter. In any case, it wasn't really food he was worried about. He would deal with that later.

It was time to get to work on his fighting skills. He knew that he could now use any of them, even if they weren't all fully developed. But his main ally was the Pump. He could just keep going and the Pump would do the rest.

Alex looked at the creatures thoughtfully. Maybe he could throw something else at them but, apart from the spear, there was nothing to hand. Or if only he could just set them on fire. Now, that would be a good skill to have! He'd love to see if they would burn.

Alex snapped himself out of this daydreaming.

"I need to get cracking," he thought to himself as he checked the container.

There was only about ten percent of what had been in there before. It wasn't the best situation to be in, but Alex remembered what they'd told him in training that prospectors could always use their internal supply for training if they had no other source to turn to. It wasn't as efficient and would take longer, but it might just work in these circumstances.

The technique was extremely simple, a prospector would direct his attention to a point just below the navel and, fixing all his attention on that one point, would try to do something with it. This method was especially useful to people who'd trained in Martial arts and many prospectors had become well versed in that practice since the discovery of the Other Side. It wasn't a method that helped everyone, but Alex was prepared to give it a try.

Alex fixed all his attention on that one point of his body and imagined energy shooting out of it. Predictably, nothing happened straight away but, if it was that easy, people would have conquered the Other Side a long time ago.

After three long hours of monotonous training, Alex's energy had decreased ever so slightly. He looked at his interface .

[Energy: 34/35]

"Fantastic!" He rubbed his hands together and his eyes lit up with glee.

It was exactly the small result he'd been trying to achieve. Normally, it would have taken him one or two days to reach it, but, the main thing here was attention and concentration and he had all these qualities in abundance.

This small loss of energy showed that he had somehow managed to detect his energy storage and could therefore interact with it further. Now he just needed to increase the flow rate. Strangely enough, in this case, energy loss was a good thing. If it was going somewhere, that meant it was being used on something.

Other prospectors used energy infusions to refill their energy supply but, fortunately for Alex, he had the advantage of the Pump.

But the end result still depended on luck. Some people took months of training to get anywhere at all. Only a few lucky ones with talent could get results quickly. The only question was what they would get in the end.

Alex couldn't afford to spend a long time training here so he decided to get started on the caterpillars straightaway . Sitting down on his backpack, he looked at them and thought about what exactly he would do. He needed something simple, but effective.

If he'd been at the base camp, he could have asked the other prospectors to show him a trick or two. It would have been easier than developing his own skill and he'd also have a better chance of learning something useful instead of some rubbish. But there were some advantages to Alex's position. If his idea worked, Alex would get his own personal ability, rather than a copy of someone else's skill. Such a skill is often stronger and easier to develop.

"Ok, here we go," thought Alex. He gathered his thoughts and started focusing on the area of space around the monsters.

Last time he'd tried to feel the excess energy

around, but with there now not being any, he tried to focus on the space itself. What did Alex even know about space? He remembered some general information from training, but nothing specific and useful. Then he thought about it from another angle. His talent wasn't based on theory, but on physical sensations, so he should try and use that as much as possible.

But what kind of physical attack could be based on a sense of space? How could you even attack with space?

That's when he remembered the Barrier. There was a reason it was called the "Spatial Barrier." Alex started it up, trying to feel all of it. He tried to feel the shield in front of him, but his hand simply passed through to the other side. Of course! The Barrier acted selectively, it only worked on enemies and their attacks. Then he imagined he had a knife in his hand and brought his hand to his chest. There was a strange sensation as his fingers touched the shield. It was as if they weren't touching it at all but were being gripped by something. It was a small interference but when Alex applied a little more pressure, it intensified. The shield was not like an invisible wall, but like a viscous, impenetrable space.

That feeling was all he had to go on. It was the only bit of information he had to cling to and Alex knew that using this skill was probably his best chance of getting out of here.

The caterpillars hadn't noticed Alex's struggles. They hadn't moved a muscle in all this time.

He looked at one of them and concentrated all his attention on the space around it while thinking about activating the Barrier. He was trying to activate the shield just at the right point so that part of it would enter the creature's skin.

*   *   *

He continued working like that for the rest of the day. Alex could work like that for hours with full concentration, but by the evening, he was completely drained and had no energy left at all. He knew all this monotonous work wasn't ideal, but Alex didn't have the luxury of being able to loaf around and do what he wanted and he knew from his meditation training, that hard work pays off.

By the end of the day, his head was throbbing and his eyes were watering. Utterly exhausted, he lay down on a rock and looked up at the dark vault of the cave. Although it was dark, Alex actually found that quite comforting. He loved darkness and had often meditated at night, gazing into the starry sky. Now the darkness and silence soothed him and helped to relieve his tension.

Memories of people he cared about came back: his parents, his sisters, his doctor, a couple of friends. In recent years Alex had paid little attention to these people as he became more and more wrapped up in his own little world, only really communicating with his doctor and, even then, only because it had been absolutely necessary. It was wrong. He'd been too absorbed in his own problems and forgot about those closest to him.

Alex made a promise to himself there and then that if he got out of this cave and somehow survived this crazy place, he would find time to visit his family. A man can't be only concerned with his work, he has to keep in touch with his loved ones. At that moment, he fell into a deep sleep.

CHAPTER 12

ONE AGAINST EIGHT

THE NEXT DAY ALEX WOKE UP fresh and determined. After a quick stretch and a bite to eat, he went down to the lower boulder, trying not to make too much noise. He'd decided it was best to keep the noise to a minimum, just in case there was something else lurking nearby in the darkness.

He hadn't come up with any new ideas overnight so he went straight back to his training from yesterday. He felt like a marathon runner. If he'd had a choice, he would have trained for two or three hours a day and the rest of the time he would have been hunting. That style of living would have done wonders for his development out here.

Maybe the problem was the low energy reserve, he thought, trying to remember how much energy a standard fireball requires. If memory served him right, it was about a hundred units per shot, which was more than his reserve capacity. It would be difficult to have such a skill at level zero.

Alex believed in his talent. He just didn't have enough energy for the initial activation. But how was he going to find a skill that was both powerful and remote and, at the same time, not cost too much energy? And all this without any support, surrounded by monsters.

*   *   *

Unable to come up with anything groundbreaking, Alex continued his training. However, despite the efforts, his training led to nothing. Day after day, Alex continued the training but there was no improvement. He was slowly starting to lose heart but he stubbornly continued, just as some lonely traveler, wandering through the desert, knows that it is necessary to continue moving in one direction.

Alex knew it was important to sustain his effort. His growing tension was just a sign that he was approaching his limit and that meant he was definitely getting closer.

By the eleventh day, Alex knew he only had enough water left for two days. He'd been saving it as best he could but he knew it wouldn't last much longer. Once that ran out, dehydration would set in. With that he knew that his concentration would inevitably drop and the chances of forming a skill would greatly diminish. He decided that if nothing happened by then he would make a run for it. With a bit of luck he might find some water before the monsters caught up to him.

Realizing that he was running out of options, Alex took out the last of the powder. He felt like every ounce counted right now.

He sprinkled it out onto the nearest stone. There was so little left that it was almost impossible to see. Alex swayed back and forth a little to find his balance, straightened his shoulders, relaxed his body and focused all his attention on the nearest monster. Having tensed his body as much as he could he once again mentally created the Barrier next to it.

Whack!

A cut appeared on the stone grey skin of the crawler. And this time the creature was not indifferent. It didn't scream, but began rolling around on the stone floor.

"Yes, I got it!" exclaimed Alex, but he immediately cut himself short as he whispered quietly: "Status!"

[Signatures: Rare: *Scissors of Space (1%)]*

Scissors. The name was a good one, even if it wasn't entirely accurate but Alex didn't care. It wasn't about the name, it was about the result.

The interface showed that the reserve was completely spent:

[Energy: 0/35 units]

Although the skill was useful, it was quick to use up energy. A predatory smile lit up Alex's face. It was time to test out this ability he'd worked so hard for.

Despite his stamina and calm behavior in all situations, Alex was not a robot. He was a human being and success after a long series of failures caused jubilation and euphoria. Suddenly the gloomy cave with its dull green twilight didn't seem so oppressing.

The tension of the last few days was replaced by excitement. It was still unclear exactly how well it would work, but now at least there was something that could make a difference. And when a man has both a plan and the means for its realization, it changes him. Alex suddenly felt like a predatory eagle, not the lost prospector he was half an hour ago.

A thirst for action seized him and Alex set about his revenge. Whack! Another cut appeared on the caterpillar's body. The scissors themselves made no sound, but when they struck, there was a thud, as if someone was driving a knife into a sandbag. No blood flowed from the wound as the monster writhed in pain.

The wounded creature jumped back deeper into the cave. His companions paid him little attention.

Whack! It started to crawl away a little more. Alex tried to strike again, but it turned out that the Scissors only worked at a certain distance from where he was standing.

The next eight hours were spent practicing. Alex tried opening the Scissors to hit a nearby stone until the skill got to thirty per cent, after which the development stopped. As with the Barrier, a fight with a real enemy was required for further progress. But at least now, Alex could summon the Scissors instinctively with a simple mental effort.

Though the day was almost over, he wanted to keep going and set to work on the other creatures around

Whack! ... Whack! ... Whack! The blows came one after the other. He tried to hit the same spot every time but, usually after a few attacks, they ran away and he never actually managed to kill one.

But Alex didn't believe that his ability was weak, rather the monsters were too strong. Even a spear hadn't made much impression on them before. Their skin was tough and it was going to take more than that to do some more damage. Fortunately, judging from their wounds, these monsters didn't have high regeneration rates.

He tried to draw them closer, hanging his feet off the cliff, but the creatures didn't react. Then he activated the Barrier, jumped down and immediately climbed back up. It worked! The stupid creatures took the bait. Whack! ...Whack! He made connection with one of them but they soon realized the trap and slithered off to where they'd come from.

Looking at them retreating, Alex decided that

they weren't so stupid after all. But why didn't they crawl away completely? Maybe it was some instinct they had that sooner or later their prey would try and venture out again. So maybe it was time to do just that.

Alex jumped down and straightened up, but the monsters were still wary. "Not as stupid as you look," thought Alex. But as soon as he took a step towards them, they cautiously moved forward. Without waiting any longer, Alex scrambled back up the rock.

Sadly, they remained where they were. So he activated the Barrier, went down again and walked forward. Once they started moving towards him, he backed up until his back was against the rock. They were inching closer every second. Suddenly one of the caterpillars rushed forward towards him.

Seeing this Alex turned round and climbed back up again. There was only one of them approaching and he could have hit it with the Scissors but he didn't want to take such the risk. It was time for the second part of the plan.

Reactivating the barrier, he sat down on the edge of the boulder and slowly lowered his foot, keeping his gaze fixed on the monster's face. The creature was clearly excited and even arched his whole body in anticipation.

Alex felt like he was a stuntman sticking his head into the mouth of a lion.

Bang! He didn't register the moment of the attack, the sting came out too fast. But the barrier held! A moment later, the Scissors were activated and the monster's stinger fell to the stone floor with a low squelching sound.

The monster began to wriggle and roll around on the floor, no longer paying any attention to Alex. The other creatures took fright and started to crawl away.

After a few minutes the monster started to calm down but it was still very much alive. However, Alex was almost dancing with excitement. He was ready to jump down and beat the creature with his spear! He would have strangled the bastard with his bare hands if he could. These eight freaks stood between him and everything he cared about.

Having calmed down, Alex had to admit that in many ways he'd got lucky. He'd risked everything, but managed to unlock several individual skills. And that was worth a lot! Although this ordeal wasn't over, he felt like the end might be near. All he had to do now was deal with the rest of the monsters.

He looked around and, once again, used the Scissors on all the creatures he could reach. They crawled away. The monster who'd just lost his sting had crawled away slightly, but it was just twitching and lying down now. The loss of the stinger had obviously taken a heavy toll on its morale, if the cave creatures had any.

"So much for this proud subterranean kingdom. All running away like cowards. At least one of them won't get away from me," thought Alex to himself with a smile on his face.

His body clock told him it was evening, but he didn't want to rest. After so much effort, adrenaline was racing around his body.

Alex got down and brazenly headed towards the monsters, not forgetting to activate the Barrier once more. The creatures, sensing his determination, slowly crawled away. He rushed after them. Even at level zero, his speed was faster, so the monsters couldn't escape, but the whole pack, except for the wounded one, moved in a single formation towards the dead end where Alex had first appeared after his crossing to the Other Side.

That suited him just fine. Without waiting for the reserve to be replenished, he attacked the wounded creature with all his strength. He stabbed him with the spear as hard as he could. The monster hardly resisted. It could only move haphazardly in circles as the blows rained down on it. Finally, after the tenth strike, the creature went still.

Having quickly collected the pollen, Alex made his way towards the rest of the group. Hearing his approach, the whole group turned around in one movement and rushed forward. Alex immediately ran to shelter, but there was no need to climb up. The monsters had stopped.

"What, too scared now!?" he shouted in fury, forgetting about his promise not to make any noise.

For the next half hour Alex ran around the pack, trying to separate them, but nothing worked.

They resolutely stayed as one. Then he chose one of the caterpillars and started targeting it with the Scissors. In half an hour, after a lot of activations, the creature had died. By that time, they'd given up trying to reach him and now just moved from place to place trying to avoid him. This turned into a pattern and went on for several hours. Alex ruthlessly kept going, he didn't plan on sleeping. He wanted to finish them off, by any means he could. He didn't want them crawling away while he slept.

So he chased them around the cave, not letting any of them escape until the last one was dead.

Once he was finished, Alex was exhausted, mentally as well as physically. After collecting pollen from the last creature, he went to sleep on the rocks without even looking at the interface. He'd figure out the rest tomorrow.

CHAPTER 13

LOOKING FOR WATER

ALEX WOKE UP AND MADE A REVISION of his supplies. There was enough water to last till the evening, so he would have to go look for some more today. At least, since his enemies were dead, there was nothing to stop him from doing that now. He was about to go down, but then something stopped him. Something in the surrounding rocks seemed strange.

"What the hell!" Four camouflaged cave crawlers stood directly below him.

The creatures were well hidden but, in a short time, Alex had learnt the surroundings so well that he knew the position of almost every rock. He took a closer look. They looked like ordinary crawlers, just like the ones that had kept him pinned down for so long. The scanner confirmed his suspicions:

[Cave Crawler: level 1]

A familiar enemy had taken the place of the previous pack. Maybe there was a reason for that. Did the monsters somehow sense that there was potential prey hiding here? Alex was the only human in the whole cave, so maybe they were just drawn to him. He could imagine them drooling right now in anticipation of a potential victim.

He was partially glad to have new visitors. At least this time they wouldn't surprise him out of nowhere, they were clearly there in front of him. Encouraged by this fact, Alex decided to greet them with his new skill the Scissors. They didn't really appreciate this welcome and, after receiving a few painful blows, they crawled away from the rock.

He had already learnt that it took seven or eight blows to kill a single crawler which, in itself, was an excellent result and proof of the Scissors' strength.

In general, prospectors ranked attacking skills by their effectiveness per use, in other words, how many times you needed to use it to kill a monster. Alex remembered how the rankings worked. An attacking ability was considered strong if it killed a human-sized enemy in one or two blows, or four to seven blows if the monster was a level higher.

According to this scale, Scissors were an excellent attack skill, as seven uses was all Alex had needed to kill these cave crawlers. It would be even more useful on something smaller.

Eager to continue the fight, Alex proceeded to exterminate the pack. This group was smaller and weaker than the last one. The creatures quickly ran away, but they were easily cornered by Alex who then finished them off without mercy.

By this time, the bodies of yesterday's victims had already started to rot. It was hard to even recognize what they had looked like. It didn't take long for remains to decompose on the Other Side and in a few days there would be nothing left of them. The same applied to human corpses, they also quickly disappeared and relatives back on Earth were often left without bodies for burial. In general, everything decayed quickly. It was believed that this was the Other Side's way of returning energy to itself. Fortunately, everyone knew about this, so prospectors took extra care when bringing food over. Only certain food was suitable as most ordinary rations just didn't last.

But there were a few practical advantages on the Other Side. Alex had been on the rock for almost two weeks in difficult conditions and his whole body seemed to be functioning more or less normally. On Earth, he was sure it would have been a different story.

After collecting all the pollen, he climbed back up the rock. Now he could go for water, but first he needed to check his progress:

*[**Level:** 0*
__Energy:__ 35/35 units.
__Transformation:__ Body: 10.8% / Structure:

14.4% / Brain: 10.3%
  Signatures. Simple: *Walker (15%)*
  Rare: *Space Barrier (34%), Space Scanner (38%), Pump* (52%), Space Scissors (42%).*
  Talents: *Touch of Death, Sense of Space]*

The energy structure had transformed more than any other aspects. That was thanks to his newfound skill Scissors, which he'd made plenty of use of. The skill matrix relied heavily on energy, so it was this aspect that benefitted the most from killing all these monsters.

But it was the star next to Pump that caught his attention. The skill had crossed the fifty per cent mark. But how? Alex remembered the skill getting to fifty per cent, but it had frozen there. For further development he needed to create some special conditions, but he wasn't sure exactly which ones. Had he somehow managed to do that without realizing?

Alex started to go over the events of yesterday and today and after a few minutes realized that it was all about the increased energy background. When dying, creatures emitted pollen. This evaporated and increased the energy background. When fighting, Alex didn't always have time to collect all the powder, but the Pump never stopped for a second. So, the conditions for the growth of the skill were excess energy.

But that wasn't all, Alex wanted to know what the original strengthening of the most valuable ability gave. Reinforcement meant matrix transformation and new possibilities. And what's most important to the Pump? Of course, the speed of filling the energy reservoir. To test it, he drained all the energy on the barriers, took out his watch and checked the refill speed. Yes, the time had decreased. If before, the reserve had been filled in five minutes, now it only took two and a half.

Boosted by this news and the new possibilities that went with it, Alex packed his rucksack and moved towards the sound of water.

In a few minutes Alex had reached the end of the section, beyond which the cave widened. The walls were hidden in darkness, and the ceiling was so high that its outlines were lost in the black gloom.

The glowing moss grew in significant quantities on the walls, lighting the way forward. But go a little further away and you were plunged into complete darkness where the small specks of moss dotted on the infrequent boulders did little to illuminate the surroundings.

Last time, Alex had gone to the right and that was where he'd first encountered the cave crawlers. This time he chose the left, as that was where he could hear running water.

The rucksack, though thin, was pressing heavily on his shoulders. Alex dropped it, deciding it would be easier to do some scouting without it. He ventured out in each direction, taking care not to move too far away.

With spear in hand, he walked along the wall. He scanned everywhere for suspicious rocks, but all the monsters seemed to have disappeared. The central part of the cave seemed the most dangerous. Looking in that direction, Alex really couldn't see anything and decided he wouldn't go there under any circumstances.

He walked very slowly, taking extra care, because even with enhanced skills, scanning took a lot of time. Alex advanced slowly but surely, at no more than a mile an hour, but he still hadn't seen a single monster.

He thought about the universal law of averages and as soon as he thought about it, a sound of pursuit could be heard from behind. He'd almost missed the sound as he'd been dragging his rucksack at the time.

Alex turned round sharply and saw two undersized figures running towards him, exactly the same creatures that had attacked him on the first day. Out of surprise, he activated his scanner instead of Scissors

[Cave Goblin Sniffer: level 1]

"Dammit!" His own voice brought him back to his senses. Alex hurriedly dropped his backpack, and thought about what to do

The monsters approached quickly, so Alex turned tail and ran. Unfortunately, these creatures were faster than the caterpillars and they slowly began to catch up to him.

As he ran, Alex gained energy and as soon as the reserve was full, he hit out at his pursuers.

Whack! The leg of the nearest figure was sliced off and he rolled around on the floor, squealing in pain.

The second monster froze. Even during the first fight, Alex had noticed that these creatures were cowardly and cautious. As the creature froze, Alex turned back around and ran towards the dead end. The monster's slight pause had given him a head start and he managed to reach the shelter and climb up.

The goblin reached the rock and tried to jump up after him. He would have succeeded if the rock hadn't been so sloping, but instead it just clawed at the rock face and rolled back down.

Alex cursed himself that he hadn't thought to hit it with his spear.

The interface showed that there were only fourteen units in reserve, which meant he had to hold out for another minute and a half.

The monster noticed the corpses of the crawlers and it stopped as if it had been shot.

It stiffened and drew back slightly, bearing its fangs. The creature's face, normally without expression, now looked as if it was twisted with anger.

Alex was glad of this effect, as it gave him that little bit of breathing space to refill his energy reserve. After a few moments, the monster gathered itself to leap onto the rock again. However, it was no longer a cautious, slightly cowardly opponent that it was a moment ago. It had become something akin to a rabid dog.

It was rushing at him frantically, but Alex couldn't hit it with his spear. The monster couldn't get to him but Alex didn't want to get too close to the edge, for fear of falling off.

Once it realized that it couldn't reach him from there, the monster stopped and started running around the rock. In a swift movement, it rushed to the other side and tried to take Alex by surprise. Fortunately, Alex was ready for it. He quickly jabbed at the creature with his spear, catching him full on in the face. The creature slithered down the rock, writhing in pain. He hadn't done much damage with the blow, but he had clearly made it even angrier.

"That pissed him off," thought Alex. He would gladly have gone back to fighting the cave crawlers in that moment.

In rage, the goblin-like creature tried jumping up again, but Alex responded in the same way. The more time went on, the more annoyed the monster was getting. Things were escalating quickly and Alex knew he would have stood little chance if he hadn't had the high ground to save him.

Finally, the reserve was filled. Moments later, the Scissors were activated. At that very moment, the monster was moving and he ran straight into one of the blades, piercing his body right through. Alex noticed how the blades of the Scissors seemed to hang in the air for a few seconds before disappearing.

Once they disappeared, the monster fell to the ground, rolling around in agony. Just to make sure, Alex activated the scissors a second time to finish the job. Thinking everything to be over, he approached the corpse to gather pollen.

To his surprise, despite what it had been through, the creature was still alive. Seeing Alex, it started hauling itself towards him. It was moving its arms frantically and looked completely mad.

But now Alex had the upper hand. Despite its rage, there wasn't very much it could do lying on the ground. Whack! The scissors hit the base of its neck, but, miraculously, it still didn't die. The blade wasn't able to cut through the neck in one blow as Alex had hoped.

Once the energy reserve had been restored, the Scissors struck the wheezing enemy for a third time. Its head finally separated from its torso and rolled onto the floor. Finally, the monster's body went still as its head stared vacantly somewhere into the darkness of the cave.

* * *

This latest encounter had shown that Alex was far from safety. As much as he didn't want to, he had to move to find water so, after a short rest, he got up, loaded his rucksack and walked on.

Although Alex felt unprotected near the cave wall, he was afraid to go into the darkness, so he kept the wall close to him, moving forward gingerly. The more Alex advanced, the more he could hear running water. It sounded like an underground river or maybe there was some kind of waterfall up ahead.

After a minute or two, a glow appeared ahead of him, and the closer he got, the brighter it became. Eventually, the wall curved round to the right which brought him to a turning. Looking around the corner, he saw a remarkable sight. The walls here were almost completely overgrown with this luminous moss which illuminated the cave much more than further back. The moss here had grown so thick that the rich, almost emerald light it emitted filled the darkness of the cave. Alex blinked, half dazzled by the bright light.

Now he could see everything clearly, all the suspicious rocks and bumps were much easier to make out. However, his experiences since crossing over had taught him to keep his guard up. The Other Side still wasn't a place to get too comfortable.

Alex's scanner worked at a range of a hundred feet, so from where he was, Alex tried his best to scan everything he could. Sitting behind a rock, Alex watched everything for a long time, but he couldn't make out anything suspicious.

The only thing he did see was a large crack in the very corner of the cave. It was a dozen feet wide and went vertically upwards towards the high ceiling of the cave.

On Earth, life usually gathered in places where there was water but that didn't seem to be the case here, as no sign of life appeared in the next half an hour.

"Maybe I just don't know enough about the inhabitants here," thought Alex to himself. During training he'd been more interested in how and with what it was easier to kill them, not in how they lived. But surely, they'd need water at some point? Having said that, he did recall how the caterpillar-like creatures hadn't needed much sustenance in their long watch over him.

Unable to see any hidden surprises, Alex made his way to the crack in the rock. It started several feet off the ground so Alex threw his rucksack up, then climbed his way up after it. Once he'd got up there, Alex could see it wasn't much different in here than from the rest of the cave. There was just more moss and, therefore, more light. The passage was about two hundred yards long and from the other end he could hear the distinct sound of running water.

Alex put aside his rucksack, took his spear in both hands and slowly moved taking care with every step. At the very end he came across a section of wall completely free of moss. He activated the Scanner:

[Creature: level 1]

Just a creature? It wasn't like any of the other creatures he'd seen before. However, Alex didn't know all the properties of the Scanner yet. There was obviously something there. But no matter how much he looked, he couldn't see anything. Just a bare rock face. Maybe it was detecting the moss as a possible life form, but it had never done that before. Besides, there was no moss on the wall. Alex was puzzled and now felt even more on edge than he had before.

Moving away from this suspicious area, he walked to the edge and looked out. A dark expanse of water came into view. A river was flowing beneath him and from somewhere below came the sound of a waterfall. Between him and the river was a narrow bank, only a dozen feet wide. Oddly enough, there wasn't a lot of moss near the water and there was only enough light to see the rocky shore. The other side of the river was so far he couldn't make out the other side at all.

The gigantic river flowed gently and leisurely and all Alex wanted to do was go down and get a drink. But first he had to deal with the suspicious area on the wall. He activated a Barrier and came close to it. Suddenly something flew out of the wall and hit the screen. Alex quickly recoiled. Looking over himself he could see he wasn't hurt and the impact hadn't affected the Barrier either. He quickly grabbed his spear and lunged forward with all his might. It was only then that he noticed something, some small layer of translucent material on the rock. Maybe the scanner was analyzing it now. Then it came up on the screen:

[Transparent Polyp: Level 1]

So there was something in front of him. Something with level one, but very small and clearly very weak. Strange that the name hadn't immediately come up.

From a distance Alex hit the polyp once more, this time with Scissors. They made a dent on the stone surface, but that was it. As far as Alex could tell it was still there

Out of curiosity he approached again, holding the Barrier at the ready. He waited a little, then the polyp struck again. This time, Alex was ready and he pierced it with his spear. He tried to pin it down to the floor but even there the transparent creature merged with the surface. It was a little bit like trying to impale a lump of jelly.

Next, Alex tried hitting it with the spear shaft. This killed it immediately and then the small, lifeless corpse began to emit pollen. But there wasn't much use in collecting it as the amount was so tiny.

Satisfied with his work, Alex straightened up and started scanning the shore. The Scanner immediately detected several more polyps lying on large boulders. The creatures, though small, were a worry, as they were numerous and well camouflaged. He also thought about how he would have to kill them by hand as the Scissors were too bulky for such a small target. At least they wouldn't aggressively attack him, but he still needed to get to the water. Alex decided to activate the Barrier several times to form a large circle of defense. Once he'd fortified himself in this way, he started making his way to the shore. He saw two polyps right in front of him as he moved. The nearest one was only a few steps away. Alex picked up a large rock and threw it straight towards the creature. It was a direct hit and the transparent creature fell to the floor, apparently lifeless

It was still moving, but Alex could see that the blow had split it in two and there was no chance it would last much longer. Alex switched his attention to the second creature. There were no suitable stones to hand, so he just ran closer and knocked the creature down with his spear. This one didn't offer much resistance and was dead after a couple of blows. They definitely weren't as serious opponents as the ones he had encountered before.

"That's it," he whispered contentedly. "The way is clear."

But just as he relaxed, a sharp pain burnt his shoulder blade. Alex cried out in surprise, turned round and saw a small ripple on the wall.

"Where the hell did that come from?" thought Alex as he turned around.

Out of the corner of his eye he saw a couple more polyps and realized he was in trouble. It turned out that the creatures could move and fast. Fortunately, when they moved, they lost their invisibility.

"Dammit! I think I've pissed off the whole colony," surmised Alex hopelessly.

At that moment, three polyps shot from the wall almost simultaneously. The barrier deflected them, but it was slightly damaged after that. The next shots could really do some damage, so he had to run. It didn't matter where, he just couldn't stay there waiting for them to attack.

The path back to the original cave was not an option. As well as the trio of polyps who'd just attacked, there were fresh creatures crawling along the wall that would gladly welcome a victim like Alex. He had no idea how they'd appeared so quickly.

Thinking quickly, Alex spun round and in two jumps reached the river, noticing several more polyps on both sides. They seemed to be everywhere now!

Without stopping, he hurriedly jumped into the river and ran a couple of yards. Luckily it wasn't too deep where he'd landed.

Looking back, Alex took stock of his situation. At least fifteen polyps surrounded him. That was the bad news. The good news was that they weren't getting into the water, just sitting motionlessly on the shore. Another five polyps were hanging on the wall, blocking any potential escape route.

The wound was no longer bothering him, there was pollen to deal with that, but it still felt numb. If it got any worse, he'd struggle to climb back up where he'd come from.

He tried walking downstream, but the polyps tenaciously followed his step. They did move slowly though, which gave Alex a glimmer of hope. If he could draw them away, he could run back quickly to where he had come from before they could chase him. But then there were still the five at the cave entrance he'd have to think about.

He thought about throwing rocks, but as it turned out, there were only heavy boulders around, which he could hardly lift, and even if he did, he wouldn't be able to throw them far.

He'd also noticed a slimy residue on his shoulder left over from the hit he'd just taken. It was eating away at his clothes and the fabric had split around the wound on his back. So even if he decided to step on them, he'd have no shoes left at the end of it! So, of all the options, he was left with only a spear.

An idea popped into his head. What if the Barrier could be used on his feet? That way he could step on them with everything well protected. To test his idea, Alex made a large shield out of the barrier and moved a dozen feet along the riverbed. The polyps followed him as he moved.

Then he formed another barrier under his right foot and jumped on the nearest monster.

Bullseye! His foot landed right on top of it. The other creatures lashed out, but the defensive shield held! He moved back in the water, once again out of their range. That was one down. Now, he just had to deal with the others

Feeling slightly rejuvenated, Alex stood in the water and started gathering energy for a second attack.

Although Alex had managed to kill several polyps, they'd been quickly replaced as more of them arrived. He still had a lot to deal with.

"It's better not to rush," Alex said to himself. "I *will* get through them."

Having gathered energy, he prepared to go again but, suddenly, he received a stinging blow in his leg.

"Ahh you fucking..." the blow wasn't strong, but it was extremely painful.

He looked down and saw a fish splashing in the water. In a rage, he struck it with his spear and killed it straight away. He pulled it out of the water to look at it closer. It was just a plain-looking eel.

The scanner confirmed just as much:

[Eel: 0 level]

Alex recognized it because he'd heard this creature could be found in two places, the Plains and the Foothills and it could also be eaten. Because of its small size it wasn't hunted for pollen, but it was hunted for food.

This was the first piece of food that Alex had managed to find in this godforsaken place. He began to think about how he would cook it when another stinging blow interrupted his musings.

"What the hell!" He screamed out, looking into the water where another eel was swimming.

Without waiting for another attack, he rushed along the shore. The time for standing in the water was over, he had to get back into that cave. Looking further down the river, Alex could see the water bubbling as if something bigger was lurking there and, suddenly, he had no desire to stay in the water whatsoever.

He jumped out onto dry land and turned towards the pack of polyps. Gathering some energy, he put up a shield of the Barrier, then another one. The pack was getting closer. But he didn't want to fight them, he just wanted to draw them away from the crack in the cave wall. A little more and they were exactly where Alex wanted them to be.

He started to rush back at full speed. He ran through the water, just out of reach of the polyps, all the while, noticing how the water was bubbling away not far away from where he was.

Moving swiftly, Alex ran away from the river and back towards the crack in the cave wall, still guarded by five of those small, now well-known to Alex creatures.

They were still hanging there on the wall, their bodies shaking slightly so they could just about be seen. One sat in the center, and two others guarded the edges. Alex cursed his luck that they seemed to be guarding the cave so well.

"It's now or never!" he thought feverishly as he sprinted towards them. Bang! The barrier didn't fail him and he rushed straight through them as they scattered on all sides. He felt one of them strike out but, again, the Barrier came to the rescue.

Alex struck out with his spear in anger and saw it fall to the ground, lifeless.

Without looking back, he scrambled up and hauled himself through the hole he'd come down from.

Once he felt like he was in the clear, Alex sat down and leaned against the wall. With sweat running down his back and his heart threatening to jump out of his chest, only now did he feel safe.

He quickly took a swig of water from one of his water bottles as he thought about what to do next.

CHAPTER 14

The Fishing Trip

TIRED, WET AND HUNGRY, Alex decided not to relax, but to finish off the remaining creatures that were crawling below. But it was dangerous to go down — his usual tactics of "hit and retreat" wouldn't work here.

Prospectors usually hunted in groups, against an enemy of their own level. A few coordinated blows were normally enough to kill a monster in a flash. Uniting as a large squad was always a very efficient way to deal with lots of enemies. Of course, there was never enough loot for everyone, but the risk was always low.

In addition, they normally had the benefit of some protective gear or armor so they often felt very safe going out into combat situations.

Alex had neither armor nor companions, but he had the Pump. Besides, he could evolve faster on his own. He kept his eyes on the passageway until the first polyp appeared.

"They don't give up easy," Alex thought to himself. "But no matter. Now it's time to get even."

They slowly started to appear as they came crawling up from the shore. He didn't have to lure them this time. They seemed to be coming straight to him.

With the protection of the Barrier, he jumped up and struck the nearest polyp with his spear, immediately drawing back out of reach of the others. The monster he struck was killed instantly.

"They don't attack quickly," Alex noticed happily.

It seemed that he just had to kill them as quickly as they came and, if there were several of them, the Barrier would help to repel any unwanted attacks.

After a few minutes of repeated attacks, the wave of monsters dried up. Alex walked cautiously to the edge of the cave and looked around carefully. There were no polyps nearby and the river looked flat and calm.

Tired but satisfied, he went down to the river and scooped up some water in his hands. It was so refreshing to drink! He had been told before coming here that any river water was safe to drink. There was also no winter, an always mild climate and very fertile soil. If it wasn't for the monsters, the Other Side might have actually been quite a pleasant place to wander.

Having filled the water bottles, he returned to

the rock crevice and wondered where he could spend the night. The crevice in the rock was about five feet from the ground, so he was out of reach of a lot of creatures. But he knew there were still plenty who could scramble up there while he wasn't looking.

Despite all these thoughts running around his head, he was too tired to think of a better plan. In the end, Alex just made a bed in the center of the passage and went to sleep. The latest events had tired him out so much that he instantly passed out.

Alex woke up and immediately checked his status.

[Level: 0
Energy: 35/35 units
Transformation: Body: 12.4% / Structure: 16.5% / Brain: 11.7%
Signatures: Simple: Walker (15%)
Rare: Space Barrier (42%), Space Scanner (46%), Pump (54%), Space Scissors (44%)*
Talents: Touch of Death, Sense of Space]

He saw that the Scanner and Barrier had grown by ten and eight per cent respectively. The first thing to do was to strenghten both skills, and there was no better place for that than the riverbank.

While the Scanner could be used anywhere, the Barrier could be developed only in combat, and it was much more preferable to fight polyps than anything larger. Even if one of them managed to break through his defense, Alex knew their attacks wouldn't be enough to kill him. In short, they could be the perfect sparring partners.

He also wanted to try and catch some fish in an effort to mix up his diet a little bit. He'd also been told that eel on the Other Side tastes much better than any fish you could find on Earth.

Having made up his mind, Alex walked down to the shore. There were no polyps nearby. Unlike crawlers and other monsters, they were known for normally staying in one place. He looked further upstream and he saw a group of them gathered closely a few hundred yards away. That would be a good place to start.

Alex reactivated the Barrier and calmly approached the nearest monster. It, like many others, was sitting on a small boulder. For some reason, they seemed to prefer resting on boulders than on the ground.

The polyp fired as soon as Alex was in range. Again, the Barrier did its job. It continued to strike out at him, but the Barrier was equal to everything that was thrown at it. Alex stood there letting his defenses take the hit, until he felt the Barrier weakening. Then he took a step back and the polyp immediately followed him.

Yesterday's experience showed that it was better to kill them individually away from the pack. That way the rest of them were more likely to ignore one death and Alex wouldn't have to deal with the swarm of revenge that would no doubt come his way. As soon as he thought he had drawn it far enough away, Alex finished it off with one blow to the head. The pump quickly refilled his energy reserve, then he went back for another one.

After repeating this cycle for six hours and fifty-three polyps, Alex looked at the Interface:

*[**Transformation:** Body: 14.3% / Structure: 19.1% / Brain: 12.9%]*

Sadly, killing a whole horde of polyps hadn't led to any groundbreaking changes. Even though they were a level above him, they were just too small to bring about any change in his development. He looked further down at his skill development:

*[**Signatures. Rare:** Spatial Barrier* (50%), Space Scanner* (50%)]*

The two skills there had definitely increased their capacity. Alex took a closer look at the Barrier

At first glance, not much had changed; the size, energy expenditure and lifespan had all remained the same. But there was a difference. The Barrier could be controlled. Earlier, when Alex wanted to increase his defense, he'd just used the skill, and its area doubled. But he knew that he couldn't double the shield. He could just pour energy into it, as if he was refueling it. And he could also choose whether to increase its life-span or the size of the shield.

Alex had also noticed how the Barrier had become more flexible and movable. He could stretch it in different directions and he could even wrap it around himself in the form of a ball. However, in doing so, the density of the screen decreased, and with it its protective properties. It was understandable, the larger the area, the thinner the screen. He knew that he'd have to spend a lot more energy to get more protection.

He created a sphere around himself and immediately tried to infuse it with energy. He could see the Barrier getting stronger and stronger but, eventually, the energy consumption for its upkeep equaled the flow drawn by the Pump. As a result, all the energy was going to the Barrier. Alex knew this was not practical. He had to find a way to better distribute his energy.

After dealing with the first skill, he moved on to the second.

"What do we have here?" thought Alex as he activated the Scanner. "Something rare but not very handy."

The previous Scanner had simply shown the name and level of monsters and for each detection it spent fifteen units of energy. It was more like a locator with a distance of a hundred feet. This new version had a range of a hundred and fifty feet.

But it wasn't enough for him, he wanted something more. Luckily, he had something. There was a new mode which, when activated, scanned everything in its radius. Once it was activated, Alex could feel all living creatures at once. The only downside was the energy consumption as it used up ten units per second. As good as this skill was, Alex just didn't have enough energy to make full use of it.

However, Alex wasn't completely discouraged. He knew his energy reserve would grow several times once he reached the next level and then he'd be able to make more use of it.

Having finished looking at the Interface, he finally got down to fishing. Nothing extraordinary happened, he just took off his shoes, walked into the river and switched on the Scanner.

For five minutes, he scanned the water around him and then an eel appeared from upstream. It hovered nearby, wary of swimming too close to the shore. Then Alex switched off the Scanner and waited a few seconds for his reserve to refill. Whack! The scissors cut the eel in half. He picked up what was left and threw it on the shore. A few minutes later, another one swam up to him.

Alex continued this process for a few minutes and, by the end of it, he'd killed five of them. Fortunately, they could be eaten raw so Alex didn't have long to wait before he could enjoy them. Also, the people teaching him had been right, they did taste better here than on Earth.

After he'd finished eating Alex set about doing another task he'd been neglecting. Washing himself. After two weeks of rough living his clothes and body were in serious need of a wash.

Once that job was done, Alex sat down contentedly and just thought about resting. Sitting back in the passage facing the river, he thoughtfully looked into the dark waters, feeling the fatigue and tension floating away with the stream. He did nothing else, just contemplated the water's surface, ignoring the noise of the distant waterfall, until his thoughts, doubts and worries were gone and only peace and calm remained.

CHAPTER 15

HUNTING IN THE CAVE

BY THE EVENING Alex had decided to return to the big cave. Although there were less big monsters here, the polyps were still a problem. Besides, the Barrier and Scanner had strengthened since he'd been here so he decided he'd rather take his chances with the Cave Crawlers.

At the thought of meeting them again, Alex was filled with a burst of excitement and confidence that he could now cope with a pack of these beasts without having to take cover like he had before. But he knew he still had to be careful. Despite his newfound capabilities, he was still far from invincible.

Another reason to go back to the cave was to gather all the pollen he could from the bigger monsters. With enough energy powder, he could activate the Walker. This skill worked quite simply.

Once activated through the interface the user would be transported back home. You just had to have enough energy. It was a useful skill to have, especially when one needed to escape from mortal danger. Alex knew that he'd have to kill at least a couple more cave crawlers before he had enough pollen for that.

*   *   *

In a cheerful but serious mood, Alex returned to the cave. He restocked his pockets with as much as he could for his next foray into unknown territory. He knew he would need everything he could get if he was going to go monster hunting!

He climbed down to the cave floor and looked left and right. He remembered he'd come from the right, but the path to the left led to uncharted territories. He ruled out walking away from the wall. Out there in the darkness he would be far too open to attack.

Alex was almost ready to go to his old refuge place, but after a short hesitation, he changed his mind. He had to push on further. One way or another he had to find out what was out there so, taking a deep breath, he moved slowly along the cave wall.

Alex prayed that he would meet more cave crawlers. They were much more preferable to the human-like goblin creatures he'd had to deal with. Alex felt the threat of something looming over him. He couldn't even rely on the Scanner as the range only went so far.

"Be nice to see them in the dark," he said to himself thoughtfully.

He needed a new skill, otherwise he knew he wouldn't survive here. After thinking over his options, Alex went for a simple solution — sight. It was a quick, cheap skill to acquire and, arguably, one of the most fundamental skills for anyone on the Other Side.

Having made his decision, Alex directed his energy reserve to his eyes while looking into the darkness. In this way, prospectors could easily get a simple ability related to the senses. So, just as they had all been told in their training, after half an hour of concentrating in this way, Alex felt a surge of energy, and a new line appeared in the interface:

[Signatures. Simple: *Night Vision (1%)]*

Straight away, Alex could see much better. Everything around became a little more discernible and he could suddenly make out a lot more than before. The outlines of distant boulders emerged from the gloom. Looking deeper into the cave, Alex could see clusters of green dots. It reminded him of the starry sky at night.

It took ten units of energy to activate the skill, and then two units every ten minutes. For any prospector, that was a very respectable exchange rate.

Alex was glad he'd discovered such a simple skill. It was ideal for his situation and the skill itself wasn't complicated, so he didn't need to worry about overspending on his energy structure.

Prospectors were advised to take no more than three or four skills at level zero and no more than two or three for each subsequent level. The number of skills depended on their complexity and how well they fit together. As the level increased, these restrictions decreased.

Instead of getting a new skill, it was always better to find a new use for the existing abilities, especially those related to talent. That's why Alex was so glad about Night Vision, because of its simplicity. It should hardly affect his development. He knew that the Scanner was probably a more useful long term skill but right now, stuck in this cave, Night Vision was a very welcome aid.

Alex had planned to form several classes of abilities: attacking, defensive, masking and strengthening the body and senses. In short, everything that a prospector might need for hunting monsters. Thanks to his efforts, Alex had nearly all the skills he needed.

"Not bad for a newbie with no support," he thought to himself.

He also wanted to get a healing ability but that wasn't a priority. He could heal a wound with pollen, that was enough for now.

Now that Alex could see more, he was able to move a lot quicker. He no longer shuffled forward step by step but was now able to move forward in swift movements while scanning the area around him. He'd also moved away from the wall and was now more in the open. Armed with the Night Vision, he felt like less of a target as he advanced in the darkness well away from the lighted cave wall.

As soon as he'd walked out into the open, his Night Vision proved its usefulness. Hiding behind a boulder just in front of him, Alex spotted a pair of goblins. Two of them were walking leisurely near the wall, occasionally stopping as if sniffing something out.

It was clear they preferred lighted areas, unlike the crawlers. They were much closer to humans than the cave crawlers.

They were slowly approaching where he was. Judging by their path, they were going to pass right past him, but Alex was sure they would smell him. He readied himself for another fight.

But they didn't notice him. They sauntered past, completely unaware of his presence. Alex wondered what they were looking for, why were they wandering around the cave? There was no food or water here. They couldn't be looking for people all the time, could they? Alex had ended up here by accident so he was sure that they weren't looking for other people like him.

As soon as the goblins moved away, Alex followed them, taking care to keep his distance. He wished he had a crossbow with him instead of a spear. Killing monsters from afar wasn't good for development, close combat was what he really needed to boost that. But, all the same, Alex wouldn't have refused a long-range weapon at that moment.

Thinking it over in his head, Alex decided just to go for it.

"Come on you little fuckers! I've got you now!" he shouted, running out at them from behind his cover.

From previous encounters, Alex knew that the goblins would be lost in an unfamiliar situation like this, but as soon as they got into a frenzy, they would go completely berserk. He hoped he'd finish them off before that.

They froze for a few seconds which gave Alex enough time to get close enough to strike out with the Scissors

Whack! The blade partially severed the neck of the first creature and it wheezed, clutching at the wound as it began to fall sideways.

Without stopping to think, Alex went straight to the second one. It stared at the approaching man in silence, its eyes empty, as if they were sizing him up. It didn't even look at its dying companion.

Whack! The blade of Alex's spear hit the monster full on. Just like before, it didn't have enough force to pierce through the body. The goblin waved its hand at Alex as if in a farewell gesture as it fell to the ground hopelessly.

Alex had almost won this one, but he still had to act carefully.

First, he checked to see if anything was running to help them. He had cried out after all. Fortunately, the crack in the cave wasn't far away and the sound of the river had drowned out his shouting.

The first monster had stopped wheezing and was now just lying there silently twitching its legs. The second one had a bit more life left. It was trying in vain to get up with a look of madness etched on its face. But Alex's spear was planted firmly in its belly. He remembered how thick the flesh of these creatures could be, so he waited for his energy reserve to refill before trying to pull it out. He didn't have to wait long.

Whack! The blow sliced the creature's throat and it lay there writing in pain on the ground. Its claws carved deep furrows in the stone floor as dark blood gushed from the wound.

But it didn't give up. Amazingly, it was still trying to inch towards him as it lay there dying. It was a strange sight — with a spear sticking out of its belly, the creature wriggled forward, the emptiness in its eyes replaced by wild rage.

Alex just looked at the creature with indifference and, as soon as his reserve was full, he struck with the Scissors again. The blade hit the same spot and the creature's head rolled away into the darkness.

Thankfully, nothing came to the monster's aid. Alex noticed that the monsters hadn't screamed as were dying. They moaned and wheezed, but never screamed.

Having collected the pollen, Alex decided to look around. Over the next four hours he found and destroyed two more goblins. They seemed to always move in pairs and they almost always stayed in the lighter areas.

Why were they so afraid of the dark? Did that mean they never came across the crawlers? Also, what else was out there?

After dealing with the latest set of monsters, Alex didn't see any more of them. He started to relax a little.

Alex summed up his results for the day: four creatures, half a gram of pollen and a leg wound. He decided he'd done enough for one day and it wasn't worth tempting fate anymore. A lot of time had gone by and he didn't want to go too far into the unknown.

With these thoughts, he treated his wound with more pollen and started walking back.

CHAPTER 16

BACK TO THE CAVE

ALEX GOT BACK TO THE CAVE tired, but his wound had stopped aching.

It was still early so he decided to go fishing. He'd wanted to ever since he'd first seen the river. Besides, the previous catches had shrunk over the day and now looked very unappetizing. Ideally, Alex wanted something he could cook so why torture himself, he thought, when he was next to a huge river teeming with eels

He chucked the remains of the eels to the polyps but they didn't pay them any attention. The food chain of the Other Side was still very much a mystery to humanity.

In some ways, he had an advantage over the other prospectors. The cave was a closed ecosystem and here he definitely had a lot more interaction with the wildlife than he would have done on the surface. It would be nice to find out what they want. But not all creatures feed on energy, do they? Otherwise, why do goblins have teeth? To scare the prospectors? Alex just didn't know.

He only knew that some creatures on the surface ate plants, but almost never each other, except for the most primitive ones. But this was knowledge that had been acquired after years of research by scientists.

It was also known that this world was not dead! On the contrary, in every drop of water, in every inch of soil and even in the air there was a living substance. But no one had been able to take it to Earth and study it there. In the buffer zone it dissolved without a trace and, on the Other Side, nothing more sophisticated than an optical microscope worked, so scientists were limited in their research and ended up deciding that this living substance was basically like plankton for monsters.

And how do they reproduce? Alex tried to remember what he knew. In the reviews he'd read they'd said that simple monsters, like shadow cows, reproduced by budding. More complex ones had a hive structure. But how complex life-forms reproduced remained a mystery, because the obvious signs of division of male and female individuals in most of the local inhabitants simply weren't there. Some scientists assumed that their numbers were regulated by the world directly and if necessary, the population of monsters was increased by non-biological methods, but this was purely hypothetical.

Basically, it was still a world shrouded in mystery and not many clues to go on. But one thing was clear — any monster would gladly attack a human no matter how it reproduced.

Alex went into the river and waited for an eel to appear. Once the first one came along, he caught it quickly, but he didn't go straight back to the shore. He was thinking about crossing the river. He remembered the shadow of something bubbling under the surface when he had been fighting all the polyps and thought better of it. He still didn't know the river well enough to head into the depths without protection.

So he set about trying to attract the monsters. Time passed and after ten minutes five fish were circling around his feet, with the Barrier keeping them at bay.

"There's always a bigger fish." Alex muttered to himself.

The huge river flowed leisurely past him, its surface smooth and calm. It should be easy to spot something big coming towards him. Seconds later, a vague silhouette appeared, moving under the surface towards him. Fortunately, the scanner saw through the river surface and picked up what it was:

[*River Bulldog: Level 1*]

The name surprised and alarmed him at the

same time. Without thinking, Alex dashed to the shore and stared at the river creature with excitement. He didn't want to miss it. He had to catch it, now that his skillset gave him many more options than if he'd had a simple fishing rod.

From the water's edge, Alex started pounding the water with his spear. He was waiting for his energy to refill, but he didn't want this new creature to swim away so he did everything he could to keep it interested.

The monster silently swam in circles about fifty feet from the shore. Finally, the reserve was filled!

In a second, the half-circular blade had ripped through the water and immediately disappeared, but it was enough — the water surface erupted as a huge creature with a large head and long crooked teeth jumped to the surface. Its body was covered with scales the size of shingles. Small fins completed the creepy image and made the monster look more like a toothy reptile than a fish.

Despite its huge frame, the monster moved fast. It thrashed its tail in a fury, twisted and fell back into the water racing away into the depths. Alex watched it disappear back into the unknown river and thought to himself how he really didn't want to follow it there. Now he'd seen a few of the river creatures but he was sure there were plenty more out there under the seemingly peaceful surface. He still had every right to feel cautious in this new world.

* * *

The next day Alex followed yesterday's route. He wanted to find out two things: where the route would lead to and would he meet any goblin pairs this time.

He walked for several miles and, seeing no one, started to relax. But as he came to the end of the path, a couple of goblins spotted him and immediately started rushing towards him.

Fortunately, he had enough energy to deal with them. So without thinking he hit the first one with Scissors, then, once the other one reached him, he jabbed it with his spear. That was enough to finish them both off. He was definitely getting better at dealing with these creatures, he remarked to himself. He hadn't even had time to be frightened and once the adrenaline wore off, he collected the pollen and continued on his way.

The familiar route ended after half a mile or so. Having learnt from his last encounter, Alex moved farther into the darkness and moved parallel to the wall while keeping in the shadows. He kept going like this until he saw the cave wall turn and disappear from sight. The cave must be widening, he thought as he rounded the bend in a great arc, but he quickly saw that wasn't the case.

It wasn't a turn, but a huge tunnel. The bend became a corner leading into the tunnel and Alex remarked how everything here seemed to take on a strict geometric shape. But the most remarkable thing was that each of the corners had a path leading outwards: beyond the crack had been a river, and here there was an unknown tunnel.

The darkness made it hard to see details, but Alex couldn't hear anything suspicious. It was much brighter in there as well. Maybe it was an exit to the surface. But after looking closer, Alex discarded this idea as he realized the light was just from the glow of the moss he'd already seen in the cave.

But the most interesting fact was that the path was guarded by goblins! As many as three pairs of them were sitting near the passage, two on each side and one pair right in the center. Just sitting there. From time to time one of them got up, scratched his head and walked around, but they quickly sat down again.

Alex was ready to bet that there was a reason they were guarding the passage. They looked like they didn't want to be there but they clearly weren't going to leave either. As if they'd been told to stay there by someone.

Bad news. The last thing he needed was those guys working as a team against him.

As much as Alex wanted to find out what was beyond the tunnel, it would have been suicidal to go that way. He could deal with two at once, but six would have been a stretch.

Also, the thought of these creatures being organized was a frightening one.

However, there was no need to panic. Alex knew that most of the monsters here had the simplest structure like a herd or a pack, just like animals on Earth would have done. It was unlikely that Alex had stumbled upon an intelligent species. Besides, the goblins hadn't exchanged a word or gesture in all this time.

However, the thought of more developed representatives of this goblin tribe didn't leave his head, even if they couldn't talk. But they were definitely more of a threat than the caterpillar creatures. With all these thoughts whirling around his head Alex lay behind a rock, surveying the sentry-like goblins.

A few hours later, a couple of goblins appeared from the side of the corner and quietly entered the passage. The new arrivals weren't even greeted with a glance from the others. Alex decided he'd seen enough and headed back.

The return journey was uneventful. As he approached the river he could hear it from afar which helped to get his bearings. But, as useful as that was, Alex didn't want to develop any hearing skills, so he climbed back into the cleft of rock, sat down near his rucksack and thought about what to do next. What if all the goblin creatures were accounted for and sooner or later the ones he'd killed would be missed? What would happen then? Would they send out a pack of them to search for him? Or would they just think something else had done it?

There was also something between the goblins and the cave crawlers. Alex remembered how one of the goblins had recoiled on seeing one of the crawler's bodies. Maybe they'd divided the cave and each species lived on its own land. It all seemed logical, but Alex was worried that the goblins didn't go into the darkness even in their own territory.

He could just stay near the river and not have to worry about either of them, but Alex knew he had to do more than that. He had to go hunting. After all, he'd need more than water if he was going to survive.

Tired of over-thinking, Alex ate dinner and went to bed.

*   *   *

Another morning came, even though it was hard to tell what time of day it was. Alex could only tell the time of day by his watch. He wanted to keep a routine as much as possible as he knew that would only aid him in trying to survive.

After getting himself ready, he picked up his spear and headed for the cave.

The third week of his stay on the Other Side was coming to an end. His rucksack was noticeably thinner, the standard rations were over and only energy bars remained in abundance.

A few hours later Alex approached the shelter. Glad to see the familiar rocks, he dragged his rucksack up there, then went for a look around. Just like the first day, coming out of the dead end, he turned right. Last time, he'd seen plenty of crawlers here so he expected the same again.

He walked along the illuminated wall, searching for camouflaged enemies. Knowing what the monsters looked like, he relied more on his Night Vision than the Scanner. That skill was actually growing by the hour and had already reached thirty-eight per cent. That was the beauty of simple skills, they grow quickly from simple use. All Alex had to do was look around with it while wandering round a dark place.

Even near the wall, the Night Vision came in handy. The greenish glow of the moss couldn't be called bright, but having activated the ability, Alex began to notice more details not only at a distance, but also up close. After walking about half a mile, he didn't find anyone and decided that he met the first flock near the wall by chance.

But he kept walking. If there was no one to disturb him, why not look around a bit. Maybe the exit to the surface was just around the next corner...

After a few more minutes the wall suddenly began to move to the right. The cave was widening and even started to look a bit artificial. What was the origin of the shape of the cave and the shape of everything else in this world? Alex really wasn't sure of anything.

Walking a little more, he turned around and started to go back, this time keeping away from the wall in the shadows. It quickly became clear that this was where the cave crawlers lived. It only took him five minutes to meet the first pack.

"Finally!" Alex grinned.

Last time the crawlers hadn't given anything away until he'd almost tripped over them and, this time, they were just as motionless. It was obviously their modus operandi.

"All right, you little fuckers, now it's my turn to surprise you!" whispered Alex gleefully.

Feeling calm and collected, Alex checked the monsters' levels, then literally felt the surroundings with the Scanner. He activated the Barrier, waited until the reserve was restored and then, he attacked.

Whack! Alex turned around and ran towards the wall. He ran without looking back, he knew the rustling behind him could mean only one thing. Like the first pack, the creepers moved in one group. One for all and all for one. Well, they could all die together, thought Alex.

The reserve had filled up, but there was no point in fighting here. If he hurt them badly, they would try to escape and he didn't really want to fight in the dark either. So Alex hit another monster, then a third — just to annoy and weaken them a bit. So he kept running, striking each pursuer in turn. After a few minutes, Alex and his pursuers reached a dead-end.

Then he began the now familiar process of dealing with all of them. First, he attacked them from the high ground and when they crawled away in fright, he came down and drove them into a dead end. The roles were reversed with Alex now hunting the monsters. It only took him several minutes to deal with all of them

After an hour's rest and a small snack, Alex had restored his strength so decided to go in search of some more victims. This time, without wasting time close to the wall, he immediately moved deep into the cave, checking the area inch by inch. He didn't trust his eyes, so the Scanner was an invaluable asset here. Two hours later he spotted a new group of them, just five hundred yards from his rock. This group took a bit longer to kill, but he managed to deal with them all the same. Adrenaline filled his body with a false sense of strength, but Alex wasn't fooled and decided that that was enough for today. No need to risk it.

*   *   *

The next day he made another foray and found a large pack of them within just half an hour. By the time he'd finished with this lot, the area looked like a slaughterhouse, with sixteen corpses covering the stone floor. Alex thought it strange that the crawlers kept coming to this part of the cave in such numbers but he was glad they didn't give off any smell once they died.

If anyone had told him before that he would single-handedly destroy sixteen level one monsters in two days while still on level zero, he wouldn't have believed them. And it was all thanks to the Pump! He had a lot to thank that skill for.

He felt a feeling of light euphoria and looked favorably into the future. He climbed up onto a rock and nodded contentedly,

"I could get used to this."

Despite his triumphs, Alex was still tired and knew he should rest. But first, he looked at the Interface:

"Status!"

[Level: 0

Energy: 35/35 units.

Transformation: Body: 20.5% / Structure: 28.2% / Brain: 19.8%

Signatures: Simple: Walker (15%), Night Vision (48).

Rare: Space Barrier (50%), Space Scanner* (54%), Pump* (70%), Scissors* (56%)*

Talents: Touch of Death, Sense of Space]

The Barrier and Scanner hadn't grow much, but Scissors had got its first boost without Alex even noticing. He never would have thought they could progress that quickly.

While he'd been fighting, it had seemed that he had more range than before and, on checking, he could clearly see that his range had increased to a hundred feet. The lifespan of the blades had also increased a bit, now they existed in fractions of a second rather than a blink. Now Alex felt like every skill he had was being fine-tuned to perfection.

CHAPTER 17

A Crawling Surprise

ANY PROSPECTOR WOULD HAVE BEEN HAPPY to evolve as Alex had done. Pump and Scissors gave him a fantastic combination, but Alex knew that wasn't enough to survive. When fighting several opponents he still had to be very careful. If he slipped up once, that would be it.

Most prospectors tended to hunt in groups to minimize losses. And usually, every group was made up of people with different profiles. The central figure was normally someone with the ability "Strong Body", "Iron Skin", "General Reinforcement" or something similar. Such abilities increased strength and stamina.

They were normally all equipped with the most advanced equipment and armor. As a result, these groups could normally hold back a small horde of creatures without too much difficulty. As a rule, they would also have some kind of defense ability, which increased their capabilities even more. Groups like these could defend and attack simultaneously due to the diverse pool of skills they had as a unit.

Of course, many prospectors were still killed in these group outings, but the overall risk was greatly reduced. Armed with equipment and skills, these groups of men were like tanks, almost impervious to outside attacks from the monsters.

Sadly, Alex didn't have the luxury of being in a group and, as a result, had taken his fair share of risks since coming to the Other Side. But it had all paid off and, after two days of hunting, he'd collected enough pollen to take off for Earth. Knowing this he calmed down and relaxed a little bit.

But Alex wasn't sure he wanted to go back to Earth just yet. How long did it normally take a prospector to level up? Maybe a year? And that's if you were lucky. Alex couldn't afford that. The cave may be dangerous, but Alex had reaped the benefits of being there. If he returned to Earth now he wasn't sure if he'd come straight back to the cave again. Usually, prospectors would end up returning to the same place every time but this place was so unusual Alex wasn't sure he'd end up here a second time.

Of course, he would still have the same skills if he was in a different place, but there he would have to look for new victims and, most importantly, he would probably have to share it with others. And here he just had to climb off a rock, go a few steps and the monsters would find him themselves. Nice and easy.

He'd found the cave crawlers to be fairly easy targets and, if it wasn't for them, he probably would have left without hesitation. But he was still very proud of himself. He wanted to show everyone that he could fend for himself while gaining new skills and levels.

Alex weighed up all the factors in his head and decided that, in spite of everything, it was better to stay. He had to develop here while he could. One skill Alex had thought about was General Body Enhancement. This skill would be a big help against all the creatures he'd encountered so far. As soon as he had more energy he'd think about getting it.

General Body Enhancement depended on energy, the more energy you put in, the stronger you became. Night Vision would use about two units every ten minutes, but General Enhancement uses energy as fuel for the body, so you couldn't get away with using small measurements like that. Alex remembered this, as it was something he'd particularly focused on studying during all his training.

But Alex knew that this was still a long way off. He didn't have the right equipment or the right level so obtaining those was the priority right now. It was a gradual process but, step by step, Alex was getting there.

*   *   *

The next day, Alex got up early and decided that today was a day for scouting instead of hunting. Since the crawlers lived in the dark, it was safe to walk along the wall, so Alex did just that to avoid any unwanted surprises.

He didn't want any more unnecessary encounters and he decided that, if he came across any more patrols like the one guarding the cul-de-sac, he would do his best to leave them to it. But he knew that venturing out like this was essential if he was to continue discovering more about the cave.

With these thoughts Alex set out. He was expecting a lot of walking, so he renewed the Barrier before he started. He started walking with a new feeling of exploration, ready to see something else in this new, unusual world.

As he walked, he tried to evoke a sense of space, just like he'd done back on Earth. But it just wasn't the same here. But he wasn't too upset about that. Before he'd been sitting on a chair concentrating with every fiber of his body, but now walking in a dark cave he still had plenty to think about.

Getting to the curve in the wall, Alex slowed down. Just like before, he would stick to the wall to keep his bearings.

The atmosphere was no different from the other parts of the cave. Still the same moss, cobbles and darkness. The noise of the river had gone, but it wasn't completely silent. There was a quiet sound of wind coming from somewhere, as if from a tightly closed window. Perhaps the ceiling had outlets to the surface, or perhaps the cave ceiling was so high that natural air currents had formed here.

The breeze didn't disturb him, rather it helped to muffle the sound of his footsteps. Remarkably, there were almost no odors here. It seemed the air was completely sterile, despite the presence of live creatures around. Some of these phenomena had been explained to Alex during the training course, but some of them were totally new to him.

For another few miles, the cave wall continued to twist to the left and right. Alex didn't wonder about the shape of the cave any more. He just stomped further and further until the terrain started to change. He started to come across some large boulders, similar to the ones he'd seen before. Most of them had been no more than a few feet high, but now there were boulders about three times the size of that but they seemed to be evenly spaced out in the cave, as if someone had taken care to place them there.

Another oddity was that the moss was thinning right before his eyes. Earlier in the cave they'd been growing in abundance, but now there were only small, pathetic clumps and Alex found himself straining his eyesight more and more.

Gradually, the cave turned into a dark labyrinth where it was hard to make out anything at all. Fortunately, Alex could just use Night Vision and the surrounding darkness became a little brighter. But the boulders were blocking his view, so Alex was constantly using the Scanner, checking for any hidden enemies behind the rocks.

He also looked around for some high boulder he could climb up in case of danger, but he couldn't see any suitable ones. The rocks were smooth and sloping so most of them were harder to climb than the one he'd managed to find before.

Alex continued at a snail's pace, trying not to lose sight of the wall. Gradually, the stone forest began to thin and, having rounded another boulder, Alex suddenly found himself on the edge of a huge clearing several hundred yards wide.

Alex felt a slight sense of danger as if a sixth sense was telling him something was out there, even though he couldn't see anything at all. On the other side of the clearing he could barely make out a dimly lit wall.

Then something clicked in his head and Alex noticed a huge body of something in the center. At first glance it looked just like a rock but on closer inspection it was anything but. Its size was astounding. It must have been about fifty feet long. He'd heard of such giants before but he hadn't expected to encounter them so quickly. He felt underprepared as he definitely wasn't anywhere near ready to fight one.

After a few more seconds, Alex's eyes adjusted to the dark and he could make out what was surrounding the carcass. There were dozens and dozens of cave crawlers strewn around the giant's body. It was a good thing Alex had got used to seeing the crawlers already, as it was a rather unsettling sight.

The monster's torso was twelve feet in diameter. Alex wouldn't have noticed all the crawlers dotted around if they'd been in disguise. They were just lying there in their normal state and hadn't even thought to hide. Now that Alex was scanning the whole area, he noticed there were three smaller giants just a short distance from the original one he'd seen.

While taking all this in, Alex slowly crawled back behind the nearest boulder. He didn't want to let any of these creatures know he was there. The Scanner didn't reach the biggest monster, but even if it did, Alex was slightly apprehensive about investigating it. There was no telling what kind of capabilities this monster had. In any case, Alex knew he had absolutely no chance against it.

On the Other Side, size mattered. The bigger the creature, the more energy and power it had. Increasing one's level only gave new abilities and strengthened skills. That's why an earthworm, even if it was several levels superior, would be no match for a human. A human could easily just crush it despite the difference in levels. Even if the earthworm had special abilities, it wouldn't help because size would win out every time. A small but strong creature would always lose out to a larger creature with less abilities.

Killing a small creature wouldn't lead to any

advancements either. If you wanted to develop quickly, you had to look for an opponent at least your own size. Alex's experience with the polyps had taught him as much.

Therefore, giant monsters were the most beneficial, but also the most dangerous inhabitants of the Other Side.

It seemed that Alex hadn't been noticed. As he quietly retreated, the giant and the other crawlers didn't even move. Finally, he hid behind a boulder, exhaled slowly and thanked his lucky stars that he was still safe. Then he turned around and started making his way back through the stony forest.

The exploration was over for today. Once he thought he was out of earshot, Alex quickened his step. He was afraid that such a huge monster would be able to track him. Although, he hadn't been able to scan it, he was sure that this monster had more than the first level.

Alex was trying to get out of this stony forest quickly, but he was only halfway back when he heard a familiar squelching sound. Except that the sound was much louder than anything he'd heard before.

The wall was to his left and the sound was coming from his right, out of the darkness and it sounded as if it was heading straight towards him.

"They've got me," Alex thought resignedly.

He'd been slightly apprehensive before when he felt like he was fleeing but, with the realization that a fight could no longer be avoided, he felt a strange sense of calmness.

No longer worried about being quiet, Alex ran forward. The invisible pursuer somehow sensed his movement and accelerated too. Its acceleration was accompanied by a deafening noise. Rocks started crackling and crumbling all around. It sounded like the creature was rushing forward without really looking where it was going, scattering rocks left, right and center.

Alex was sure he wasn't being pursued by the giant he'd just seen, that one was too big to move that fast through all the boulders. So he was probably being chased by one of those smaller figures he'd seen. How had they spotted him? Maybe just bad luck. Before now, Alex had thought that goblins and river-dwellers were the most dangerous, but now he wasn't so sure.

In training, Alex had been told that larger creatures could move surprisingly fast when going in a straight line. But here, Alex could hear the creature constantly stopping and picking up speed again, probably due to all the rocks and boulders dotted around.

Unlike the monster, Alex could run faster here. His human body was better adapted for sharp maneuvers. He knew he should make use of that as much as possible.

The sound of pursuit was getting closer. Alex hadn't looked back yet but he was sure there was only about fifty yards between them.

As he hurtled past another boulder, Alex stole a quick glance behind and saw a fifteen-foot long monster in hot pursuit. It was basically an enlarged copy of an ordinary cave crawler. From the quick glance Alex got, he could see it had a thick, powerful body. While running, he couldn't really scan it, but there was no doubting its size at this point. The small cave crawlers he'd seen had been able to throw out a stinging tongue, but he had no idea what these larger versions were capable of.

Looking at its size, he wasn't even sure if the Scissors would have any effect. Suddenly, his interface flashed up:

[Cave Crawler-Worker: Level 2]

"Shit!" Alex almost tripped when he saw the number on the screen. Just his luck, not only had he come across a huge creature but it also had level 2! However, he shouldn't have kidded himself. A monster like this was always going to be tricky to fight. At least it was only level two and not three or four.

This huge creature and Alex weren't even close to equal. It wasn't a small goblin, but a monster weighing at least half a ton, if not more. The peaceful name "crawler-worker" shouldn't deceive either. The additional word in the name usually meant some kind of specialization or new abilities, which only spelled bad news for Alex.

Suddenly, the creature froze and raised the upper part of its body. Alex felt a shiver go down his spine. This bastard's gearing up for something, but what!?

Without waiting too long to find out, he took a giant leap to take cover behind the nearest boulder.

BAM! A deafening crash echoed through the cave resounding from wall to wall. Something hit Alex's hiding place with such an immense force that it felt like the boulder should have collapsed straight on top of him. But it didn't. It stayed where it was while Alex was showered with rubbish and debris.

His body was instantly filled with new strength and he rushed on, hearing his pursuer close behind.

While running, Alex's mind was racing.

"It shoots, but with what? It's definitely not a sting! And does it always have to stop like that before it shoots. Whatever it is, not sure the Barrier would save me! Damn it, why did I come here!?"

Alex knew the odds were not in his favor. Whatever the monster had fired, he had no protection against it. At the moment, the only advantage he had was the boulders strewn around which helped him to move faster than his bulkier pursuer behind him.

He decided to take a chance and channeled all the energy collected by the Pump into his body, distributing it all over. He concentrated as hard as he could, trying to get every fiber of his body to focus. He urgently needed to get an ability that would give him an advantage here and he knew how to do it. He just needed to stay alive long enough.

Now that he'd got used to doing this, he could even feel the energy inside him. It was like a cool but warm fire flowing through his veins.

Thanks to this feeling, Alex had learnt to determine exactly how much energy was in his reserve, without even turning to the interface. And in addition he could mentally direct the energy to any part of his body, which is exactly what he was trying to do in that moment.

As he raced through the darkness, fleeing for his life, Alex felt like his body was in overdrive. He was simultaneously tracking the enemy's position, monitoring his internal state, distributing energy throughout his body and choosing a path to run through the boulders. It required absolute concentration and a very developed attention but, thankfully, they were two things Alex was very used to using.

Complete concentration on a task also helped him to stay extremely calm. Even though he was fleeing for his life, Alex literally had no time for any unnecessary thoughts or worries about the future. Whether he survived or not didn't matter right now.

He was going to unlock a skill that would increase his strength and help him break away from this monster. Doing all that while running wasn't ideal, but Alex was used to acting under pressure.

The stone forest was starting to thin out, so Alex knew he didn't have much time left. To buy more time, he dashed to the side trying to run in a circle to stay among the protection of the boulders.

The monster froze for a moment, trying to weigh up what to do, but it only paused for a moment before continuing to follow the way that Alex went.

The lighting had deteriorated dramatically, but Night Vision was helping Alex along. After half a minute of desperate running Alex turned again, heading back towards the clearing with the giant figure he'd seen before. He didn't want to get close to this monster, but he didn't see any other way out.

As he ran, he prayed that another crawler-worker wouldn't jump out at him. He wasn't sure he'd be able to deal with two of them. But it looked like only one of the guards had been sent out. If they were even guards. Maybe it wasn't a guard at all, but rather a messenger, whose task was to bring back the head of the poor guy who so carelessly came to the monsters for lunch, but decided to run away before the feast started. Maybe, the main giant had measured him in some way, weighed him up and decided that one crawler-worker would be enough. It actually wasn't far from the truth...

Alex raced on, cutting the corners as he went. He could feel the monster still close by but he was starting to get further away from him. Suddenly, the noise from behind him stopped and Alex instinctively dashed to the right.

BAM! Something flew past Alex and exploded just a dozen feet away, showering him with debris. The shot hadn't made any connection but it had been close enough that Alex could feel its force and he knew that the Barrier would do little to stop it.

All of these thoughts seemed very logical to him as he was fleeing for his life. People often react in this way when under severe stress and Alex was no different here. All his observations were immediately followed by conclusions and his thoughts never lingered on anything unnecessary.

Alex had survived the second shot, but realized that he was starting to run out of breath. The physical and mental strain of being constantly pursued was wearing him out.

Rounding another boulder, he came across a pack of four cave crawlers. One of them began to turn around and Alex was sure it was about to attack. Thinking quickly, Alex checked his run and sprang behind the nearest boulder. Luckily, the jump was a good one and he was quickly behind some cover. His quick thinking and speedy actions surprised him slightly. He glanced quickly at the Interface:

*[**Signatures: Normal:** General Body Enhancement (1%)]*

That was it, General Body Enhancement! Although he didn't want to start this skill while still at level zero, he couldn't do without it now. Now he could focus more instead of just running in circles.

Running suddenly became easier and he didn't feel nearly as tired now. The body seemed to forget that it had been tired at all. But Alex knew that this would only last as long as there was energy.

Alex could see the clearing in front of him but he didn't feel worried now. With his new-found strength he knew he could get away much easier. He turned and rushed away from the clearing.

For a brief moment as he turned, Alex was suddenly in the line of sight of his pursuer. It geared up for another shot but Alex kept running, confident that it couldn't be accurate from where it was.

Sure enough, the shot rang out but it flew well past him.

After a few more minutes of running, Alex emerged from the stony forest clutching his spear still followed doggedly by this tenacious pursuer.

Thanks to his new ability, Alex even found himself putting some distance between himself and the monster now that they were both out in the open. But, in a quick move which took Alex completely by surprise, the creature started shooting forward at an incredible speed. Its massive body seemed to be literally flying, making a good fifty feet seem like a couple of steps.

This was another peculiarity about the Other Side which Alex had forgotten about. The muscles of the animals here were so developed that they were able to move in a way that ordinary earth animals would never have been able to. All species here were just a completely new prospect to anything Alex had ever seen before.

Alex had spent most of his energy on strengthening his body but, until the ability was fully developed, there wasn't a lot else he could do. He was running out of options.

Thankfully, he spotted some more rocks up ahead of him so he headed straight for those. Once he got there, he went back to the familiar tactic of weaving in and out of them so as to slow down his bulkier pursuer. Just as before, the creature had no choice but to slow down to maneuver around these obstacles which gave Alex that little bit of time he needed to put some more distance between them. He couldn't completely break away, but he could make sure the monster didn't catch up to him.

Alex knew it wouldn't take long to get back to his shelter. He had to decide what to do before then. Could he hide on a rock like before? No, the creature would destroy it in one shot and then he really would be in trouble.

Alex knew he couldn't keep running round in circles forever. He could deal with fleeing one of them but what would happen if more started chasing him. He knew he wouldn't last long then.

Then something occurred to Alex. The goblins and crawlers he'd seen before hadn't entered each other's territory. That could be the answer! He would try running to where the goblins were and, just maybe, the pursuing crawler would fall behind. If not, he would rush to the river and try swimming for his life.

Of course, it was an insane idea but it seemed quite logical and reassuring to at least have a plan. After all, he had to try something.

Out of the corner of his eye, he noticed that he'd just dashed past his shelter. Unfortunately, he was still being chased. So it wasn't afraid of other creatures' territory. The unlikely plan suddenly became a little more likely.

Alex kept running as hard as he could. He was panting heavily as he fled but he could hear the creature behind him making even more noise. He wondered what would happen if they suddenly came across a few goblins. Would they run away just as Alex was doing now?

But he didn't see any of them. He reached the crack in the rock face and quickly flew up it. The monster behind hadn't even fired any shots at him. Maybe it had run out of ammo, if that's the way it worked.

Alex ran along the stone floor and could hear how the creature behind jumped up and continued its pursuit. Alex reached the end of the passageway and froze. This was the moment of truth; would the monster follow him all the way?

Crouched in a gap in the wall, Alex watched the giant crawler. It had stopped at halfway along the passageway. But it wasn't standing still. It began to sway with its whole body as if either angry or nervous. It was like it was trying to get a better look at Alex before its next move.

Alex watched it breathlessly, ready to sprint away at any second...

CHAPTER 18

BETWEEN A ROCK AND A HARD PLACE

FIVE MINUTES WENT BY. All this time neither of them had moved. Alex was still crouched down watching as this crawler creature swayed mysteriously just fifty feet away from him.

Suddenly, it lunged at the nearest boulder, opening its jaws, and biting into it. The rock split in two with a deafening crunch. The monster had enough strength to simply bite off and swallow a piece of rock.

Having got what it wanted, it turned around and assumed its familiar stance.

"It's going to shoot!" guessed Alex and he crouched even further behind the rock.

BAM! The shot landed close to Alex and it shattered with a deafening crash. Fortunately, Alex had enough cover that he didn't have to worry about the flying rock splinters. But the shot hadn't been wide of the mark. A little further to the right and Alex wouldn't have been so lucky.

He thrust his spear upwards and looked into the wide polished blade which allowed to see perfectly what the creature was doing now. He was doing much the same thing he'd been doing before, just swaying in the middle of the cave, but he didn't look like moving forward.

Alex waited and prayed for a miracle that it would just get tired and go home. All this time, Alex hadn't stopped concentrating on the Barrier. He knew it wouldn't save him from a direct hit but it would save him from any debris or splinters which came his way.

Another twenty minutes went by. Suddenly the creature began to sway faster. Alex didn't understand but then he saw a polyp in front of him. The little bugger was crawling along the floor just a couple of feet away from him.

"I do not need this," he thought to himself and prepared to strike it with the shaft of his spear.

But the polyp was behaving strangely. It didn't react at all to Alex's presence and it seemed to be trembling.

With the help of the scanner, Alex could see that the river side below was filled with dozens of polyps.

"They must be defending their territory," surmised Alex.

In a few minutes a fragile truce was established. The monsters didn't attack Alex or each other, but they didn't sit still either. The crawler was swaying and the polyps were shaking. Alex didn't understand how long it would last and decided maybe now was a good time to jump back to Earth and let the monsters figure this out amongst themselves.

His container held four grams of pollen which was a great result for three weeks of work.

The Walker was an unusual ability. But even when compared with other unusual skills, this one was impressive. First of all, all prospectors had it. Secondly, people didn't acquire it on their own through training or insight, but received it directly from the Other Side. Did that mean the Other Side took care of people coming over? Alex wanted to believe it.

The third peculiarity was that the Walker worked on pollen, rather than using energy from someone's internal energy reserve like most abilities did. Logically it was understandable. Alex's modest reserve would hardly be enough for a whole transfer back to Earth so an external source was needed. But why did it work like that? Why couldn't he directly feed other abilities with pollen, but with this one he could?

Another important point was how it was activated. The ability was triggered by starting up the interface and mentally selecting Walker. All these features pointed to the artificial nature of the ability, that it was somehow implanted in the prospectors.

Alex took out the container, unscrewed the lid

and poured all the powder on his palm at once. This was no time to be stingy so Alex wanted to use everything he had. Maybe a smaller amount would have been enough but he didn't want to take any chances.

After waiting a few seconds, he brought up the interface, selected the Walker ability and just thought about activating it. Just to be sure, he said out loud,

"Walker! Home!"

The item blinked, confirming it had been activated and Alex relaxed a little. Now, according to instructions, he should only have wait for a couple of minutes and that would be it. He would disappear from here and find himself in the buffer zone and from there to Earth it was only a couple of steps!

However, five minutes passed, then another five, but nothing happened.

Alex was sure he was doing everything correctly. The rules of transition were very simple and clear. Normally, there were no problems with this kind of thing. But despite all these reassurances, he was still sitting in a cave on the Other Side, surrounded by monsters on all sides.

"Dammit!" He cursed. He wasn't sure what to do next, but seeing that the energy background had increased, he moved into action. He didn't know why things weren't working but he thought he'd make the most of the situation.

His main enemy was the crawler, so he'd start with that. He could always deal with the polyps later.

Alex looked at the reflection of the crawler in the blade of his spear. As best he could, he tried to hit it with Scissors, but it didn't work. He needed to look directly at the creature but he didn't want to risk that right now.

He tried activating the Scanner, to sense the creature's exact position without having to break cover. Thanks to his development, Alex was able to get a clear picture of it. Now he could see its size, body position and even the tilt of its head.

Without opening his eyes, Alex got the necessary amount of energy and hit it with Scissors. He managed to strike it first time. The Pump quickly replenished his energy and then he hit it again, then he did it again.

As he kept on striking out at it, Alex tried to check what was going on in the reflection on his spear head. At first, the crawler didn't even react. Its neck was like a chopping block for wood as it kept taking blow after blow. But after about the thirtieth strike, the monster started freaking out. It didn't go berserk like the goblins, but simply started spinning on the spot faster and faster. The polyps also got excited and started trembling even more. Looking around, Alex was surprised to see that they'd even increased in number. Now there was about fifty of them. Where had they all come from? Even when he'd killed a lot of them before, they hadn't come in numbers like this. Apparently defending their territory was more important than getting revenge.

Alex could understand their instinct. This was their home after all and when something big comes along to threaten that, why wouldn't they do everything to defend it.

A crazy idea popped into his head. What would happen if he picked up one of them and threw it at the crawler? But he quickly discarded this option. For now, he'd stick to using the Scissors.

For the next thirty minutes, Alex continued to attack the creature with the scissors while it just stood there swaying but, apparently, taking the hits. It was cut all over its body. Alex kept thinking that all he had to do was hit it in the right spot. If he could find that weak spot he was sure he could kill it straight away.

After another ten minutes, his energy levels were dropping. If he'd known this would happen, he would have kept some of that pollen in the container. But how was he to know the Walker wouldn't work. Maybe this kind of thing had happened to prospectors before. They just hadn't lived to tell anyone about it.

After all the attacks the monster was tired, exhausted and could barely move. Alex decided to take a risk and stood up to see it better. Things suddenly became a lot easier and Alex even started to enjoy himself as he could direct all the blows much better now he could actually see the creature with his own eyes.

After a few more attacks the monster couldn't take it anymore. It stopped swaying, turned around and crawled back down the passage.

The polyps instantly calmed down so, without waiting for them to come to their senses and give Alex some attention, he started following the crawler.

It reached the edge of the crevice and, without stopping, clumsily slid down. Alex followed it down, striking relentlessly as soon as his energy had refilled.

The crawler was moving slowly now, its mighty leaps a thing of the past, as it struggled to drag itself just a dozen feet. Some of the cuts were very deep and, if it had been like any animal on Earth, it would have died a long time ago.

Did they have brains, Alex wondered. Either they made do without them or just did a good job of hiding them. He remembered opening the corpse of a crawler after one of his first kills and he hadn't found anything then. He thought he knew where the head was but it was hard to tell.

The monster crawled slowly into the darkness, clearly preferring to die in the dark than the light. Alex followed it without fear. After everything he'd been through with this creature he didn't want to miss its inevitable demise.

The monster died after about three hundred yards. Quickly collecting all the pollen, Alex went back to the cave wall and moved towards the rock where he'd left his backpack. He thought he'd let the polyps calm down a bit before venturing back over there.

He started walking back to his old camp with his mind now completely at ease. On the way he almost hummed, happy that he'd managed to survive again. He was starting to get used to this feeling of euphoria after surviving yet another near-death experience. He was glad of everything now, the dim light of the dungeon, the sound of the river, the sound of the wind beneath the ceiling, even the stony floor seemed to spring beneath his feet. He was in good spirits despite being thoroughly exhausted. Having reached the old camp, Alex climbed up onto the rock, had dinner and quickly fell asleep.

CHAPTER 19

WRESTLING WITH DARKNESS

The other side. The coast
Hunting for Shredder
Peter Kuznetsov

ADRENALINE AND EXCITEMENT rushed through his veins, calling him to action, as if demanding him to rush forward with a cry on his lips and a sword in his hand. But Peter held back, not taking his eyes off the giant in front of him. His hands were white on the hilt, but a weapon like that wouldn't help today, only long-range abilities were needed here. It was for that very reason that Peter, with his unique skill Air Bullet, had been invited to this hunt.

"It's time! Why don't they start? He'll get away!" he whispered to no one in particular.

No one heard Peter. Everyone around, just like him, couldn't take their eyes off the Shredder.

The Shredder was a giant creature with its very own name. That's how the Other Side identified particularly dangerous and large monsters. Only they were entitled to a special name.

The monster was indeed huge, almost a hundred yards long. It looked like a huge overgrown whale. The word monster didn't even seem adequate for it.

Two and a half thousand people were surrounding the reservoir where the legendary Shredder had just been lured.

Planning for this operation had taken many months. Five base camps from the Other Side had united with Sergey White at the head of operations.

To build the trap, all the prospectors had had to dig a small reservoir with a long canal that connected it to the sea. They'd chosen this place because it was at the very edge of the Shredder's hunting ground and he was known to swim this way once every two months.

For several years, this nightmare giant had terrorized half the coast. It had the ability to cause huge waves which swept away everything in its path once they reached the shore. The monster could also move quickly and was well known for attacking prospectors who hunted along the coastline.

Thousands had been affected by it. But so far, despite their efforts, the authorities had struggled to deal with it. It just carried on causing hardship for the coastline prospectors, while they did their best to live with the constant threat. Its level wasn't crazy, it was only level three, but, as every prospector knew, size always won out in the end.

Anyone who ended up in the water with the Shredder lurking nearby didn't really stand a chance. Also, this giant didn't swim alone. He was accompanied by a retinue of dozens of cuttlefish scavengers who travelled everywhere with him and they were the ones who finished off any poor victim who fell into the water.

Ideally, nobody would even attempt to destroy such a creature but the prospectors here had no other choice. The coast was a good place to hunt and they didn't want to give up such a rich area to this Leviathan creature.

Once everyone's patience had run out, the five base camps had joined together and set about dealing with this creature for good.

A canal was dug several miles long which ensured that once the Shredder was in there, it would be difficult for him to escape quickly. Once the canal had been dug, scouts on the coast with long-range communication skills quickly relayed news of the monster's location.

Once everything was in place, it was surprisingly easy to trap it. The people onshore made a bit of noise and that was enough to entice the creature to come closer. The Shredder almost instantly shot up the canal, dived into the reservoir and immediately started thrashing around causing a mini tsunami all around. But that was exactly what the prospectors wanted.

The huge waves swept over the embankment, hit a pre-built system of diversion channels and flowed away harmlessly into the distance. The Shredder was furious and tried summoning several more waves, but each one was smaller than the last. In its rage, it didn't realize that it was running out of water and, after a few big efforts, began floundering in the shallow water like a fish in a shallow puddle.

The water from the canal had been cut off by a pre-built sluice gate which had closed directly behind the Shredder once it had entered the reservoir. It was a clever system, helped in no small part by an excellent team of prospectors with a wide range of abilities and skills. People had been gathered from all over for several months in preparation for this task.

The reservoir had been further equipped with an internal drainage system which allowed the prospectors to slowly drain the reservoir, leaving the Shredder floundering desperately in slowly disappearing water. It only took about twenty minutes for the lake to be completely empty.

With almost no water left in the reservoir, the Shredder was completely stranded. It was trapped just as everyone had planned.

As soon as this became clear, it was time for action. An army of prospectors, including Peter, made their way to the shore of the reservoir. Everyone had been well trained for this moment.

"Fire!" shouted Sergei White.

Thousands of attacking skills rushed into the huge creature as all the prospectors unleashed everything they had.

As powerful and resilient as the Shredder was, it couldn't stand this kind of attack forever. For a while, it managed to take a few of the hits that came its way but eventually it succumbed to the inevitable. A few hours later, the prospectors set to take to work as they divided the spoils of this great creature between them.

*   *   *

The Other Side
The Cave
Alex

Alex's day began with sorting out the spoils from yesterday. He was proud that he'd killed something so big so he started by checking the Interface.

[Transformation: *Body: 24.9% / Structure: 35.8% / Brain: 25.9%]*

Fantastic! The fight from yesterday had seriously increased his progress. Alex wondered what would happen if he ever managed to kill something even bigger. But he was getting ahead of himself. He knew he was a long way off that.

He shifted his gaze to the skill scale:

*[**Signatures. Simple:** Walking (15%), Night Vision* (65%).*
__Common:__ General Body Enhancement (2%).
__Rare:__ Space Barrier (50%), Space Scanner* (55%), Pump* (74%), Space Scissors* (66%)]*

His Night Vision and Scissors scores had increased noticeably, especially the Night Vision. Alex figured that this skill had grown on its own, without really requiring any special conditions. All it needed was some darkness and there was plenty of that in the cave.

Apart from that there was nothing groundbreaking, but Alex was pleased that his energy reserve now filled up in half the time it had taken before. Maybe there were some prospectors on the fourth or fifth level who could do that quicker, but Alex felt like a master refilling his energy reserve almost at will.

He knew that collecting pollen was still essential but, at that moment, the Pump was definitely his most valuable asset.

"So... Where should I go? The coast or the cave? The polyps or the crawlers?" Alex scratched the back of his head thoughtfully.

After running through both options in his head, he decided that crawlers were the more favorable option right now. The rewards would be far greater.

Activating his General Body Enhancement, he headed out into the cave. For the next two hours he moved stealthily around the cave, constantly scanning his surroundings. But he couldn't see anything. Maybe there weren't many left to kill. He continued searching, but he kept his wits about him.

The interior of the cave was like the depths of the ocean. If it hadn't been for Night Vision, Alex really would have been completely lost. And, just like in the depths of the ocean, there were plenty of creatures there well suited to this dark, desolate environment.

Alex took all of this into account and knew he was at a disadvantage, even with his acquired skillset. While the Scanner still had a relatively short range, it was too dangerous to go really deep into the darkness.

Returning to the wall, he walked three hundred yards along it, then headed into the darkness again. He still couldn't see anything.

However, Alex didn't hurry. He kept moving cautiously and finally, a few hours later, he came across a flock of six crawlers.

One good thing about crawlers was that they didn't attack first. Alex shuddered remembering yesterday's creature but, luckily, this group was a smaller bunch.

They didn't cause him any problems and, after a few hours, Alex was able to collect some more pollen. He was also getting used to using his spear alongside the Scissors as General Body Enhancement improved his strength enough that he could now pierce through the skin of one of these creatures.

Having collected all the pollen, Alex headed back down where he came from. He went a little deeper into the darkness, sat down on a boulder, activated a few skills and, after a few hours, went to sleep.

For the next five days Alex lived an existence of hunting crawlers and developing his skills. He encountered less and less creatures but every day he managed to find at least one group. Every day, he tried to work his way further and further down the cave wall.

At the end of the fifth day, he reached the point where the wall turned. He knew if he went any further, he would encounter the stony forest again.

He hesitated. Was it worth going there? He didn't really want to meet another crawler-worker and, this time, he was afraid of meeting more than one of them. He knew the goblins, for example, actively sent out patrols and he could imagine the crawlers were no different in certain areas.

Weighing everything up, Alex decided he didn't want to go near the stone forest again. Even though he'd ended up with a rich reward the last time he went there, he didn't want to tempt fate any more than he had to.

The transformation indicator for the energy structure had crossed the fifty per cent mark. A great result!

The leading abilities were Scissors and Night Vision. Scissors had gone up by eight points, but the Night Vision was on the final step of completion.

[Signatures: Simple: *Night Vision** (99%)]*

In the coming hours, he expected to bring it up to a hundred percent. The last step was the most difficult and time-consuming, but Alex was hoping a few hours would be enough.

There was no point hunting anything at this key moment. He could give the crawlers a break. Alex moved away from the illuminated wall, sat down on a flat stone and started to relax.

As if in a huge crypt, alone with the cave and darkness, he sat quietly and looked into the impenetrable darkness. The deathly silence wasn't at all frightening now. Gradually he calmed himself down and, with that, went away all his cares and worries. Everything froze around him. He had reached the perfect state for some meditation.

Alex fell into a deep trance and concentrated solely on the task at hand. Two hours passed like this. Suddenly he felt a surge of energy, and his entire reserve evaporated at once.

"Interface!"

[Signatures: Normal: *Night Filter (max)]*

The matrix for the Night Vision had transformed into something new. Alex was glad at the change, even though he wasn't quite sure exactly what it was yet.

"Didn't see that coming," mused Alex as he looked at the Interface.

The change of the name wasn't strange in itself. It was just surprising that such a simple ability was able to transform, but Alex would take it. He wasn't one to look a gift horse in the mouth.

To check it, he directed some energy to the matrix of the Night Filter and started decreasing and increasing the flow rate. He wasn't going by feel here, as he still wasn't quite sure how it all worked. He hoped the matrix would adjust itself as he went along.

In a few minutes it became clear how it worked. Actually, the name was a clue. It turned out there were two modes. In the first one the quality of vision was doubled, at the expense of one point of energy per minute. But the second one gave completely new possibilities: colors disappeared, and the surrounding world became light grey, exactly like a filter. It allowed him to see objects in almost complete darkness at a distance of up to five hundred feet. However, it cost him five units of energy per minute.

The "max" shown on the Interface meant that the skill couldn't be developed any further. To be more precise, further development wasn't out of the question, but it would require special conditions and huge investments of effort and time without any guarantee.

For a while Alex, contemplated the cave now completely devoid of color. It was nice to have a break from the monotonous greenish glow. Finally, he could see the ceiling. As he'd thought, it looked like a dome, which started a hundred feet up from the wall, went up to over a hundred, then went higher and higher until it was lost in the darkness. Alex was delighted with this new acquisition, but even this didn't help him with finding out how big the cave itself was or where he could get out.

Armed with this new skill, Alex decided to take a chance. Now it was a lot more possible to explore the depths of the cave without having to foray out and get lost.

And he knew he needed to explore. After all, he had to get out of here somehow. Maybe he'd even be able to jump back to the Earth if he got out to the surface. Maybe the cave was an anomalous zone, where the Walker just doesn't work and he needed to try again on the surface. He thought about moving along the river but then thought better of it, as the river could stretch for miles and would probably only flow deeper into the cave.

He gazed up at the patterns on the ceiling,

"I'll check the center of the cave first, then I might try the riverbed."

Alex thought to himself there might be some kind of riddle to answer or a magic staircase to freedom. Stupid thoughts, of course, but after all the time he'd spent here he wasn't sure what to expect. He turned around and headed back to camp.

* * *

Back at the camp, he counted his supplies. There was plenty of food, but only about a week's worth of water. The meagre rations worried him. Fish and dry rations weren't the best option if he was going to be travelling for a long time. Of course, the energy bars he had contained something, but they weren't enough to survive on alone. If only he could just gain another level. Alex knew he was closer to that than when he first arrived, but he still had to get there.

The next thing Alex did was check the pollen storage. According to the marks on the inner wall of the container he had about four grams of powder left. Not bad, but deep down, he would have preferred a lot more.

When he'd finished counting, Alex lay down to sleep, but sleep didn't come. His mind wouldn't stop spinning as he thought about everything that lay ahead of him. He was torn as, part of him just wanted to find a way out, but another part of him wanted to find out what lies in the center of this gloomy realm of darkness and monsters...

CHAPTER 20

EXPLORING THE DEPTHS

The Other Side
Camp Silver

THE MONSTER, NICKNAMED GRASSHOPPER for its long legs, poked its nose out of the dense undergrowth and peered out. About two miles from the edge of the forest stood a huge defense complex, and its presence wasn't welcomed by any of the local inhabitants of the Foothills.

Beady eyes stared at the gleaming walls, looking past the field riddled with huge pits. Once there had been shrubs and small trees growing here before they'd been replaced by these hand-dug pits surrounded by huge, incomprehensible structures with heavy grids between them.

If the grasshopper had wanted to, he would

have torn through the metal bars in an instant, but this creature wasn't interested in the fortifications, only in the people behind them.

Despite its rage and anger, the five-foot monster lay motionless. Restrained by instincts that had never awakened until this hour, it waited for the signal. Not for a second did the creature avert its gaze from the gleaming walls bristling with the muzzles of large cannons. It had never been known to stay still for so long.

But then came the signal! It was a shrill sound which only sensitive ears could hear, just like the grasshopper's. It was time!

The grasshopper's legs burst into action as its body hurtled forwards at breakneck speed. It landed on the roof of an obscure structure and then took to the air again.

There was noise from all sides, but it was nothing for the grasshopper to be afraid of. He wasn't alone. Thousands of creatures just like him were running forward in attack.

Dani twitched and swallowed nervously at the sight of the army of monsters.

"Oh my God, not again! When will they stop!?" She whispered barely audibly while clutching a pencil and notebook between her fingers.

From where Dani was sitting, she could see everything. She was separated from the monsters by strong walls, cannons and special forces, but she was still afraid. And with good reason, the camp had been invaded three times in the last two months.

Three bloody times! Each time the base commander had promised that it wouldn't happen again, but no one believed him. The commander probably didn't even believe himself, because he'd introduced a special plan in case the enemy broke through.

As a result, all personnel there had an untouchable stock of powder for jumping back to Earth, which they guarded more than anything. Panic rooms had even been installed at the base of the tower, which allowed everyone enough time to escape to the material world. In theory, this would give everyone enough time to escape…

Dani had always thought that Camp Silver was very unfortunately placed. It was surrounded by the forests of the Foothills on three sides and, as a result, it was constantly under attack from a variety of monsters. If it wasn't for the portal between Earth and the Other Side, the government wouldn't even have considered building a base there.

Thanks to its location, Camp Silver became a testing ground for automated weapons. Dani's duties consisted of collecting statistics. From her post she observed the behavior of every creature, counted losses and assessed the effectiveness of newly created weapons.

Prospectors were constantly looking for replacements for medieval weaponry, but only the big guns were successful. However, they were expensive to maintain. The cost of compressed gas cylinders and reusable pollen-enhanced darts rose every month. Dani had seen the cost chart and it was basically a straight line going upward. Camp Silver could boast that it had long ago become the most expensive of all the bases on the Other Side.

Though, it had to be said, it hadn't always been that way. At first, the experiments had been so successful that the officials were euphoric. After preliminary research, they thought it would just be a matter of time before ordinary prospectors would be able to dispatch monsters with weapons manufactured from Camp Silver.

Every month new weapons were tested. Everything was used: thermal charges, bullets, poisons, acids and alkalis and more. But the Other Side just wasn't an Earth-like environment and that made it hard. The best method remained fortified darts. They were expensive to produce, but at least they could be collected and reused after they'd been fired.

Materials which were flammable on Earth didn't always have the same properties on the Other Side. Wood and coal burned excellently, but most complex materials weren't flammable at all. Generally speaking, the simpler the substance, the less problems it had.

The biggest disappointment was gunpowder and other explosive substances. It just didn't work in the same way on the Other Side, so all the engineers had never been able to make a working version of a firearm. But, what infuriated the gunsmiths and engineers more than anything was that skills and abilities always proved to be a better option than one of their firearms. A prospector with a simple power-increasing ability could kill an opponent faster by stabbing him with a stick than by using one of their firearms.

On top of that, as a result of killing a monster, prospectors transformed their abilities and, sooner or later, they became even stronger. Almost all firearms were useless.

And the worst part was that the operators of combat units couldn't transform their abilities in the same way as the other members of a unit. Even when operators went to finish off wounded monsters after a battle, their rewards were negligible in comparison with the other prospectors who had fought them. It was necessary to get close to an enemy in a fight in order to get any kind of reward from it. So even if effective firearms were invented on the Other Side, they wouldn't have been much use for those wanting to improve their abilities quickly.

However, that didn't stop the engineers from trying. Camp Silver had always functioned on a small income and survived, in large part, due to its pollen catchers. But, over time, the monsters had become more and more powerful. Dart costs multiplied and expenses began to exceed income.

The camp started to become a drain on resources. But as it was quite a large base, it wasn't so easy to throw away. In the end, they decided to carry on with it, simply for the fact that it was a good point from where prospectors could jump back to Earth. But there would be no more experiments. All the cannons and fortifications that pissed off all the monsters would soon be removed and then only fighting prospectors would remain in the camp.

After an hour of attacking, the monsters were repelled and scuttled off back into the forest. Seeing all this, Dani breathed a sigh of relief. No need for the panic rooms today...

* * *

The Other Side
Alex

Alex left the shelter in the morning and headed for the center of the cave. After he'd walked about half a mile, he stopped and stood still for a while. He looked around, thinking about what he might find today. It felt like a good day to find out something new. With this thought in mind, he set out walking, feeling more determined than before.

Fortunately, Alex couldn't see any goblins. Either they were being cautious or it was the wrong time to meet patrols.

To get his bearings in the darkness, Alex turned the Night Filter to maximum. The pump gave enough energy to support everything he needed. As long as he walked slowly, he'd be fine.

So that's what he did, walked slowly, stopping at regular intervals. It was a snail's pace, but Alex was only planning to walk a couple of miles at the most. He didn't want to explore the whole area inch by inch. He just wanted to walk in a straight line. He figured he'd be able to do that in a day.

The Night Filter turned Alex's view of the cave into a black-and-white picture and everything started to look more and more mysterious. He felt like an ocean explorer who was diving deeper and deeper, every minute expecting to meet something unknown.

This new skill helped a lot. Now he didn't have to look at every suspicious rock. No unwanted surprises from the Crawlers this time.

The landscape changed gradually as he went. The cave floor remained flat, but there were more boulders, especially large ones, several feet high. They weren't too numerous to start with but they didn't help with blocking Alex's view to the far wall.

As he walked, Alex noticed that the moss was becoming a lot more scarce and it was no longer growing on every stone. A lot of the rocks were getting a lot harder to make out.

Alex remembered a lighter he had in his pocket which he'd taken from the survival kit. The refueling fluid had a special composition and could burn for a long time on the Other Side. He hadn't used it before for fear of unwanted attention, but in his current situation a fire could definitely help.

He left signs along the way, trying to memorize the route. After a few hours, he decided he'd walked enough. He reckoned he'd walked about a mile and a half. He'd found nothing interesting and hadn't met any new enemies. It was time to go back.

Alex chose a boulder with a few handholds and scrambled up it. Up there, it was completely pitch black. He couldn't make out anything at all.

There was no way he could see the ceiling from here. The darkness overhead seemed even denser than below.

After a few minutes, Alex was just about to come back down when he turned on the Scanner. There was something above him!

All the time he'd been walking, Alex had been carefully scanning the surrounding rocks, but he'd completely forgotten about the ceiling. He hadn't even thought to. After all, all the creatures he'd seen so far had been on the ground.

He raised his head and looked up. A dark silhouette was falling from above. Without hesitation, he jumped from the ten-foot high boulder. He hit the ground hard and, while he didn't feel injured straightaway, he knew he wouldn't be able to run far after that.

"For fuck's sake," he cursed. He didn't even have any energy left as he'd been using so much for the Scanner. Alex held out his spear and shuffled backwards. He kept his eyes on the rock he'd just jumped from. Now he could see a huge spider-like creature hanging just above it. The Scanner could pick it up from where he was, but it couldn't tell him its name or level. It was holding onto a thread of web that disappeared up into the darkness and, from where Alex was, it looked like a large black ball about three feet wide.

"What if it's not alone!" A panicked thought

flashed through his mind.

He looked around frantically but he couldn't make out any others. Even if they had been there, he wouldn't see them until they were close anyway.

He thought about what to do. He didn't have any pollen to use and he knew it would take a couple of minutes for the Pump to fill his energy reserve. As he was thinking all this, Alex moved slowly backwards where he'd come from, the whole time keeping his eyes fixed on the hanging creature.

As he moved away, the monster just watched him until suddenly, in a barely perceivable movement, it shot out something towards Alex.

Luckily, the Barrier in front of him was still activated, but this wasn't an attack like he'd been used to before.

He suddenly felt a sticky substance envelop him, sticking to his body. The Barrier had stopped the whole substance from covering him but he felt its effects almost immediately. He was still able to hold his spear in front of him, but he knew he was in trouble. The spider had shot out some web.

"Damn it! It *is* a spider!" Alex cursed as he tried to jump back. The web clung to his limbs, so he stumbled and fell straight on his back.

Feeling desperate, Alex used the energy he had to jerk his body and managed to completely free his left arm. To hell with saving energy. Swearing like crazy, he let out some energy with a sharp jerk and completely released his left arm. Just a little more and he'd get out... The spider, however, had started moving. It spun around mid-air and started calmly crawling back up the web dragging Alex with it across the stone floor.

The monster seemed to be making no effort at all, but its legs were working non-stop, like a fine-tuned mechanism, pulling the swaddled prospector towards itself.

Eventually, the web stretched tighter around Alex and he was lifted off the ground swinging like a pendulum.

Alex saw an approaching rock, tried to turn towards it with his feet, but at the last moment the cocoon that he was trapped in started spinning.

Whack! He was swung head first into the rock ahead of him.

"Aaah!" Alex screamed in pain.

Slightly dazed, Alex threw a look up towards the monster, trying to find a weak point, but it was still quite far away. But what could he even do while wrapped up in a cocoon like this?

He wriggled like crazy, trying to get out while, unsuccessfully, trying to come up with a solution that would help him here. Meanwhile, Alex continued to be hoisted up, suspended in mid-air. Alex knew he was running out of time.

He thought through everything he had in his arsenal. A Night Filter, General Body Enhancement, a still working Barrier and a nearly empty energy reserve. That was it, so not much. He thought about using the Scissors but, by the time they'd be ready to use, Alex would just end up falling back down and collapsing on the rocks below.

Thinking quickly, Alex remembered that his left hand was free. Using that, he fumbled around for the knife in his belt and managed to pull it out.

Dangling in the cocoon, he frantically cut at the nearest threads. The knife kept getting stuck but he gritted his teeth in desperation. It seemed hopeless as he got closer and closer to the spider.

Suddenly it dawned on him. Fire! He had a lighter in his pocket.

His fingers hurriedly fumbled in his breast pocket, found the lighter, pulled it out and stared frantically trying to light it.

Amidst the vast darkness of the cave, a dozen feet above the ground, a small flame appeared. It seemed weak and harmless, but as soon as it appeared, the spider froze.

"Please don't go out," Alex prayed, bringing the flame to the thread of web.

The web instantly burst into flames, which engulfed Alex and his cocoon. Luckily, the Barrier managed to save him from any serious wounds.

Seeing what was happening, the spider started swinging the thread from side to side, leaving Alex feeling like he was on a swing. But it didn't last long. The flame quickly travelled upwards, the web blazed alight and, seeing the danger, the spider let go of its victim.

Alex was almost free. As he dropped to the ground, he saw out of the corner of his eye, the edge of a rock approaching him. At the last moment he instinctively tensed his body and used all his remaining energy to activate at least some sort of Barrier.

BANG!

"AAhhh!" Alex screamed in agony.

The barrier had activated, but only on his thigh. His lower leg was protected by nothing but his trousers. Of course, trousers are great. These ones could even be called a triumph of technology with their protective inserts specially designed for the Other Side, but that didn't save Alex from an excruciating blow as he came crashing down on the rock. A sharp pain pierced his ankle. He rolled down the rest of the boulder and landed flat on the ground with a crash.

With a groan he rolled over on his back and looked down at his body. The remains of the web were burning, his right hand was clutching the spear and his left hand was clutching the precious lighter, which, by some miracle, was still burning. The spider was nowhere to be seen.

He crawled slowly towards the rock from which he was still in pain. He tried to sit up and grimaced. His leg was probably broken. By an effort of will Alex pushed away the pain and tried to concentrate.

The main thing was light! As far as Alex could tell, the creature didn't like the light and that was what he would use to drive it away. With these thoughts, Alex tried to pull himself together. He switched the lighter to night mode, that way it could work for hours, and started to calm down a bit. He took out a flask of alcohol, tossed the pollen into his mouth without looking, and took a huge gulp.

For several minutes Alex sat with his spear in his hands, looking up and draining energy on re-activating the Barrier, but the spider didn't appear. All the scans he did, didn't detect anything either. Where the hell had it gone! Was it scared or just waiting for another attack?

Once his reserve was full, he switched off all his skills so that he had enough energy for the Scissors, picked up the lighter and, leaning on his spear for support, started hobbling back. His Body Enhancement had to be switched off and all he had left were tired legs, one of which was broken.

As he waited for an attack, he kept looking up, but the spider was gone. Unlike goblins and crawlers, this creature, for some unknown reason, didn't pursue its prey in the same way. Although, it could have been right above him at that moment, crawling along the ceiling, ready to jump down and attack at any second and only the light from the lighter was keeping it away.

So much for scouting around the cave!

After struggling to go a couple of hundred yards, Alex realized that he wouldn't get to the camp like this, so he used all his remaining energy for General Enhancement. After that he hopped to the nearest wall with all the strength he had. Although his left leg was in a bad way, his right leg could still do some work.

* * *

In the end, it took him two hours to reach the camp. Strangely enough, he hadn't been attacked once. It was like the cave was taking pity on him.

He took a long look at the crack in the rock before he thought about going up there. It wasn't that high and there could very well be something lurking up there for him. He still wasn't quite sure to what lengths these creatures would go in his pursuit.

Putting out the lighter, Alex struggled to climb up the rock. Before he had hidden here from crawlers and fought with the goblins, but now he didn't feel safe. Earlier the high ground had given him some peace of mind but now he knew there were spiders here he felt like a sitting duck. At any moment they could just descend silently and carry him off into the darkness.

His only defense was fire, but he knew that the lighter couldn't burn forever. He thought about gathering some moss and spreading it around, but he knew that it wouldn't keep illuminating once torn from the walls and stones. Besides, he wasn't even sure if the light from the moss would scare away the spiders in the same way the lighter flame would. Right now, he trusted only fire.

He didn't even know the level of this new creature. Most likely, just like the other creatures he'd met so far, it had the first or second level. In any case, Alex wasn't rushing to go to the center of the cave anymore. Right now, he'd much rather meet a pair of goblins than a spider. At least you could fight them on the ground.

Having rearranged his supplies, he made a splint and took some painkillers. The burns he'd received were treatable. Now he'd have to heal for a few days and then go to the river. He felt like he'd explored enough of the cave. He'd been in both directions and at both ends it seemed like there were enemies there lying in wait for him.

"If you go left there's goblins, if you go right there's crawlers, if you go straight you'll probably die and if you stay here, you'll run out of water!" Alex thought aloud.

He stared gloomily at the ceiling for another hour, until fatigue, alcohol and medicine did their work and he passed out.

If the spider came now, he'd find a very easy target. Completely exhausted and defenseless, he slept soundly in the silence and darkness. He dreamed that he was fighting with a horde of spiders and cutting their threads with his Scissors. As he fought them they all fell to the stone floor, spilling blood everywhere. It was quite a sight! Alex didn't even want to wake up.

CHAPTER 21

No One Goes Unnoticed

The Other Side
The outskirts of Camp Apache
Steve Dever

"WHAT, JUST LIKE THAT?" Steve nodded towards the covered corpse.

"Yeah, that's where we found him, the poor bastard," said a large man in worn leather armor.

"Yeah, not exactly a lucky guy... Had you seen him before?"

"Don't think so. I reckon I'd remember. If I saw a jacket like that, I'd pay attention," said the prospector, with a touch of envy. "Who'll get that d'you think?"

"The quartermaster of the nearest camp probably," Steve shrugged his shoulders.

The two men were talking in quiet tones. Dead people were quite commonplace on the Other Side so the sight of a corpse didn't bother either of these men. It was the kind of thing everyone was used to seeing, so it didn't seem strange. Anyone who didn't get used to it soon went back to a warm and easy life back on Earth.

But there was something different about this corpse. The knife in its back and the absence of his pollen container indicated the work of human hands.

"Has anyone else seen the body," Steve continued, writing down everything in a nice leather notebook with the logo of the Ministry of Law Enforcement.

"The whole team saw it," the man explained, pulling a cigarette out of his pocket. "So that's five of us."

"Hm..." Steve glanced disapprovingly at the man's homemade cigarette.

The man noticed Steve's look and hurriedly explained,

"It's not like that sir. I actually don't smoke while on duty, it's just a tradition in our brigade. You have to smoke a cigarette after a successful outing. It's good luck for us. And we need luck at a time like this, otherwise we'll end up like him," he gestured towards the corpse.

"I don't mind you smoking, I mind the monsters smelling it. But it's ok. There shouldn't be any of them around right now. Smoke away. How did you spot the corpse?"

"Thank you. I just saw it by chance. We were coming back from an outing, completely knackered, then I saw someone's legs sticking out of the bushes. At first, I thought it was someone injured or attacked by the monsters. But once I got closer, I realized it wasn't the creatures that had done it. Well, not the creatures we're used to fighting!" the man spat on the ground in disgust.

"I see. Where's the rest of your crew gone? You said there were five of you," Steve said.

"Well, they're at the camp. Why should they wait? Answered the prospector. "We'd been on our feet for five days."

"Where had you been?"

"To Grey Lake. Twenty-four hours there, twenty-four hours back, plus the hunt itself, that was another three days. The guys were exhausted, it was their third trip, so I let them go. They'd rather have a drink than look at a dead body. But I'll round "em up if you want. You gonna interview them?"

"Of course, I need to talk to everyone!"

"Ok, well when we get back to the camp, I'll send them to you at once," the man promised.

"Alright. That's all for now. What were you hunting for?" asked Steve suddenly, trying to strike up more of a conversation.

"Shadow cows. That's all we can hunt at the minute, the man said with regret. "For something more serious we'd need more skills and equipment and, so far, I'm the only one with the first level. The others are still pretty green."

"Aren't you afraid to go that far?"

"Why should we be afraid? The area's cleared and I know it well enough," the man sat down on the ground and leaned against a tree.

He took a last drag of his cigarette with pleasure, then put the remains away in his case. Having finished this ritual, he continued in a more relaxed voice.

"We were specifically looking for these cows. We applied to go there about a fortnight ago and, so as soon as we got permission, we rushed to the lake."

This guy liked to talk. He talked about hunting, the pursuit of prey, and just generally about anything and everything. He complained about the ever-decreasing cost of pollen and the lack of weak monsters.

Steve listened leisurely, without interrupting him. He'd written down everything he needed and now he had to wait for his assistant with the fingerprint equipment. There didn't seem much sense in doing all this as the body was decaying quickly but, nevertheless, Steve knew that the formalities must be observed. He didn't want to have to create more paperwork later. That was one thing he hated more than ever.

As the man chatted away, Steve was reminded of his own past. He too had once been a prospector but, after a short time, he'd had enough and decided to return home. There, he knew he could get a nice, cozy job in the police interrogating detainees. He had done this before, as he was a psychologist by trade.

At first glance, the jobs looked similar on the Other Side as they would on Earth, but they were wildly different. Thanks to the tracking chip and the inevitability of punishment, citizens rarely committed crimes on Earth now. Citizens there would break the law more often by accident than by design so, often the police were tasked with no more than a few minor arrests to deal with.

On the Other Side, however, there were no tracking chips. So when the authorities were suddenly faced with cases of murder and robbery, the camp commanders begged for help. It took the officials a long time to figure out what to do. In the end, the Ministry of Law and Order decided to set up police stations, just like they had on Earth. They started taking anyone who had at least some experience of police work and at least the first level. So that was how Steve became a detective on the Other Side.

He was the first to admit that he enjoyed the work. To him it was much better than chasing monsters. And, luckily, the job fit him like a glove. His attention to detail and ability to get witnesses to talk made Steve one of the best detectives in that area.

*   *   *

The Other Side
Alex

Alex hadn't been disturbed during the night. He woke up with his leg still hurting, but it was definitely better than before. Annoyingly, a fracture like that could have been healed in a couple of hours back on Earth. But unfortunately, on the Other Side, medical equipment didn't quite work in the same way, so he'd have to wait a few days for it to heal.

"I'll just have to sit tight for a bit," thought Alex, gingerly looking up at the ceiling.

He didn't want to lie on the rock for long. He felt quite uncomfortable where he was. But he knew that it was dangerous to move when injured like that. He could move on some crutches, but he didn't want to run into a goblin patrol.

In order not to waste time, Alex decided to develop his skills. He weighed them all up as he looked at them on the Interface. The Pump influenced the energy structure, General Enhancement strengthened the body, and the Scanner could help developing his brain. So he could use all of these skills while lying down to develop them just like that.

However, there was one disadvantage. The growth of aspects was possible only due to the potential that Alex had accumulated in battles with monsters. And this potential was still relatively small. He could only grow everything by a few points at most. Then the progress would stop and Alex would either have to wait for everything to accumulate new potential or go hunting again to replenish everything.

Usually prospectors didn't do that, because none of them had as much free energy as the Pump gave Alex. It was easier for them to just hunt the creatures.

He took a long look at the ceiling, then took out a pinch of pollen and sprinkled it on his fractured leg. Afterwards, he sat up straight, trying to get concentrated as he tuned his body into training.

As a training cycle Alex decided to strengthen his body with energy and periodically started the Scanner. The pump would be working constantly. So all three necessary matrixes were working, and through them all the aspects were developing.

* * *

By the evening of the first day, the progress had slowed down and, by the second day, it had stopped completely. But he had achieved some development:

[Transformation: Body: 42.9% / Structure: 52.1% / Brain: 36.2%]

"Not much," he said to himself.

His leg still hadn't recovered yet, so he decided to focus on the Scanner. It was an annoyingly impractical skill. The volumetric scanning required a lot of energy so Alex found himself wishing for a larger energy reserve so that he could run the skill at full power.

He also wanted to use the space perception he had developed on Earth. But he'd never quite managed to do it over here the same way he had on Earth. His perception of space on the Other Side just wasn't the same. If he'd been able to, it would make his life a lot easier when it came to surviving in the total darkness of the cave.

Having sat in a comfortable position, Alex relaxed his body, closed his eyes and tried concentrating on the area around him. He waited until the small area around started to feel like an extension of his own body.

Without losing focus, he activated the skill. The scanning field covered the rock and then disappeared instantly, expending thirty units of energy. After a while the Pump collected enough energy, and the action was repeated.

Alex kept doing this again and again, making sure that his own perception of space was not disrupted between the acts of scanning. He kept doing that till the end of the day. As he kept doing it, he saw more and more clearly that there was a clear connection between the Scanner and his perception of space.

Gradually it became clear that the Scanner was a kind of additional structure that amplified the signals coming from sensations and converted them into vivid images. However, in the process of this conversion a part of the information was getting lost. Alex was determined not to let this happen.

* * *

The next day passed without incident. Nothing interfered with his work, neither goblins, nor crawlers, nor spiders. However, by the evening he felt that he had reached a dead end. He was utterly exhausted. The growth of a skill was like the growth of muscle. Over time, more and more effort was required for less and less progress. But there was a key difference. Muscles grew from monotonous training, while skills on the Other Side could come on in leaps and bounds from something as small as a moment of clarity. But to reach that moment, one had to work for it. So Alex did just that.

He was sure that the Scanner wasn't being as efficient as it could be. It was like the energy matrix here was draining the potential he already had. So he'd just have to work even harder now!

Perhaps, with constant practice the skill would transform itself in time, but Alex couldn't wait. He needed some results now.

* * *

After a good night's sleep, he resumed training,

but this time he meticulously checked how the Scanner and his spatial perception worked together.

The training cycle went on and on. Alex completely concentrated on his work and almost forgot about the dangers of the cave. Without thoughts or words, he ran the energy through the Scanner matrix over and over again.

After several hours, he felt like his spatial perception was back to the levels he'd had on Earth. Now, Alex could easily perceive the contours of objects and even the slightest movement of air around him. It felt good to be back!

Finally, his spatial sense and the Scanner felt as one and could now work in unison with each other. They worked together like a pulsar, working around the body to detect everything that was going on around him in a way that Alex had never felt before.

But Alex knew this was no time for rejoicing. He barely had any reaction. He just wanted to keep developing and get out of this cave.

He decided to check the Interface.

"Status," a hoarse and slightly tired voice broke the silence of the cave.

[Signatures: Rare: *Space Scanner* (65%)***]**

Surprisingly, the skill hadn't changed its name or rank, but its progress had jumped up. The second major change surprised him, as his brain transformation increased by more than five points:

[*Transformation*: *Brain: 41.7%*]

Unexpected but Alex would take it.

But that wasn't the main thing. Most importantly, Alex had managed to regain his spatial awareness skill that he had worked so hard to attain back on Earth. He wiped the sweat from his brow with satisfaction.

As soon as the meditation was over, fatigue set in. His body was tired and his leg was aching just as much as before, but Alex didn't care about that. He was overflowing with joy and satisfaction at everything he'd managed to achieve while lying there on the rock.

With some apprehension he started to test the renewed skill, though inside he already knew that everything would work out. With his first effort he could see that there wasn't going to be a problem. With the consumption of only two units per minute he was able to feel the space around him, even in complete darkness. Right now, for example, he could sense that there were no threats nearby. This was exactly what he'd wanted to get. No more cunning spiders were going to take him by surprise.

"Thank you Donid!" Alex thanked the long-dead creator of the Way of Emptiness.

He grinned to himself. He felt proud that he could now manage to recreate the same skills he'd had on Earth. But now, he had other skills to go with it.

Alex had more abilities at his disposal than

any of Donid's other students had ever had before. He was just starting to realize just how significant this simple meditation method could be...

CHAPTER 22

RETURNING THE TERRITORIES

THE WATER WAS RUNNING OUT and there wasn't much left in the way of normal food. There were still some energy bars, which Alex was sick of, but he knew that he was going to need them more than ever.

But his leg had almost healed and would be back to normal in a few days. Alex thought about what he would do after. He wanted to do something active after such a long period of sitting like hunting some monsters, but it was too early and there was nothing around anyway.

But he felt like he needed to do something. If he were taking a leaf out of Robinson Crusoe's book then he would have started planting crops or engaging in some other useful activity. But he didn't have any task like that. He didn't need to get food just yet, he had a sleeping bag instead of a bed and even his clothes didn't need much repairing. Or rather, they did, but that would only take about half an hour. Standard equipment could be repaired easily, some self-adhesive tape normally did the trick. Everything he had was, broadly speaking, functioning.

In the end Alex decided to do some physical exercises to help with his General Body Enhancement. He started off by walking until he felt confident enough to run short distances between stones, building everything up bit by bit.

Once he got more mobile, he then started doing practice battles with his spear, as if fighting an opponent. It was important to get used to the increased strength and new sensations in his body. If he didn't do it now, he might not realize just how much strength he actually had.

One clumsy swing and he might fall over in the heat of the battle.

His General Body Enhancement had reached 42% and was growing rapidly. Alex wanted to boost the skill as much as he could in the next few days, then the way to the river would become easier and the battles faster.

Having heard plenty about the ability before, he knew exactly how fast it would grow at different stages and, after two days, he really started to notice the differences.

[Signatures: Normal: *Total Body Reinforcement* (50%)]*

"Great!" thought Alex. Now with only two units of energy per minute he could increase the strength of his muscles twice as much. That would definitely come in handy when fighting a few more goblins.

With the faster creatures Alex still had a bit to work on, but he could catch up on that later. For now, he'd have to just kill them from a distance. There was no point in investing too much in hand to hand fighting skills right then. For now, he just needed to develop the skills he had.

Closing the interface, Alex continued training with his spear. After the skill upgrade he wanted to get used to the changes in his body again. He wanted to master everything.

The next day, Alex had a light breakfast of an energy bar and a few sips of water before preparing to move out of the camp. During his recovery he had used up half his pollen supply to heal the fracture and now there were only two grams left in the container. But the expense had paid off, his leg felt much better and he could walk freely while carrying his rucksack.

Having finished packing, Alex looked round it for the last time. It had served him well. Here he'd found shelter, made a base and became stronger. But it was time to move on. A long journey along the river awaited him. Praying that he wouldn't meet any new creatures there, Alex set off on his journey.

As he walked, he followed the familiar pattern of moving slowly while trying to make out any potential threats around him. Alex walked about a mile until he saw a trio of what looked like a goblin patrol.

"Dammit, there's more of them!" Alex cursed, taking cover behind a rock. He wasn't sure if them walking around in threes had anything to do with him or not, but he knew that he didn't want to stick around too long to find out.

While Alex was hiding, the goblins strolled calmly along the wall towards him. Their empty arms were almost dragging on the ground. One of the goblins, who looked like the main one, occasionally twisted his head to look round. Was it him they were looking for or maybe they were just scouting for crawlers? Alex wasn't sure, but he was sure of what would happen if they saw him.

Maybe they weren't looking for anything and Alex was busy making up all these theories for nothing. After all, the monsters on the Other Side had lives of their own and he didn't know what they were thinking. Humans had only recently begun colonizing this world, so maybe the patrols were the locals' response to human invasion? Millions of prospectors were flooding into this new world regularly so this had to bring about changes of some kind.

But now was not the time to think about these things. Alex pushed aside his inner researcher and the hunter returned in his place. The patrol was too far away if he wanted to attack it with Scissors. If he wanted to do that he'd have to wait for them to get a bit closer. Alex, sheltered by the darkness, sat still, waiting. Darkness was his ally now. He needed all the help he could get. This was going to be a difficult fight. But he couldn't just let them go. There might be more of them up ahead and if he got pinned down on both sides, he'd be killed for sure.

The level of goblins was higher, but they weren't particularly strong. Alex had killed them with just a spear before and now, with his Body Enhancement increased, he was hoping it would be even easier to deal with them. Or so he hoped.

Preparing to attack, Alex stood up, but the patrol suddenly turned round and went back the way they came.

"Maybe that's the end of their route and they're just going back and forth," he thought to himself.

Waiting for them to move away, Alex cautiously followed, taking care to stay out of the light. He looked above as well. He didn't want another surprise now that he knew what was up there.

So Alex kept tracking them until they got to a crack in the cave wall which they gave a very wide berth.

"Well if they don't want to go there, maybe the others will stay away from the river too." Alex thought hopefully.

The roar of the waterfall could be heard from afar, drowning out all other sounds. No longer needing to worry about being quiet, Alex began to walk faster towards the goblins. Alex was just about to attack when they turned again and completely changed direction.

"What the hell!" Alex didn't get it.

Maybe they were just patrolling a small area and that was why they kept turning. Alex was suddenly afraid that there might be another trio patrolling nearby so he took a step back. It wasn't worth the risk. From where he was hiding, Alex could see that the patrol would pass right by him and he prayed they wouldn't pick up on any smell he might have given off.

But despite his worry, they passed by and Alex decided to continue his silent pursuit of them.

He waited until they'd gone back down where they'd just come from and, when he was sure they were quite alone, he got their attention with a shrill whistle.

Straightaway, the goblins turned round and made their way straight towards him. Alex counted down the distance between them. A hundred and twenty feet... a hundred... eighty... seventy-five... Whack!

Alex hit the leader with Scissors and he fell down writhing in agony. The other two stopped and looked around as if trying to work out where the invisible attack had come from.

As they hesitated, Alex counted down the seconds. Maybe he'd have time for a second strike. But no, they both turned towards him and resumed their sprint towards him. Even if he used pollen, he still wouldn't have time to use the Scissors a second time. Alex watched them approaching.

"Plan B," said Alex, holding his lighter up to

some paper he'd scrunched together.

Once the paper was lit, it acted as a kind of flaming torch and he jumped forward while holding it in one hand along with his spear in the other. He couldn't shout, so having the torch was a good substitute to have something which might momentarily stun his opponents before he made his next move.

Once he got to them, Alex threw the improvised torch in the face of the goblin on the right and, without stopping, rammed his spear into the chest of the other one as hard as he could. It didn't completely pierce the bone but it was enough to send it running away at full speed. Thanks to his strength, Alex could easily hold onto the spear now without it being dragged out of his hand. He turned to the other goblin.

The paper was still burning and Alex saw the stunned look on the goblin's face. Without hesitating, Alex struck it in the stomach with enough force to plunge the blade deep into its belly. That was enough to snap it out of its stupor and its eyes suddenly filled with pain and rage.

Pulling out his spear, Alex struck again. That was enough to finish him off for good.

The third goblin, who'd run off after being struck by Alex's spear didn't take long to find and Alex quickly finished him off.

Having dealt with all of them, Alex decided not to leave the corpses out in the open so he dragged them deeper into the cave so they wouldn't be so obvious to find. There was still blood on the stone floor, but there wasn't much he could do about that.

Picking up his rucksack, Alex paused and listened. He was worried that the sound of fighting might have attracted a few others, but nothing stirred in the darkness.

He made his way back to the break in the wall, the whole time expecting some new trouble to appear before him but, fortunately, it was all quiet.

Before hoisting himself up into the crevice, he double checked but everything was clear there too.

"The little buggers must have scattered!" Alex hoped as he slowly made his way down to the riverbank.

The Scanner was in detection mode, Alex was leaving nothing to chance. With less than fifty feet to the river bank, the Scanner lit up in warning. Three polyps were up ahead in the curves of the wall.

"All right, let's start the clean up," said Alex aloud. Apart from his own voice he hadn't heard anything human for a while now so it was good to remind himself what a human voice sounded like.

Alex suddenly wondered. How long had he been here? Was it a month or more than that!? How time flies. He also wondered how much longer he would have to be here.

With the Barrier activated and his spear in hand, Alex approached the nearest polyp and struck it twice in quick succession. It was dead almost immediately. The other two polyps, sensing some kind of action, headed for the scene of the crime. Alex, once again, marveled at how these creatures, seemingly unfit for movement, could move so fast when they wanted to.

They were crawling towards him and Alex could see there was no way around them to the river. He wasn't too worried about dealing with these two creatures, he just didn't want to wake up the whole herd because that really would be a problem.

He managed to kill the first one without too much trouble, even managing to gain some energy from it. He used that to finish off the other one, but he still wasn't sure if there were any others waiting for him in the background.

"Shit! I've had it now!" Alex swore when he saw another polyp appear in the distance. "Well, here we go again!"

The last visit here he'd made use of the Scanner, the Barrier and the Pump all at once, but then he'd lured the polyps out one by one. Now, it seemed they were coming at him in droves. The Scanner showed only fifteen of them up ahead and Alex prayed that was all.

Last time, Alex had either crushed them with his foot or he'd waited till they were close enough that he could hit them with his spear one by one. But both tactics weren't an option here. If he crushed them, he would ruin his shoes and, if he tried dealing with them one by one, that would take far too long and who knows what other monsters would turn up in that time.

Thinking quickly, he decided on something

else. He ran to the first line of polyps and began to quickly pound the monsters with his spear as fast as he could. The whole time he tried to focus all of his energy on the Barrier and the background energy from the polyps he was striking just about kept that going to defend him from all the shots coming his way.

In this way he managed to kill several of them while moving slowly back to where he'd just come from. This turned out to be a good move as the polyps didn't want to get too close to goblin territory. After he'd gone back about fifty feet, they just didn't go any further with him.

"Fantastic!" Alex breathed a sigh of relief. He'd been hoping for something like that.

After that, his task became a lot easier. The polyps stayed huddled together in a small group, so all Alex had to do was rush up to them and take a few of them out.

Gradually he made his way through all of them and it seemed almost a bit too easy. He decided to leave one alive, purely for experimental purposes. With his Barrier still activated, Alex sat down next to the monster and watched as its poisonous spittle hit the invisible screen and fell to the floor, leaving no trace. Nothing was sticking to it. There was no lack of energy around, so the Barrier could clearly withstand a lot of power. Once the creature started to give up, Alex quickly finished it off and then finally went to the river bank.

He walked without fear. He now knew that the corrosive substance they loved to spit out disappeared about an hour after it was discharged. For him, it was proof that the corrosive properties of these jelly-like monsters were an ability, not some substance secreted by their bodies. So when they die, their energy runs out, and with it all danger from their corpses.

Having descended to the river, Alex looked around. The nearest polyps were sixty feet away on both sides and didn't react to him in any way, but he knew that all he had to do was piss off one of them and they would all come running. Taking a deep breath, Alex began the long process of clearing the area.

The second round of killing polyps took several hours. He used the rock crevice again to protect himself and to deal with the sheer numbers that came rushing after him.

By the end of the day, all the polyps within a hundred and fifty feet were dead.

"Finally!" said Alex, stretching with satisfaction.

He was glad that he'd come back to the river. It was somehow more pleasant here than in the cave. Maybe the dark waters concealed some dangerous secrets but here he felt calm and even peaceful, a rare and valuable feeling in these underground adventures.

When he was done with the polyps, he got to work in the river. Refilling bottles and cleaning his clothes. Now that the Scanner was more efficient, Alex didn't worry too much about the river monsters. As soon as he felt danger approaching, he immediately checked what was swimming towards him and, if he needed to, got out of the water.

Fish, fresh water and rest by the river were all Alex needed to round off the day. Once he'd finished by the river, he went back up to the rock crevice to spend the night.

* * *

The next night passed by quietly. Alex was no longer afraid of the goblin patrols now that he was high up. He knew that the polyps could get up here but that didn't stop him from falling into a deep sleep. He really needed something which would wake him up if there were any dangers either an ability or a comrade. As he had neither of them, he dozed off, having disguised himself for the night in a small hollow.

Once he woke up, he began to think about which way he should go up the river. It was logical to go upstream, the exit to the surface was bound to be in that direction. But he also wanted to look at the waterfall. He was sure that if he went there he'd have more chance of development with all the skills he'd managed to accumulate so far.

* * *

For the next two days, Alex made his way towards the waterfall. The number of polyps decreased sharply as he walked. Apparently, they only seemed to hang around that opening in the cave where he'd first come across them.

As he moved, Alex also changed his tactics of dealing with any polyps he came across. As there were less of them, it was easier to come across one of two stray ones who he could then kill with a single blow. With the force of Body Enhancement behind him, Alex dealt with several of these creatures as he made his way towards the waterfall.

"This isn't a fight, it's just hard work," Alex complained after dispatching another polyp. "I can see why they call us prospectors."

Every time he killed one, he collected the pollen and moved on. It took him ten to fifteen minutes to deal with one polyp, most of which was spent on recharging the Barrier and scanning. It was a slow, but safe method.

Alex constantly used volumetric scanning, otherwise he couldn't see exactly where his enemies were. The new mode didn't help. It reliably showed him there were monsters nearby, but not the exact place where they were hiding.

While resting, Alex sat down and let the polyps bombard the Barrier around him. Despite destroying a large number of polyps, he only got about a gram and a half of pollen out of it. Unfortunately, small creatures remained far from the best creatures from which to get pollen.

By the end of the second day, Alex finally reached the waterfall. Here, the powerful stream of falling water drowned out all sounds. Alex didn't need to speak here, but if he had, he wouldn't have been able to hear his own voice.

The waterfall itself was huge. It was unlike anything he'd ever seen on Earth. Another thing he realized on seeing the waterfall was the astonishing size of the cave. From where he was stood, Alex couldn't see the other side of the river, nor could he see the ceiling. It was mind-blowing as he stood there looking around.

Near the waterfall, the bank narrowed and Alex struggled to walk along the slippery path. Afraid of falling into the water, he tied a rope to a large boulder for safety, just in case.

At the end of this short part of the river bank, a stunning view opened up before him. A waterfall at least three hundred feet high fell straight into a gigantic lake, the size of which Alex couldn't see due to the darkness but he could see it was big. He could have been standing on the edge of a sea for all he knew.

"I wonder if there are any eels in there," he contemplated to himself.

He switched to the Night Filter mode and looked at the shore of the lake. There was glowing moss growing below, but only on the rocks near the water. How far away the dry land went, Alex couldn't see. The lake, on the other hand, wasn't illuminated in any way. It was just a huge black mass of water. The water mist created by the waterfall further reduced visibility.

For half an hour Alex watched the lake and the shore, but didn't notice anything suspicious. In the end he decided to test the surroundings. He took out a piece of paper, wrapped a stone with it, set it on fire with his lighter and threw it further down the river bank.

The throw turned out just right. The object landed about a hundred yards from the water's edge, still burning thanks to the substance from the lighter fluid. Alex strained to look down. As far as he could see, the shore was deserted covered with cracks and fissures, but there was nothing alive but moss.

When the light was just about to go out, Alex noticed how suddenly the water close to the shore bubbled and a huge round silhouette appeared on the surface. Alex strained his vision, but he had no way of making out what it was. From afar, the monster looked like a giant crab with a strange head shape. Alex was cursing the fact he didn't have any binoculars with him.

The monster jumped sharply onto the shore. Usually you wouldn't expect high speed from large creatures, but this one could move fast. It only took a few seconds for it to reach the burning object. It clearly wasn't frightened by flames.

Reaching its target, the creature froze and then turned towards Alex.

He immediately ducked, not daring to stick his head out again. It might have seen him and who knew what it would do next? What if it could climb steep walls as well?

Alex lay clutching the rope, cursing his curiosity and passion for exploration. Twenty minutes passed, but nothing happened.

"Maybe, it's gone," he whispered as he peered

cautiously out from his hiding place.

He couldn't see the creature anymore so it must have disappeared somewhere. Alex decided it was best not to linger here any longer. He didn't want to provoke anything else like that. In any case, he was sure it was suicide to try and go further. He was sure there would be more huge monsters down there to whom one lonely prospector would be like an insignificant piece of plankton.

Alex felt like a tiny ant, walking against the wind and fighting against fate. What could he do against such giant creatures? He was sure that humans couldn't survive here, not even a large and well-trained group. What was the use of being a few times stronger. Size really did matter down here. Good tactics or skills would count for nothing against such size. The only consolation would be that he would die quite quickly if he did come up against a beast like that.

Having come to his senses, Alex pushed away all these dark thoughts. He would survive, become stronger and get out of here. He had to believe in himself. He'd been in hopeless situations before and he'd managed to get out, so why couldn't he do the same now?

On the face of it, it wasn't difficult. All he had to was go back up the river as going any further down was not an option.

In the end, it didn't take him long to get back. The dark waters of the river didn't seem so serene anymore now that he'd seen what was in there.

* * *

Returning to the passage, Alex decided to make a cunning move. Approaching the polyps, he beckoned some of the creatures from the right side of the crevice and walked in the opposite direction. The five monsters crawled briskly after him along the shore.

He continued walking without attacking them until he led them a hundred yards further away from the entrance to the crack, closer to the waterfall. Then he quickly ran around the shallow water and hid from them in the crevice itself.

After a few minutes, he peeked out to check where they were. As he'd expected, they'd stopped a hundred and fifty feet from the tunnel and weren't moving.

"Stay right there guys," he whispered.

He wanted to rebuild a barrier against the goblins. If there was nothing left near the exit from the crack in the rock, then a few curious creatures might wonder what was going on here. But if there were a few polyps clustered there, any other creatures would keep to the boundaries just like they had before.

It wasn't foolproof, but Alex figured it was the most reliable border he could have had.

Having finished doing that, Alex checked the large cave once more, peering cautiously out of the rift, but he couldn't see anything. The cave was quiet, dark and serene, but he knew that there was probably something lurking there in the darkness.

After eating dinner near the water, he moved his camp closer to the river and went to sleep.

249

CHAPTER 23

ALONG THE RIVER

The Other Side
The Cave
Goblin camp, 7 km from Alex's camp

ON THE BORDER NEXT TO THE GOBLIN CAMP, which Alex hadn't risked going into, there was a lot going on. Hundreds of goblins were crowding at the entrance, while more of them just kept coming and coming. They weren't sitting still either. They wandered about, growling and scratching themselves and there were so many of them that there was almost no free space left.

Judging by the numbers here this wasn't just any other patrol. Their normally dull faces were all lit up with excitement and anticipation. They were clearly here for something out of the ordinary.

The bulk of the crowd were standard first-level creatures, the same kind that had given Alex so much trouble. But among them were also larger, more dangerous creatures who looked much more powerful and ready for action than their comrades. Unlike their smaller brothers they gave the impression of speed and strength and their faces carried a slightly more meaningful expression. Another thing they had, which wasn't obvious from first glance, was a vastly superior intelligence which made them a formidable opponent to even experienced prospectors.

If Alex had been here, he would have assumed immediately that these goblins were a force to be reckoned with. This was exactly what he had feared to encounter, second level goblins.

The reason for the horde's gathering was clear. Not far from the cave passageway was a blue-black pillar about ten feet in diameter. Any prospector would have seen straightaway that it was a portal. The goblins, however, weren't interested in what it was, they just knew that it paid to hang around objects like that.

The pillar vibrated, emitting a low hum that echoed off the walls and reached far into the cave beyond. This was what brought the monsters together. This was what stirred up even the more powerful and intelligent second level goblins. None of them could resist being drawn to it.

At that moment, Alex was sound asleep, the noise of the mysterious pilar being drowned out by the roar of the waterfall.

Once the crowd of monsters was nearly overflowing, they all began to slowly make their way towards this mysterious object. One by one, they approached its vibrating surface and stepped into it without hesitation. Once they stepped into it, they didn't come out again.

But it wasn't actually a portal in the traditional sense. It didn't work the same way all the time. A large ripple would run across its surface from time to time and the next goblin simply couldn't enter. But each time, after a second's delay, it vibrated again, emitting a sharp, unpleasant squeal, and then started working again, just as it had before. Apparently, Alex wasn't the only one having trouble teleporting out of here.

At that same moment, far away from the cave, deep in the forest another similar looking portal was vibrating in much the same way.

This forest was in the Foothills and was considered the most dangerous region on the Other Side. There were a lot of high-level creatures here and any group that did venture here normally suffered heavy losses. It was often the more experienced groups that did venture out here but, sometimes, new prospectors just didn't have a choice and they would end up here the first time they made the crossing.

The goblins who were appearing from the portal were all scattering in small groups of five or ten, as if they knew where to go and what to do. In any other situation they would not have behaved so brazenly in a foreign land but here they seemed controlled by a territorial imperative. They were accustomed to defending their domain by scaring away other monsters, so they were eager not to be on the receiving end of similar treatment.

But in this gigantic forest there were actually very few creatures left, thanks to the prospectors' extensive efforts since coming over to the Other Side. Because of this, it often felt like a constant, never-ending war between the monsters and their enemies. Usually, the monsters were the losers in this war. The prospectors had improved their knowledge and bettered their techniques since coming to the Other Side and only retreated from a fight if they happened to encounter a new, unknown species.

But this world had its own rules. The Other Side didn't like emptiness, so some monsters were simply replaced by others. One wave was followed by another and the war never truly stopped.

The prospectors, however, had got used to the ways of the Other Side and they knew about the portals. They just didn't know where the constant influx of new creatures was coming from.

Any newcomers were often ill-suited to the area they'd been thrown into, so they had to adapt. This led to the theory that the monsters didn't move around of their own free will. Otherwise, they would have chosen something more suitable. It seemed to many scientists that their task was just to drive the humans away.

In any case, the constant influx of creatures was a good thing for the prospectors. Their resources never ran out, thanks to the endless supply of pollen provided by these creatures. If you killed one batch of monsters, another one would take its place. This is not fossils, which could just run out.

The only problems arose when weak monsters were replaced by stronger ones. And the faster the prospectors got rid of a batch of creatures, the stronger the creatures that came to replace them. But it did keep the prospectors busy. Thanks to the constant practice, they were getting stronger all the time.

However, newcomers had a hard time in this environment as there were fewer and fewer weak creatures to fight. Shadow cows and similar creatures with level zero had become quite scarce. Animal rights activists weren't so active on the Other Side so weak animals continued to be mercilessly exterminated for human benefit. The only rule there was, was that veteran prospectors were forbidden to hunt them. Obviously, it was hard to enforce this law, but it was a law all the same.

So the goblins kept streaming in through the portal to replace whatever had been there before. Luckily, these goblins weren't as highly skilled as they could have been but, nevertheless, they were there to cause problems.

Gradually, they all moved through the portal and scattered in different directions. After they'd dispersed, the portal melted away. The forest and the cave became quiet again.

*　　*　　*

The Other Side
The Cave
Alex

Alex had been walking along the river for a week now. Six days to be exact. He didn't feel so afraid of the giant monster he had seen in the water now. During his trip he'd only met polyps and a few eels.

He'd actually been glad not to have met any new surprises. He was quite happy dealing with the small insignificant polyps. Much easier to deal with despite the lack of rewards gained. Despite the number he'd killed he only had an extra two grams of pollen to show for it. But Barrier and Scanner were clearly developing.

On seeing this, Alex decided to focus more on developing the Pump. He'd found himself collecting less pollen from his victims so he figured the Pump would only be more and more useful as he continued.

Of course, he continued training the Barrier just as he'd done before. All his abilities were going to be crucial as he discovered more and more about this new world. He'd got quite used to training with polyps. So much so that he'd got carried away one day and just waited until a solitary polyp had run out of whatever it was shooting at him and had started climbing the Barrier as a last resort of attack. Alex just finished it off after that.

Thanks to the mass of creatures he'd come across, his development was continuing smoothly, but to distract himself from the sometimes monotonous cycle, Alex experimented from time to time. He'd tried throwing some of them into the water and it turned out they could swim. One of the polyps, he'd tried to set on fire and it reacted violently, spitting at him while bravely enduring the flames which engulfed it.

In general, he tried to amuse himself while also trying to find out something useful at the same time. Sadly, the research didn't lead to any groundbreaking results. He only found that polyps and the creatures living in the river didn't seem to mix with each other. They seemed to steer well clear of each other.

For six days the terrain had not changed. The giant river remained as dark and mysterious as it always had done. He still hadn't even seen the opposite bank. Either it was very far away or there was no luminous moss growing on that side. Either way, Alex was quite happy staying safely on this side of the river for the time being.

From time to time, the Scanner told him there were creatures swimming nearby, but they never came ashore. He didn't know what kind of creatures they were and he didn't even try to find out. Fishing was also kept to a minimum as he didn't feel like getting too close to the water after what he'd seen come out of there.

At first, he was even afraid to sleep too close to the river. Every day, once he'd finished his daily trek, he returned to set up camp at the cave wall rather than stick to the riverbank. But, sooner or later, he knew he'd have to sleep closer to the water, as returning to the cave wall every evening took up a lot of time.

At the end of the sixth day, he was getting to the end of his tether. General Body Enhancement had saved him so far, but he knew he couldn't keep going on like this. He decided to check the Interface. Both Scanner and Pump had made some serious progress.

*[**Level:** 0*
__Energy:__ 35/35 units
__Transformation:__ Body: 66.3% / Structure: 77.1% / Brain: 66.2%.
__Signatures: Simple:__ Walker (15%)
__Common:__ Night Filter (max), General Body Enhancement (60%)*
__Rare:__ Space Barrier (84%), Space Scanner** (88%), Pump** (85%), Space Scissors* (75%).*
__Talents:__ Touch of Death, Sense of Space]

The Scanner's range had increased. Now in locator mode, Alex could determine the level and name of a creature up to eighty yards away.

"Doesn't matter," he whispered to himself. "I'll level up and check it again."

But the Pump pleased him, even though the speed of filling the reserve was roughly the same for the time being. It took him some time to realize the full potential of this skill but he could now extract energy not only from the surrounding area, but also directly from pollen.

This new Pump mode made Alex much stronger than he realized. He couldn't use the ability as he wanted in normal combat but pollen suddenly became a lot more useful than it was already.

But there was a disadvantage that the Pump wouldn't really develop too much more, even with all the potential energy Alex was getting from killing all these monsters. It was annoying, but Alex realized that he would just have to find another way to further develop the skill. He was sure he could find a way.

"I guess it can't all be easy," Alex muttered to himself. "The stronger the skill, the harder the development." But deep down, he knew that one Pump was better than a dozen Night Filters.

And he was right. The complexity of a skill was a strength, not a weakness. The more complex and slower an ability was developed — the more complex and powerful it turned out in the end.

Unfortunately, Alex didn't have enough pollen just then. Hunting polyps, although easy, was not a lucrative business. He thought back to the crawlers and sighed almost nostalgically.

Now they were worth hunting.

* * *

In order not to spend the night unprotected on the shore, Alex decided to make a shelter. He spent several hours rolling boulders along the shore to where he set up camp. His new strength helped him cope with the task, but it was still hard work. He built himself a mini-fortress, half-resembling an embankment on the shore. It was only about five feet high and if the polyps attacked, it wouldn't offer much in the way of protection. It would just hide him from view and Alex hoped that would be enough for one night. So far, they'd only attacked when they felt threatened and Alex was banking on that remaining the case.

Since this was a first night near the shore, Alex decided to watch the river before he fell asleep. For some time he gazed into the calm, dark waters.

Gradually he relaxed and began to remember his journey through the cave. In almost a month and a half, Alex had become accustomed to this new way of life. So far, everything was going according to plan, but he still had a lot of questions. First of all, how did he get here? More precisely, what had brought him here? He felt that if he went all the way to the end, he would find the answer to these questions. He felt like something had called him, and he wanted to find out what it was.

With these thoughts running round his head, Alex fell asleep.

* * *

"Time to get up," Alex stretched and yawned.

The first night by the river had gone well. He hadn't been eaten so now he could go out and carry on exploring and hunting like he'd been doing before. The only thing he wanted was to get the Barrier reinforcement as soon as possible. Yesterday evening, the progress of the skill had been at 84%. He was hoping that if he tried hard enough, the polyps would help him advance this skill

Two hours later Alex was admiring the entry in the interface:

*[Signatures: Spatial Barrier** (85%)]*

The second reinforcement of the Barrier had brought significant changes. The shield had become mobile. If before Alex could only create and stretch the Barrier, now he could shift and move it and even change its shape in ways he could never have even imagined before.

At first glance, the new mobility of the skill just looked like a simple new property but, after playing around with the skill, Alex realized this was a bit different than before. It was like the energy matrix had now become integrated into his nervous system and he felt like all the nuances of the Barrier as an extension of his own body.

"That's a new feeling," Alex remarked to himself.

The only thing he couldn't do was shrink the Barrier. It only expanded and there was no way he could compress it.

Nevertheless, Alex considered himself lucky. How many prospectors could boast that their defense could hold off an attack from a monster one level higher than him?

The next two hours Alex spent training this new skill and then went on hunting polyps just like he'd been doing before. It was a never ending task and Alex found himself wondering if it would be better just to run along the shore and quickly avoid all of them. Surely if he ran fast enough they couldn't attack? But he didn't pursue this idea as he didn't like the idea of something surprising him from the river-side. He figured it was best just to continue targeting these small jelly-like creatures. The rewards were small but at least they weren't much of a threat.

"No need to get cocky. Calm, steady development is the key to success," he said to himself.

He had to kill about a dozen and a half polyps to get the same reward as killing one crawler. As long as the polyps didn't die out, he just had to keep going till he got to the next level. He hoped there wasn't going to be anything too difficult to deal with any time soon. So far Alex had been lucky. Every creature he'd come across he'd managed to deal with but if he came across even one creature that he couldn't defeat, he just wouldn't be able to get past it. He would have to just go back to the cave, assuming he survived the encounter.

By the end of the next day, his fears were realized.

Coming to the end of an easy walk, Alex looked out at the open landscape.

The narrow shore-line broke off and right behind it opened up a stony beach. As Alex approached the stones, the mossy bushes thinned out with every step until they completely disappeared. He looked cautiously ahead unable to make out anything in the darkness, even with the help of the Night Filter.

The polyps were gone too. The last one he'd encountered had been about two hundred yards ago. In Alex's mind, that could mean only one thing. A change in territory. He tensed slightly, thinking about what could lie ahead.

"There must be something out there," thought Alex, putting his spear out in front of him.

Moving very cautiously, Alex moved back along to the cave wall which turned in front of him. He peered around the turn but it was a similar story there. There wasn't even a speck of light in sight.

Alex shivered. He suddenly realized that it was cold here as well. The water on the shore-line wasn't frozen but the temperature had definitely dropped in this part of the cave.

Alex didn't mind the cold, his clothing provided comfort in a large range of temperatures. He just didn't like the uncertainty of this new place.

As he walked back to the shore, he suddenly noticed how it became warmer again. It was as if he'd crossed an invisible line between summer and winter. He moved back again a few steps and, straight away, the cold hit him. It was remarkable!

Moving back into the warmth, Alex stared into the darkness for a long time, trying to pick out some living creature with the locator. But there was nothing there. He even remembered to scan the ceiling, but there was nothing there either.

"Hey! Is anyone out there!? Come out if you are!" he shouted out hopefully. No one appeared. "Well, I'll just have to go and see for myself," he said under his breath.

Taking out his lighter, but not yet lighting it, Alex went forward. After a hundred yards, the ice crunched under his feet. He made a mental note to be careful not to slip.

After another hundred yards it was dark even for the Night Filter. The light from the shore didn't reach here. Alex shivered and remembered how the spider had attacked him in similar circumstances.

He wasn't sure what to do now. Going backwards would mean giving up. He wanted to know what was out there but, at the same time, he was apprehensive about seeing them face-to-face.

He decided to walk a little further. He moved cautiously, his vision and hearing strained to the limit, but still no signs of any creatures. One more step... At that moment Alex suddenly felt a feeling of danger and his whole body tensed up. Something was approaching...

CHAPTER 24

THE STONE BEACH

SENSING THE ENEMY'S APPROACH, Alex immediately lit the lighter. A small petal of flame slightly dispersed the surrounding darkness and revealed dozens of snake-like silhouettes quickly approaching from the depths of the cave.

"Well at least it's not giants," Alex managed to think to himself.

The darkness prevented Alex from properly seeing these new creatures, but that didn't matter. Alex had made some sort of contact with a new creature and now he just wanted to run before this contact turned into a closer acquaintance. He turned sharply but slipped on the frost and smacked his knee painfully on the ground.

"Shit!" the lighter flew out of his hand and then promptly went out.

For a few frantic moments, Alex fumbled around in the darkness desperately trying to find it. Luckily, he found it within a few seconds. He clutched it gratefully and, jumping up, rushed back to the shore.

As he ran along, he tried to get the lighter going again but it didn't seem to be working now. He gave up trying and just concentrated on running as fast as he could. The rustling of dozens of bodies was enough to drive him forward.

The Body Enhancement, cranked up to full power, consumed almost all of his energy. The ability made him significantly stronger, more enduring, and slightly faster. But he still had to think about defense. He shifted the Barrier backwards so the back of his body was completely covered. If the creatures attacked while he was on the move, at least he would be protected.

The crunching sound underfoot had now gone. There was no more ice and it was much less slippery. He tried his best to run faster, even though his knee ached with every movement. The shoreline was approaching but he could hear his pursuers getting closer with every second. From behind there was a sound like the blow of a leather belt making contact with something. A second later Alex felt a jolt that almost knocked him off his feet. Had he taken the hit earlier, he would certainly have been knocked off his feet, but now that the ground was no longer slippery it was easier to keep his footing. But, the blow had slowed him down slightly and that had only brought his pursuers closer.

Phut! A second blow hit the Barrier, weakening it slightly, but the defense held firm. Almost tripping, Alex accelerated. He was so close!

All his attention was now focused on fleeing his pursuers. Alex shifted the remnants of his shield to the likely place of attack. His legs and the back of his head were now stripped of protection and he had no energy left to renew the Barrier.

Alex wasn't even running anymore, just using his energy-enhanced muscles as much as he could. He had almost reached the shore. The first boulders with flecks of moss were starting to appear.

Alex ran across the invisible line between hot and cold barely even notching it. It was only when he felt the definite change in temperature that he was sure he was on the other side. He could still hear movement behind him but he felt for a second as if he'd actually managed to get away.

Whack! A sharp pain suddenly stung his right shoulder, and it felt like something was clinging to it. His arm was instantly numb, hanging limply by his side. Luckily he still had enough strength and energy in his legs and they were what was going to carry him to safety. Without looking back, he continued to rush forward, while clutching his shoulder.

Now he was running along the riverbank, he didn't slow down. He could definitely feel something clinging to his shoulder now as it was reaching down and trying to beat his back and legs as he ran. With each step, Alex could feel it doing more and more damage, but he didn't want to stop with the pursuers still probably close behind.

Having reached a more lighted area, Alex stopped and turned around. The pursuers had disappeared. Had he really given them the slip or were they just waiting in the darkness so they could pounce on him when he least expected it? To hell with them, it was time for him to deal with this unwanted passenger he'd acquired. He tried to look over his shoulder but he couldn't get a good look at it. It was probably quite comfortable hanging there on his shoulder but, at that moment, Alex was anything but.

The situation was far from ideal. Although, he'd managed to shake off the main crowd there was something clinging to him that was draining all the energy he had. He wouldn't get far this way. He felt like he was being hunted. His heart was pounding frantically and sweat was pouring into his eyes as he thought about what to do.

Suddenly, Alex felt General Body Enhancement switch off. He immediately felt weaker than he had a few seconds ago. But why had it switched off? The Pump was working properly so everything should just work as normal. He checked his reserve and saw that it was empty.

"Shit!" He exclaimed loudly. He had no idea how that had happened but he could figure it out later. First things first, he had to deal with this monster clinging to him.

Alex looked around frantically. He cast his

eyes to the wall and a neat idea popped straight into his head. He sprinted towards it and then threw himself, back first, onto the cold, stony surface. He felt no sympathy as whatever it was that was clinging to him hit the wall with the full force of his body behind it. In spite of the force Alex was throwing at it, it still clung to him tenaciously.

Unable to think of any other way out, Alex threw himself on the rock again and again, not sparing himself. His Body Enhancement was finished, but his rage gave him new strength. He wanted to crush and hurt this monster more than anything else. With each blow his shoulder flared with unbearable pain, but he continued to throw himself against the wall, hoping that the pain for the monster was even worse.

Whack! After about the tenth time of throwing himself against the wall, the sharp pain suddenly disappeared and everything started to feel normal again. He leaned against the wall for a second, breathing heavily, but his legs soon buckled and he fell to his knees with a groan. The fight was over, but his body was a spent force. Alex felt like he'd run a marathon, he hadn't been so tired for a long time.

With a sigh that turned into a wheeze, he pulled himself to his feet. With horror, he realized that the creature was still on him. All he wanted to do was lie down and relax but he had to finish what he'd started. He moved weakly and his right arm had completely given up on him so, with his good left arm, he found the creature behind him and pulled down hard. He screamed as he felt the creature detach while taking a piece of flesh with it. Warm blood trickled down his back and his vision started to go blurry, but he stayed conscious. At that moment, he really had to!

With difficulty he reached the nearest rock, having discarded the clinging creature on the way. He sat down and then wrapped his arms around his knees. He began to sway backwards and forwards in an effort not to pass out. Slowly, he felt the numbness subside and his head slowly started to feel a bit clearer.

Looking back he saw what had clung to him for so long. A purple, almost black body just over two foot long lay on the floor. It looked like a snake with the eyes of a deep-sea fish and a mouth filled with dozens of small teeth, Alex could even see his flesh stuck in its teeth. He wrinkled his nose and felt like he was going to be sick.

At first glance, the monster seemed unharmed from the blows on the wall. But it was clearly dead. Fury and strength had won the fight but, truthfully Alex knew he'd won just because of his size. As he'd told himself many times before, size mattered over here. But that didn't mean it had been easy. Despite the difference in size this creature had still managed to inflict considerable pain on Alex.

A quick glance at the Scanner revealed its name:

[Ice Leech: Level 1]

The name suited the creature well. But now was the time for some research. Throwing the corpse on the floor, he began to gut it.

In that moment Alex didn't feel an ounce of disgust. He'd never been the squeamish type, but here he really couldn't afford to be. Every bit of information he could glean here would give him an advantage, so Alex was ready to dissect and dig into the innards of this creature as much as he had to.

At first, he struggled to use his knife. The blade simply couldn't cut through the top layer of skin. He was worried he was just going to break it so he started using the spear instead. He could use some pollen with the spear too so it was all round a more efficient method. It was a shame he only had one of these weapons. He thought about using Scissors for this job, but it was precision he needed here. Scissors would probably just obliterate the body and leave him with nothing to work with.

With one swift movement he cut open the leech from head to toe. A bright green substance came trickling out of its body, which started to evaporate almost immediately on touching the floor. By this time, Alex had learnt to feel the changes in the energy background and he noticed the energy dispersal here as this blood-like substance evaporated.

"So energy builds up in their blood," he quietly remarked to himself as he dipped a finger in the small pool forming in front of him.

The substance started to form an ice-layer on

his finger but, thanks to the warmth of his body, it quickly melted away. He had a hunch that the abilities of these monsters were somehow connected with sucking energy, hence the name leech. He'd felt the life being sucked out of him while it was clinging to him. Maybe they could extract energy from any life form and Alex dreaded to think what else they could do.

For the next half an hour Alex sat next to the gutted creature, catching his breath while trying to figure out how best to find these cunning beasts. As he sat there, the pool of blood almost completely evaporated leaving behind a small black residue which looked just like dried human blood.

He looked out towards the river and felt a lot calmer than before.

"I'll rest up a bit, then I'll try again," he mumbled to himself. He tried moving his shoulder but it still wasn't in great shape. He sprinkled a pinch of pollen as best he could onto the open wound and then he set about bandaging it up. It wasn't easy doing it with one arm, but he just about managed it. The sharp pain subsided but he was still acutely aware how vulnerable he was. If he was attacked right then, he'd struggle to defend himself with one working arm.

He got up and tried wandering around near the river. He looked out and tried to see if anything had changed there, but the ocean of darkness prevented him from seeing anything. He was sure there were plenty of creatures out there. He just couldn't see them. He needed to set up camp somewhere and think through his next step.

Once he'd set himself up with a makeshift camp, he treated his wound again and then he set about repairing his overcoat. It didn't resemble much of a coat anymore but it was all he had for a top layer and he was determined to make it work as best he could.

Having patched it up as best he could, he lay down to sleep. Anymore activities like fishing for some food were out of the question.

*　*　*

The next day, Alex decided to use his wound as an excuse to rest. Sitting on the rock he'd used to set up camp, he looked out at the river and thought about what to do next. He knew he didn't have long till he'd get to the next level. Maybe only a week and a half more and he'd be there. Maybe dealing with the ice leeches would be a good way to level up. He just had to work out the best way to do that.

What did he even know about them? Clearly, they were very sensitive creatures. It hadn't taken them long to sense him once he set foot on their territory. He'd even tried his best to move quietly just before he'd come up against them. So they clearly defended their territory and, seemingly, attacked in numbers. Just like the crawlers, they could move a lot quicker than expected but, unlike the crawlers, they had a lot more abilities to do some damage.

One thing Alex did understand was that they didn't like the light. This was definitely a weak spot, so Alex figured it was a good place to start.

He wished he had some other source of light apart from the tiny, little lighter in his hand. There were a few things like that which he wished he could have had with him. But it was hard to foresee everything, when making the crossing to the Other Side. One thing he had been lucky with was the energy bars. That stock of food had proved very useful as he would have struggled to get far just by catching fish.

More than anything, Alex knew that he didn't want to turn back. He would have to negotiate the shoreline again and then, after that, there were sure to be some of his old friends waiting for him back in the cave. Besides, Alex didn't believe he'd find the exit walking that way. He'd walked along the river for a while now and he'd noticed how he was walking on a slight upward slope. He figured going uphill was a sure way to find at least some sort of surface.

At that moment Alex wasn't angry at the leeches. He had no real hatred for the inhabitants of the Other Side. Yes, they could kill him, but so could a car on Earth. Whenever he cursed and swore at them, it was just a way of releasing some fear and tension. They were a serious inconvenience but, at the same time, he needed them for development. Now when he encountered them, he was much more likely to feel a sense of collectedness and inner peace which, in turn, was exactly what he needed for rest and recuperation.

He'd managed to avoid the other extreme. There were people who believed that creatures should be treated differently because it was "their" world. But such people mostly lived on Earth and, normally, quickly changed their views once they'd experienced the dangers of actually dealing with these animals. Alex didn't consider monsters as heirs of this world. He believed that the Other Side was the world of people and for people.

So for him, the leeches were just another obstacle which needed to be passed. There were plenty of monsters and, if he needed to, he would deal with all of them one by one, no matter how long it took.

* * *

First thing the next morning Alex took off the bandage and started testing the strength of his arm. A few lunges with his spear were enough to convince him his arm was back in working order. Once again marveling at the healing power of the pollen, he set out looking for more leeches.

The darkness and cold around seemed to suck out all the life and energy he had, but Alex knew how to detach himself from negative emotions. He'd become quite good at that on Earth.

He hadn't really noticed, but the long journey was changing him. The old sense of fatalism and the desire to live as long as possible had gone. The skills and sense of energy gave a new impetus and meaning to his struggle. Thanks to them, Alex gradually began to perceive himself not as a toy in the hands of fate, but as someone who was fully capable of choosing their own destiny.

However, he didn't lose focus. For the next hour he stood in the freezing cold intently watching out for more ice leeches. Nothing appeared.

"Let's try again," he whispered and walked forward about a hundred and fifty feet.

The light from the rocks on the shore made the gloom a little lighter and the Night Filter was a big help as well. He moved forward slowly, with only one thing on his mind.

Yesterday he'd thought that the Pump was working a bit slower than usual. Now he was back here, he measured the background as best he could. One look at the measurements confirmed his suspicions. It looked like the leeches sucked everything they could, not only from the moss and the visiting prospectors, but from the surrounding area too. Fortunately, they couldn't extract everything that easily. They at least needed physical contact to harm humans.

This is a well-known feature of the Other Side. Just as prospectors couldn't use skills inside monsters, monsters couldn't harm humans in the same way. Otherwise, Alex would simply activate the Scissors inside the enemy and instantly cut their internal organs. Fortunately for both sides, this was impossible. The organism of a human and a monster is a separate world, a completely different entity with its own laws. Alex's body had formed additional structures: matrixes, energy centers, channels and it required a huge excess of energy or a big difference in levels for something to break through that natural defense.

He continued to walk forward in the darkness but nothing came to meet him. In the palm of his hand Alex clutched the lighter, which he'd repaired from the day before.

Yesterday, the monsters had come from the river and the shore. So they could live both on water and land. They also seemed to settle in groups and attacked in a similar fashion. When he'd been chased yesterday, they seemed to work pretty collectively.

Thinking about it, Alex couldn't help but admire these new creatures. They'd found a suitable habitat and, when needed, could work together towards a common goal. Granted, that common goal had been him yesterday, but all the same it had been impressive.

"Now it's my turn," the prospector muttered under his breath as he trod carefully on the ice. "I can't keep running away from you."

After a couple of hundred yards of walking he stopped while scanning a hundred-and-fifty-foot radius around him. He didn't have enough energy for more. Alex cursed the limitations of his current level. If only he just had the next level now. It would make everything so much easier. One thing Alex had always been able to use in his favor was his sense of hearing. Here on the Other Side, the monsters never tried to be cautious or stealthy in hunting people. The approach of a group of them could be heard from afar and that was exactly what had saved him yesterday.

As it happened, his hearing came in handy to-day as well. About a hundred yards away he heard a splash. This sound was enough for to turn tail and run but a quick glance at the Scanner told him everything he needed to know. The ice leeches had woken up.

Just like the day before, Alex was pursued by an annoying rustling sound but, this time, he was better prepared. He ran to the end of their terri-tory, turned around and lit the lighter in his hand. The faint flame in his raised hand revealed a dozen dark, serpentine silhouettes. They all stopped a dozen feet away, but they didn't stand still. Their bodies wriggled frantically, twitching and beating their tails on the stone floor.

Keeping the lighter hand raised, Alex took a step forward, bringing the light in his hand for-ward with him. The creatures squirmed in front of him but then reluctantly crawled away.

"What's wrong, do you want some more?" Alex laughed as he slowly moved forward.

The monsters looked furious but they slowly retreated, the warm yellow light chasing them away. They looked like cockroaches fleeing from a flame in the middle of the night. But the further he drove them away, the more he'd have to go into their territory. Further into their territory, they were only going to grow in confidence.

Alex had walked about a hundred and fifty feet into their territory now, and the leeches still kept their distance. They were close enough that Alex could have got them with Scissors if he wanted to, but he still wanted to test their reaction to the light in his hand.

At that moment about a dozen of them crawled towards him. The light seemed to be getting weaker. The spot of light in his hand narrowed and the darkness started to close in around him. Alex was confused. He knew there was nothing wrong with the lighter, so what was going on? Could the leeches slow down chemical reactions as well?

Several more silhouettes appeared out of the darkness. The leeches circled around him like nocturnal predators, but the flame in his hand fortunately stayed lit.

He stretched out his hand and shook the flame from side to side. The leeches didn't like that and quickly took a step back.

As a test, Alex then covered the flame with his hand. The leeches immediately rushed forward. As soon as they got close he removed his hand and they recoiled as quick as they'd advanced. He tried this movement several times and they reacted the same way every time.

"They're not the brightest, are they," he remarked to himself.

Having exhausted this maneuver, Alex started to back away. He was surrounded on all sides but, with the help of the flame in his hand, the leeches parted like the Red Sea leaving his path free out of their territory.

As Alex moved, they started to get a little closer to him but never quite dared to launch themselves at him. The flame in his hand was just too much. When Alex was close to the edge of the territory, he stopped.

"Right, let's see how tough you guys are, shall we?"

He chose the nearest victim and, activating the Scissors, he heard how they easily sliced through its skinny body. It fell to the ground severed in two, twitching a couple of times and pouring blue blood onto the cold floor.

The pack went into a frenzy, the clump of bodies disintegrating into writhing silhouettes. The monsters thrashed against the floor with unbelievable force, making a cacophony of sounds, as if a crowd of men were beating the ground with leather whips.

Alex just stood there watching. He wondered if the death of one of them could make them blind with rage to the point where they wouldn't be afraid of the tiny flame he held in his hand. But, luckily, they all kept their distance. Now Alex felt stronger. If that wasn't enough to send them fleeing away, he could now set to work at harvesting them for pollen. But there was another surprise in store for him.

In the midst of the raging crowd, several of them began greedily devouring the corpse who had, shortly before, been a living, breathing member of their pack. They were almost fighting over it as they sucked up bright blue drippings from the rocks. They greedily sucked everything they could, not leaving a drop behind for Alex.

"Fucking cannibals!" he exclaimed irritably. His tactic of killing a bunch of monsters and siphoning energy from their corpses wouldn't work if the others just ate their dead. It didn't seem fair to him.

Having come to terms with the loss of pollen, Alex decided that enough was enough and he stepped back into safer territory. On seeing him do this, the ice leeches turned around and disappeared in the darkness of the stone beach, leaving behind them what was left of the leech which Alex had just killed.

He hadn't got everything he wanted from the latest foray but he'd confirmed the leeches' aversion to light. Now, he wished he had some kind of ability related to light or fire. That would really have come in handy.

Despite the disappointment, Alex had an idea of what to do next. He walked along the river until he found a suitable boulder heavily covered in moss. There wasn't much moss growing on the rocks next to the icy beach, so he had to move further away.

Picking up the improvised lamp, Alex headed back. He wanted to gather some moss but, if he gathered it straight off the rocks it wouldn't keep glowing like he wanted it to. So he had to get to work and drag the boulders all the way to the border of the leeches' den. It was hard work, but he needed this light more than anything.

"That should be enough," he said to himself after he'd dragged the eleventh boulder over to where it needed to be.

Here, in the dark and cold, the dull greenish glow from the moss seemed faint and lifeless and Alex started to doubt whether this was really a good plan at all. But now that he'd started, he had to go through with it.

He took out his lighter, walked a hundred feet into the cold territory he'd been in before, then stopped. They should see him here. As soon as he heard the familiar splashes and rustling, he lit the lighter and moved back. The leeches came to a halt in front of him, held back by the flame and in a large mass followed the slowly retreating prospector.

They came to the boulders and skirted around them as Alex moved through the carefully placed pattern. He'd arranged them in such a way that he could move in the middle of them but the light which came off each boulder should, in theory, keep the leeches from getting close to him. The more he moved through them, the more the leeches stayed away from the light. So far, his plan was working. Alex smirked, feeling confident that he'd chosen the right method to deal with these creatures.

When he reached the largest pile of stones, he stopped. The monsters froze nearby.

Alex extinguished the lighter, watching the reaction of the creatures around him. Would the familiar green light stop them or not? As soon as the fire went out, the dark silhouettes jerked forward uncertainly, not quite sure what to do next.

The leeches were still few and cautious, but after half an hour or so some more came to join them and there was soon a real swarm of them. In all that time, they'd swarmed to within about fifty feet of him.

This was the moment of truth. Alex picked one of the leeches just to the left of him and, just like before, activated Scissors slicing the creature in half. Just like last time, they all went berserk and the circle shrank even tighter. A few of them started devouring the corpse as well.

After about half an hour they'd all calmed down but the pack had somehow grown. With this increase, they became even bolder and, to make matters worse, the light from the moss was beginning to fade.

But Alex was happy as he stood there in the semi-darkness. His plan had worked and he was getting to know more and more about the limits of the ice leeches.

"Need to get out now, next time I'll have to lay down more rocks," he said quietly to himself.

His quiet, hoarse voice, interrupted by the endless rustling around him, sounded thoughtful and distant, as if Alex was thinking about something trivial, rather than planning an operation that could very easily end in his own death.

The dark silhouettes still moved frantically around him, unwilling to settle down. Crawlers in such a situation would long ago have curled up, waiting for the victim to come closer, but these greedy leeches had no idea what patience was. It was only a hundred yards to get out of their territory but it was too dangerous to make a dash for it. Alex doubted whether the tiny flame he had would be so effective now against such a vast horde of monsters.

Alex picked up the brightest stone he could see, lit some of the moss attached to it and made his way towards the shore. The result was a powerful source of light which dispersed the darkness and infuriated the leeches. The rustling circle broke up before him as they reluctantly made way for the light. But despite their fear of the light, they stuck as close as they could to him. Despite their fear of the light, they still didn't want to just let him get away.

The moss continued to burn, but Alex knew it wouldn't last that long. He quickened his step and started running. By the time the light went out, he was running along the shore, leaving the leeches' territory far behind.

The rest of the day Alex devoted to hard work, gathering more rocks with glowing moss. For each boulder he had to go further away than the last one, but General Body Enhancement was a big help here. The more he worked, the more the pile grew and the light increasingly dispelled the surrounding darkness.

The next morning the work continued and, by the end of the day, Alex had completely cleared a huge chunk of the shore, collecting about a hundred and fifty boulders. He'd even managed to roll in a couple of the larger boulders without damaging the moss too much. It was a pity he couldn't just strip the moss off the rocks and use it like that, but he just knew that wasn't possible.

During all this labor, his General Body Enhancement had increased by four points, which was a bonus he was very happy to take.

Satisfied with the results, Alex went to bed. Tomorrow he would really set to work.

CHAPTER 25

THE ICE MASSACRE

The other side of the Moon
Nina Farrell

A SMALL, BRAND-NEW SHIP moored gently to the automated dock on the other side of the moon. The vessel was only fifty-one feet long, so it wasn't much to look at. This model had been used to deliver cargo to satellites orbiting the Earth but now that job had been taken over by a different model.

Earth only had a small space fleet and ship-building had been in decline for a few years now. The root of the problem wasn't a lack of technology, but a lack of places to fly to. Any potential space traveler from Earth had a small choice of routes. There were a few large research stations, settlements on Mars and about a hundred small, inhabited modules scattered around the solar system. All of these places were essentially research centers rather than any attempt at colonization so there were never many free vacancies to fill there anyway. The human race hadn't had much success in exploring their solar system. And since there was no need, they did what they had to, hoping that one day they would start to populate Mars and then they could start thinking about building another fleet.

The reason Nina piloted this particular ship was the lack of hold requirements and the short flight distance. Despite the small size and simpleness of the ship itself, the crew's task was highly important. They were carrying pollen, the only "exported" product shipped outside the solar system. Humans had tried to trade other goods, but nothing else interested the aliens. The Tamedians showed no interest in any cultural values or achievements of mankind. They just politely explained to the humans that there were plenty such objects elsewhere in the galaxy and they just didn't hold the same value to them as they did to humans. But pollen was another matter.

Nina Farrell, a third-generation captain, had been mad about space since childhood. Thanks to her family's reputation and personal efforts, she was able to get this assignment and she'd been incredibly proud of her achievements. But now Nina looked enviously at the Merchant ship as she approached the outer dock. The ship itself was hidden beneath the lunar soil. But that was enough for Nina. Her vivid imagination had already painted a picture of how she'd flown to the nearest star system and even managed to find a couple of inhabited planets there.

"Captain, the tribute's been received. The big man's happy!" The chief mate loudly reported through the comm unit.

"Cargo, Simon, it's just cargo!" Nina tiredly corrected the chief mate.

"Sorry Captain! The cargo's been received. The big man's happy!" Simon immediately corrected himself.

The chief mate was an excellent specialist, but Nina feared that one day his jokes would go too far and that would be the end of his career. There were some people in the fleet who took a dim view of that kind of thing. Nina decided to have a heart-to-heart talk with him once she'd finished work. It would look bad on her too if he ended up crossing the line somehow. They were sleeping together and, sometimes, Nina believed that he treated that like a free pass to do what he wanted. She just wanted to tell him there was a clear line between personal and work life. So far, high command had said nothing about their situation so either they hadn't cottoned onto it yet or they were turning a blind eye to it as they knew a good team when they saw one.

All pollen was transported solely by warships and only by crews who had never been to the Other Side. Using commercial ships for transport was strictly out of the question. The risk was too great.

There were millions of people on Earth who just couldn't be allowed to get their hands on energy powder. There would be no telling the damage if it fell into the wrong hands. Nina had heard that after going over to the Other Side, prospectors normally came back stronger, more aggressive and unable to switch back to everyday life on Earth. In the end the authorities just accepted this and decided it was easier to just settle veterans next to each other, away from regular citizens under the pretext that all former prospectors should be given special conditions in the form of luxurious housing.

For the same reason, pollen wasn't transported centrally from one place, but from several different bases to reduce the number of movements within the planet. Each major region on Earth sent a shipment of powder to the moon as soon as it had accumulated a certain amount.

The captain glanced at her watch. The next ship would be arriving soon so it was time to call it a day. They'd already unloaded a couple of tons of "tribute," as Simon had put it. Nina cast a glance at the lunar landscape and initiated the takeoff procedure. She'd be home in a few hours, but Nina would have given anything to go on a real space journey rather than work as a glorified courier. But sadly they just didn't have the technology for that on Earth and the Tamedians refused to share it, explaining that it was still too early for humans to leave their system. The aliens said that even they themselves didn't set sail round the galaxy. It was a long, complicated procedure that was often best completed by unmanned ships anyway.

That's why the Trader still hadn't left the moon, preferring to conduct all business with humanity from there. Thanks to an agreement with the authorities, the entire back side of the Earth's only satellite was his territory, to which no one had the right to land without special permission.

Not everyone was happy about this. Nina was part of a small group of people who thought it might have been better had the Trader not found them at all. But it was hard to argue with the benefits they'd had thanks to him. Society had developed further, technological progress had soared and even the well-being of the population had undoubtedly improved since his arrival. It was hard for the human race to refuse such advantages.

The idea of long life was a huge factor that had captured the minds and hearts of people. New youth seemed like too big an opportunity to pass up, so the dream of space exploration was exchanged for plans to explore the Other Side. The government promoted it in every possible way, channeling their main resources into pollen mining and the study of this new world. Exploring what was out there in their own galaxy could wait for a bit.

Besides, even if mankind wanted to explore space, they'd struggle to find enough willing participants. Most people were quite happy not exploring outer space. Nina understood them in a way. What was the point of studying for years and then being stuck in a small module, or living on a station and staring out the window at nothing? Wouldn't it be better to take a crash course in a few months and get involved in the main mystery of Earth, the Other Side? There was also the incentive of new capabilities which gave people power, albeit in another world. This was what drew people over there, forcing them to risk their lives day in day out.

Until now, no one knew what an alien ship looked like from the inside. They didn't even know what the Trader was doing with so much pollen and, most importantly, — how he transported everything to his home world. The humans weren't fools, however, and realized that the Merchant must be transmitting everything from a distance. There was no other explanation. Transporting it the normal way would have required too much time and resources.

And indeed, this wasn't a bad guess. The Trader would transfer the pollen from material form to energy form and then send it to his home planet, where the dust would again materialize as powder. Unfortunately, about thirty to forty percent was always lost during transmission but it was still the fastest and most economical form of transport.

A quarter of an hour later, Nina's ship departed and the moon was quiet for a few minutes, until a new carrier arrived with another load of pollen.

* * *

The Other Side
Alex

Alex approached the border. He expected a long and difficult day ahead. He hoped he wouldn't have any serious wounds by the end of the day but, as ever, surviving the day would be considered a success in his eyes. He wanted to see if he could make it through the ice leeches' territory or if he had to look for a way around.

The first thing he did was to examine the pile of boulders left from yesterday. As expected, the moss had faded. If the moss continued to fade at this rate, the rocks would stop giving light in two or three days. Time was working against him.

This time he wasn't mean on the number of rocks he thought he'd need. He planned to build a safe route for retreat, for which he'd need about a hundred mossy rocks. The result would be a path about six feet wide.

Once his work was done he was ready to go.

"Great," he murmured, looking at the glowing line that led into impenetrable darkness.

This path meant that the leeches wouldn't stab him in the back if he was running away. It would also help him safely carry more stones if he wanted to extend this artificial pathway. It was hard work but Alex continued building what he'd set out to do. The result was a kind of hunting shelter at the end of the path he'd already constructed earlier about two hundred and fifty yards into the leeches' territory. The shelter was open on one side and there was enough room inside for a man of average build to fit comfortably. There was no roof, but strong walls protected his back and sides. There was an inner circle which would act as the last line of defense, but Alex really hoped he wouldn't be needing that. In reality, if the creatures broke through, nothing could save him.

The first guests began to arrive when the construction was still in full swing. They came from two directions, from the darkness of the cave and from the water nearby. Alex didn't pay much attention to them, continuing to run back and then drag more stones to where he needed them. The whole time he made his way up and down the path he was accompanied by the leeches back and forth like faithful squires waiting on him attentively. When the construction was over, there were at least a hundred of them around the fortification.

"Good turnout," Alex thought to himself amusedly.

Critically examining the circle, he sat down between the stones. A spear, a lighter, a torch made of folded paper and his powder container were all lying next to him.

The leeches around were starting to get restless and the cacophony of sounds only attracted others and soon the fortification was surrounded from all sides bar the pathway side.

"Showtime," he whispered and smiled to himself.

He picked one of them he could see not far away and got to work with the Scissors. It died almost instantly. An already chaotic jumble of creatures descended into complete bedlam as another dozen excited creatures did their best to get their fair share of the spoils.

He went for another one on the other side of the fortification. This time he was lucky, the slice managed to cut two of them at once. Things were starting to get pretty heated out there. All of them seemed to be fighting amongst themselves to get at the remains of their brethren.

Encouraged by these results, Alex continued using Scissors from the safety of his self-made fortification. Two more monsters fell to the ground simultaneously while another was only partially cut in half by one of Alex's blows and writhed on the ground in agony as his comrades descended on him. It was complete chaos. As soon as they saw that one of their own was dead, instead of running away from what was clear danger, they just made their way towards the corpse, helpfully providing Alex with more targets to aim at. They didn't seem to have enough brains to realize that they would have been better off just getting away from there.

In an hour Alex managed to destroy about a dozen more monsters. He'd been using the Pump to keep everything going. It was a shame the leeches didn't give him any time to make use of the excess energy when he killed them but Alex wasn't worried. Sooner or later, he'd kill all of them if they kept behaving like this.

Besides exterminating the whole tribe, Alex had hoped to find out a bit more about them. Surely, he'd be left with at least one corpse to look at by the end of all this.

Putting aside this idea, Alex kept dealing with these stupid, seemingly endless creatures. Surely they couldn't keep attacking forever like this?

Another hour passed and Alex continued to deal with them. He'd long ago lost count of how many he'd killed and he gave up even trying. Sometimes Scissors took one life, sometimes two. But despite all the kills, the horde didn't seem to have shrunk at all.

Everything was going more or less according to plan. Alex had wanted to kill as many as he could and he was doing just that. But there was a problem. The moss on the outer layer of stones was degrading faster than expected. With each passing hour, the light had dimmed more and more.

Alex had noticed in the last hour how the leeches were getting bolder and had got closer and closer to the circle.

"For fuck's sake! Well, you asked for it!" He shouted angrily.

It was time for pollen. At his current level, one gram of it was enough to fill the energy reserve forty times. That would instantly give him forty blows with Scissors

With this help, things moved a bit quicker. Now, he could hit them every fifteen seconds which did wonders for transforming his abilities. But Alex wasn't distracted by the Interface. He kept dealing with the monsters, meticulously making his way through the seemingly endless sea of them.

The number of corpses increased sharply and the pack became even more frantic, if that was even possible. It was as if the leeches knew they couldn't reach Alex so they took out their rage on their fallen comrades. But Alex was fine with that. He'd much rather they devoured each other than him.

After a few minutes, Alex closed the container. He'd need more pollen soon and, with levelling up just around the corner, he preferred to keep some powder in reserve just in case he needed it.

This monotonous battle continued for another five hours. All this time Alex had to sit curled up in his stone fortress. From time to time, he got up to stretch his legs, but he didn't leave the inner circle, fearing that the leeches would just jump over his defenses if they saw him move about so brazenly.

Finally, the horde started to thin out. Many of the surviving monsters had numerous wounds and were barely moving. Alex even noticed an untouched corpse which might come in handy for some research. As they dispersed, the energy background began to increase, which was a huge boost to the Pump. With all of this going in his favor, he continued hitting them with everything he had.

With eyes red from fatigue and constant strain, Alex looked at the last two live leeches cowering amongst the pile of corpses. They weren't really hiding, just chewing lazily on their dead brethren. It was disgusting to watch.

He stepped slightly out of his perimeter and hit them with Scissors, killing them both with one swift blow.

"Finally!" He said with satisfaction. It had been a long, hard fight. But no sooner had he finished them off, than dozens of new silhouettes suddenly appeared out of the darkness. It couldn't be another wave of them!?

He glared angrily at them as more of them kept coming and coming.

"Why does there have to be so many of you!?" He shrieked in frustration.

He'd genuinely started to believe that he'd cleared the area and here were hundreds or even thousands more of these despicable creatures slithering out of the darkness towards him.

"Shit, it must be the energy!" He suddenly realized.

All the dead bodies had created a huge surplus of energy in the surrounding area and, although Alex had managed to absorb some of it with the Pump, he couldn't absorb all of it. It was this surplus which had attracted so many creatures so quickly. Alex wrinkled his nose. He noticed that the light was beginning to fade.

"Oh, for fuck's sake!"

They were a lot braver than before and they'd

now come right up to the stone perimeter protecting him. Without hesitation Alex opened the container.

He immediately started slicing away with Scissors, just as he'd been doing before, only this time with a little more urgency.

Ten minutes passed. Then twenty more. Soon thirty minutes had passed, but Alex barely noticed. He felt like a worker on a conveyor belt, who couldn't be distracted, otherwise the line would stop and everything would go to waste. Like a fine-tuned machine, he filled the reserve and immediately poured it into the Scissors. The pollen was whittling away. At this rate, the container would soon be empty. Behind the line of fading light the mountain of corpses was growing and growing. Hundreds of these leeches had now died going after this one tenacious prospector.

"That's enough," Alex whispered, closing the container. He reckoned he could continue on his own now.

The fading light was a serious concern. He'd been constantly monitoring them, but he couldn't do anything about it while he was busy slaughtering leeches.

After seven hours, the entire space outside the luminous perimeter was filled with corpses. It was literally like a wall which made it difficult to see and find new targets. The living mixed with the dead and the whole area looked more like a slaughterhouse than anything else. Illuminated by the dim greenish light, the icy beach seemed especially ominous. However, Alex was so exhausted that he didn't pay attention to the dreary landscape around him.

The pack was getting weaker, and the stones, on the contrary, were glowing a little stronger. Alex didn't want to tempt fate anymore. As soon as the last creatures died, he would run away from here.

Finally, he finished off the last leech he could see and with a groan he tried standing up but could barely muster the strength to raise himself. The silence of the cave was broken by the rustling of dozens more bodies.

"Dammit! Again?! I killed so many of you. Where the fuck are you all coming from!?"

Alex looked tiredly at the arriving enemies and reckoned this new horde must have spotted his position hours ago and had just been waiting for the right moment to attack.

As much as Alex wanted to run, he couldn't risk it now, even with a torch in his hand. He tried to gather crumbs of energy from the corpses with the Pump before they were sucked up by the horde, but the leeches were faster and way ahead of him in this department. There were just so many of them.

The leeches' behavior made him angry, but then Alex seemed to come to his senses and started laughing.

"You're fucked anyway, you freaks!"

He was very tired and in his laughter he sounded almost mad. If he could have seen himself, he would have marveled at the changes that had taken place. He'd always considered himself a rational person. Not some kind of maniac who'd fight a crowd of monsters in a battle of life and death and, at the same time, actively enjoy it. However, sitting in a stone circle surrounded by mountains of corpses, nothing seemed strange to him at all.

In that moment, Alex decided to get away by any means.

Having attacked the first few new arrivals with Scissors, with the help of a pinch of powder, he got up and rushed to the shore with all his might.

The perimeter he'd set out held fast and continued to glow. Not a single leech tried crossing it as he dashed back up the path. A few seconds later and warm air washed over Alex's face. He'd made it!

Utterly exhausted, he wandered back towards the temporary camp. He'd barely even reached his sleeping bag when he collapsed and passed out. He hadn't even checked to see how safe the camp was from any unwanted visitors. He was just too tired and if they came so be it.

*   *   *

In the morning Alex called up the interface. The readings both pleased and disappointed him:

[Level: 0
Energy: 35/35 units.
Transformation: Body: 89.4% / *Structure:*

100.0% / Brain: 90.9%
   Signatures: Simple: *Walker (15%)*
   Common: *Night Filter (max), General Body Enhancement* (65%).*
   Rare: *Space Barrier** (90%), Space Scanner** (92%), Pump** (89%), Space Scissors** (91%).*
   Talents: *Touch of Death, Sense of Space]*

A day of intense combat had reaped the same reward as the previous weeks of polyp hunting. Alex was fortunate enough to have been in a unique situation where, despite the danger, he could hit enemies but not be hit back. And he'd dealt with a lot of them! Even though the leeches were small, their level was higher than his. It was no wonder that he'd grown his abilities so fast.

However, deep down Alex had hoped that after such an intense fight, all three aspects would have risen to a hundred per cent. They were all still good results. Alex just found himself wishing for better.

"So what next," he muttered to himself, looking at all the lagging aspects.

He thought back to all the advice he'd had on how to get to the next level. His situation wasn't unique. He'd been told in training that most prospectors encountered lots of obstacles as they tried to level up.

Sometimes it just took a lot of effort to get that one lagging parameter up to a hundred per cent.

"Okay, so I'll focus on the body," Alex decided. But what about abilities?

There were no surprises here. As a result of

frequent use Scissors had crossed the threshold of eighty-five per cent and got the second strengthening. He had the stupidity of the leeches to thank for that.

He'd managed to increase the range of this skill to a hundred and fifty feet.

"We'll have some fun with that." He said to himself. It would now be a lot easier to hit out at new enemies from afar. It didn't seem like much of an increase but being able to attack from such a distance gave him a massive advantage.

In addition to the range, Scissors had received a second mode. If you let a little less energy through the matrix, the wide blade transformed into miniature version of the ability. This new mode wasn't suitable for combat, but Alex wasn't upset. He figured it would come in handy somewhere down the line.

For the rest of the day, Alex tidied up his clothes, relaxed and fished until he felt the tension go. He wanted to feel well rested and ready to go again.

Once he felt well enough, he started hauling rocks again. Remembering how many creatures had appeared from the darkness, Alex wasn't lazy and collected all the boulders he could find. He really didn't want to get into a situation where he had to guess whether he had enough light for the rest of the fight or not.

After a few hours of toil, a decent mountain of cobblestones loomed in front of him. General Body Enhancement had helped him save energy, but it was tedious work. The next day Alex planned to make a new foray out of his area.

* * *

When he set out the next day, he was met with a new, but pleasant surprise.

The stones, left from yesterday, had noticeably faded, but still glowed. Although it wasn't much, it was still a good sign.

There was something else. The icy beach had warmed up! The frost on the stone floor had disappeared, and the temperature felt like it had risen to ten or fifteen degrees. By all accounts, the balance of power had changed. But why? Maybe he'd killed so many of the creepers that their power had diminished and they'd lost control of the territory?

"Hmmm... I'll see what happens tomorrow anyway. If it goes on like this, maybe I'll claim this damn beach for my own." With this thought, Alex went back to camp.

CHAPTER 26

THE PATH TO DARKNESS

The Other Side
Upper Cave
70km from Alex's camp

"TONY'S IN A BAD WAY, BOSS!" Jah said as he ran up to Thorwald.

"Is there any pollen left? I'll go check," Thorwald replied quickly and headed for the far end of the cave, where all the wounded were.

Jah could barely keep up with the long strides of his commanding officer.

Thorwald was well over six foot and, with his beard, he looked almost like a Viking.

This resemblance to a medieval warrior was completed by a shield, a huge axe, and an armored waistcoat that looked more like chainmail than a piece of high-tech equipment.

Thorwald, or Thor as he was known to the men was the commander of a small group of trapped men. He was a veteran with five years on the Other Side, but he wasn't the commander of a group of rookies here. In this group, only prospectors with level two or three stood a chance of getting in. The prospector with the lowest level in the group would have been considered elite anywhere else, but not here.

All the members of the group respected Thor and trusted him unconditionally. In any situation, his confidence always gave the men hope that they could cope.

When they got to Tony, they found him lying on an improvised bed of a simple sleeping bag on a hard, stone floor. Two men, Marta and Vika stood just beside him. Tony was not in a good way. There were no wounds on his body, but everyone around knew he was dying of poison.

It was a lipoid which had done that to him. They were called lipoids because they looked just like a lump of fat but looks could be deceiving. If they got close enough, they could do some serious damage.

Everyone wanted to help Tony but they didn't know how. A lot of them had been poisoned themselves so it was hard enough to deal with that. Each member of the team had received their share of poison. No one had managed to avoid it.

When the lipoids attacked, they would shoot a piece of foul-smelling mixture and then attack immediately. The substance evaporated quickly, releasing a thick fog, but once anyone breathed it in, they would be stopped in their tracks as they struggled to breathe and felt sick. There was no way to stop it, except to stop breathing.

So the prospectors were hemmed in by these creatures. The only way out was to go deeper in the caves but even this wasn't ideal as the monsters knew the caves a lot better than they did. And with all the wounded people, it would be hard to move them as well. Of course, there were other less dangerous creatures in the deeper caves, but the prospectors didn't particularly want to deal with those either.

The only reason why the prospectors were still alive was that some of them had adapted to the toxic gases. If someone could cope with the first dose, they would develop a slight immunity while recovering from the effects of the poison. So the prospectors tried their best to survive the first intake as much as possible. Luckily, everyone in the group had such a high level that it was a lot easier for their bodies to adapt to these new demands. But that wouldn't save them forever. The monsters were coming in waves and even for these experienced fighters, it was a struggle to cope.

It was hard for them to keep up with the relentless attacks and a single shot from one of these lipoids quickly filled the small space they were in.

Thorwald made sure that his men had at least some exposure to this poison in between the attacks. He figured it was good if they could build up a tolerance. The more often they inhaled the poisonous fumes, the less impact they had in serious skirmishes, which were starting to happen more and more regularly.

"How's he doing? Did you get more pollen?" Thor asked Vika whose hand was resting on Tony's forehead.

The symptoms of a poisoning usually included a strong rise in temperature. If that temperature stayed high, the body would shut down very quickly. Pollen helped with treating it, but it wasn't a cure. At the rate he was going, Tony had about half an hour. If it didn't get better in that time, it probably wasn't going to.

"We gave him some pollen, but he's still not looking good." Martha answered for Vika, while nodding at the container.

They'd found Tony in a side corridor three days ago. He'd only had level one when he came here so he'd been up against it from the start.

Thorwald was ashamed at how he'd disregarded him when he first arrived, but he was the commander and he had so many others to think about that he was always thinking about what was best for the group. In total, the group was made up of seven people. Four men and three women, for now.

Everyone wanted to believe the commander's words that they were going to get out. He wanted to believe them too. But there was no fooling anyone here. On the Other Side there were no guaranties and everyone had spent far too much time here to kid themselves.

Thorwald would only have said what he really thought to Martha. Even now, he looked lovingly at her. By the time Thorwald was 50, he'd been married twice. By the standards of the modern world, a man having tied himself to only two companions by that age was a rare sign. In this modern world, the institution of marriage had lost its former meaning. But Thorwald was a chip off the old block who wanted to remain true to the old Scandinavian republic where he'd come from.

It was exactly this attitude of not wanting to conform that Thorwald had given up his career as a teacher and became a prospector.

During his time on the Other Side, Thorwald had spent plenty of time with prospector women but he never imagined he'd become so attached to anyone again until he'd met Martha.

It was her he really wanted to save here. The other members of the team were just a bonus. He wanted more than anything to get out alive with her.

"Damn golems!" At the thought of the creatures around them, his blood boiled and he clenched his fists.

Stone giants were the reason they were all stuck here. The Other Side labelled them "spirits of stone', but Thorwald had no identification skill and, even if he did, he still called them golems.

The upper caverns where they were standing were huge. They consisted entirely of halls connected by passageways and tunnels. The survivors had all managed to find their way back to this small area after the trouble they'd run into. It just so happened that this was where a lot of them had ended up when they'd made their first crossing to the Other Side. It wasn't the most ideal point to end up on the Other Side for a newcomer, but plenty of them had managed to survive in spite of the difficulties.

The only ration they had left was eel. It wasn't ideal, but what saved them was the level of all the team members. With each level gained, a person's dependence on food on the Other Side decreased.

From where they were there were three exits. They'd checked out every one.

The first route was a network of tunnels and passageways connected to each other leading deep into the upper cavern. There were also plenty of monsters to worry about here. The team periodically cleared the tunnels, reducing the population of monsters around them, but they never ventured too far. They didn't want to encounter some higher level creatures they wouldn't be able to deal with.

The first humans who'd arrived at this spot had had to deal with plenty of different creatures but, in the end, they managed to carve out a small area for themselves. That didn't stop the monsters from trying to claim back their territory and every fortnight or so the prospectors had to repel a few waves of lipoid invasions.

One of the monsters there besides lipoids was another group of creatures called Profangs.

The Profangs were trickier. They would emit a

product into the surrounding area, leaving spores hanging in the air. Eventually they would settle on the rocks and from there they grew into small mushrooms. None of them really understood how they worked, but they didn't really care. Every day people went round the area and crushed these small mushrooms before they became dangerous.

The second route led to the waterfall, so it was doubtful there was a way out there. A few months ago, they'd checked this way. They'd had to deal with a lot of monsters blocking the way and, once they'd dealt with that, they'd come to a lake inhabited by some creatures shooting balls of acid. At this point, they all just turned around and went back.

The last route was a tunnel which the prospectors knew led out into the open. The only problem was it was guarded by the most dangerous enemy of all. The creatures Thorwald liked to call golems.

Thorwald had only seen them once, when they had accidentally provoked one by getting too close to the tunnel entrance. The creature had attacked and they'd lost three men that day.

As a result, they decided not to try and fight it anymore. They couldn't defeat it and they didn't try again. The previous leader, a similar character to Thorwald, had thrown himself at the monster to buy some time for everyone else to escape. The golem killed him with a single blow while the others were able to get away.

Thorwald hadn't seen where the golems came from but he'd heard from others that if you go into the tunnel, the scattered stones would begin to gather into a humanoid figure. Depending on their size they could be dealt with but when they became about a dozen feet tall, it was more difficult. As always on the Other Side, size did matter.

It would take a massive volley of dozens of prospectors to kill a creature like that, so Thorwald's current team didn't stand much of a chance. He clenched his fists again. He really hated them. That was the only thing standing between them and their route to safety. They could almost smell the surface air from where they were. It was so close but at the same time so so far away.

"Han, Oleg, Nobby," Thorwald whispered quietly to himself. He was remembering the names of all his fallen comrades.

At first, the team had only been small, no more than three or four people.

Then little by little, more people started to come.

If before, new prospectors were coming every two months, now there was someone new every two or three weeks. But the cave was reacting to this increase in numbers. The attacks were getting stronger, there were more and more high-level monsters, and there was no telling how long they would be able to keep going like this.

Thorwald was banking on some new arrivals to bolster the depleted team. He figured that sooner or later there would be someone whose skills would help them through all this. The good thing was that all the newcomers here were veterans who had spent several years honing their skills on the Other Side. Most of them had been through a lot and were more than well equipped to deal with the creatures they were up against there.

Thorwald checked over the rest of his team. Bar the poisoning, there were no serious injuries. There was still hope.

He made his way over to Tony's bedside. Unfortunately, Tony hadn't made it. Thorwald sighed. Yet another friend he'd have to bury.

*　*　*

The Other Side
The Cave
Alex

Slaughtering so many ice leeches had at least given Alex the necessary experience and understanding of how best to deal with these creatures. Their weak point seemed to be their greed. They also weren't particularly good at working together. At first, Alex had thought they were pack animals but he changed his mind after seeing their single-mindedness at work. Apparently, the Other Side had given them a lot of dangerous skills, but not much brainpower.

"Even the polyps were smarter," Alex thought to himself at breakfast that morning.

Having had a good think, Alex figured it was time to change his tactics slightly. It had taken too much time and effort to carry all those stones. Of course, the light they gave off was a great defense, but he just thought he didn't need to build such a big fortress with an escape route the next time.

The pile of building materials he'd collected yesterday was waiting at the border. Alex surveyed everything, walked around it, clucked his tongue and checked the condition of the moss. He counted up everything as economically as he could and, after a while, his head was spinning with new plans about how best to move what he already had and how best to preserve the moss. He even thought about starting some kind of farm, where he could grow his own moss, but he discarded this idea quickly as it seemed far-fetched and impractical.

His first task was to deal with the rising temperature. He took his spear and lighter with him and headed back to the place that had seen so much action yesterday.

The first thing he noticed was the light. The moss on the stones left behind was still thriving and showed no signs of going out.

"Leeches no longer rule this place," he muttered, feeling the moss on one of the nearest rocks to him.

It had warmed considerably overnight which was good for more moss to grow but Alex didn't plan on waiting for a long time. Since there were no creatures nearby, he got to work.

The work was uneventful. It was tough going but a lot safer than fighting for your life against dangerous creatures. After a few hours of carrying boulders and going back and forth Alex had made some good progress.

The second stage was a bit more difficult. He needed to move more rocks further into the darkness. He started building small piles with about a hundred yards apart.

Working in this way, he advanced about a mile and a half into the leeches' territory but he didn't come across one of them. He even began to relax a bit. He continued carrying stones until he felt like he could go on no longer. He decided to turn back and get some rest.

"There's a time to work and there's a time to sleep," Alex muttered on the way back to camp.

He was slightly confused as to why he hadn't seen any leeches. Usually, he found himself having to hide from his enemies but, now, he was almost on the verge of going to seek them out. He felt almost insulted by the fact they hadn't come to see him in spite of all the effort he'd made.

*   *   *

In the morning, he made his way back to the furthest pile of stones that he'd set up and saw that the moss had slightly faded since yesterday. This could only mean that there had been some leeches nearby which had drawn out some of the energy from the glowing moss. Alex smiled.

"So they are still around." That did seem to be the case as he even started to feel frost beneath his feet again. At this point, Alex decided it was time to build another fortification. He worked as quickly as he could while he felt strong. He was able to work fast but he was more worried about the moss in these conditions. Every extra hour in the cold worsened their condition.

After he'd set up everything he wanted to, he moved forward slowly with his lighter in hand. After a few hundred yards he heard a familiar rustling sound. Without waiting for what would happen next, he turned tail and ran back towards his fort. He'd even lit a fire there before setting out just to deter any unwanted visitors even more.

As soon as he reached it, he ducked inside and turned around. The new pack met expectations. On scanning them he could see they were all level one monsters. The more dangerous level two creatures had stayed away.

"Fantastic!," he rejoiced to himself.

Once they got close enough to where he was, Alex proceeded to unleash Scissors on them, just as he'd done the last time. Remembering that his task wasn't only to reduce the number of these local inhabitants, but also to gain a level, Alex didn't strike at random. He aimed accurately, trying to control the place of impact. The more carefully he aimed, the more the control systems were engaged and thus the corresponding ability developed.

This approach slowed down the destruction of the pack, but it was what had to be done to develop in the right way. Alex didn't even find it a stressful fight anymore, now that he'd already seen the stupidity of these creatures.

After a while, Alex finished off every single last one. No new threats appeared so he stood up and approached the pile of remains, looking at the darkness and replenishing his pollen reserves. An hour passed and the energy background returned to normal. Soon another pack of about seventy leeches appeared on the horizon. He dealt with all of them in a calm and collected manner and, after about three hours, they were all dead.

During this whole time, the glow from the moss had faded a bit but, Alex was sure it would brighten up now that all the leeches were dead.

At this point, a welcome change appeared in the interface:

*[**Transformation:** Body: 100.0% / Structure: 100.0% / Brain: 100.0%]*

This was what he really wanted to see. Once he'd decided that there were no enemies around, he went back to his camp and immediately went to bed. He needed some rest before the next step. That was a non-negotiable rule.

Raising one's level was a well-studied process that millions of people had gone through. The main thing was having enough pollen. Without that, nothing would happen. The Other Side was unmovable in that respect. If you wanted something, you had to give something.

The second thing was being able to feel one's energy structure. This wasn't usually a problem as, even the new prospectors could usually feel that after a few months.

To trigger the transformation you needed to focus the whole body and concentrate all the energy you had in one place. It was similar to the way in which Alex had activated General Body Enhancement, only this time the density of the flow would be higher and all three aspects would be involved in the process.

Usually it was done in a special chamber where the walls prevented the energy from dispersing. In this controlled environment, four or five grams of powder was normally enough to create a sufficiently saturated energy background and start the process from there.

Alex didn't have a special chamber, but he had a Pump and some pollen:

"Not like the treatment the others get, no chamber, no instructions," he complained as he pulled out his container.

Anyone else in his place would have tried to make a pollen mixture, but Alex wanted to keep the pollen he had in the purest form possible. He didn't want another substance like alcohol affecting the process. Any disruptions weren't considered ideal and, performing the whole process out in the open, Alex wanted to keep everything as pure as possible. The odds were stacked against him as it was.

He sat down, got himself comfortable and activated the Pump, directing his attention to the center of the container. That immediately managed to split some of the powder, transforming Entelechy from material form into pure energy.

The channels immediately filled up but his storage was full and there was no room for anything new. As a result, the flow of energy began to circulate around Alex's body. This was the reason one needed a developed feeling of energy channels. Without it, it was very hard to control this crucial stage of the process. It also had to be done by the person himself. Even in a controlled environment, no outside help could be used.

Now the Pump was properly capturing energy. As it did so, the amount of pollen was decreasing and the energy flow inside the body was increasing with every second. Alex felt like he was bursting with a feeling of power and joy but he didn't let himself get distracted and directed all his attention to holding and further compacting the flow. Every second he was adding new portions of energy.

This process was known to take a little time. The number one hundred on the interface didn't indicate the transformation of the aspects themselves, but the achievement of the necessary potential and readiness for a complete transformation. After the transformation, the body would be able to work with energy of a higher quality. This is what levels were distinguished by, not by the quantity of energy used, but the quality.

So, in a situation where two prospectors were presented with the same energy background, it was always the prospector with the higher level who was able to extract more.

The Tamedians hadn't explained this point,

but humans reached this conclusion after many, many tries.

Perhaps the Tamedians hadn't purposely withheld these details as they didn't have an Interface like humans did. Their thinking was just based on images. They'd told humans that they can "see" abilities, but they obviously operated in an entirely different way. Different species in the Galaxy, worked with energy in different ways and each species used the way most familiar to their consciousness . After all, the Other Side was essentially a product of consciousness.

Alex took his time, continuing to thicken the energy flow. After ten minutes he felt something change inside him, as if energy was being sucked in at tremendous speed. The Pump receded into the background and became a secondary channel.

If he could have looked inside the container, he would have seen pollen literally evaporating before his eyes. Energy was being sucked away, not only from the pollen, but also from the surrounding environment. Even the moss on the walls was fading, as if a swarm of leeches, had just arrived and were sitting on the bank watching.

The transformation was now going on by itself. It was as if all the aspects knew exactly what to do and how to change as the transformation progressed. No one really knew exactly how the process worked, they just knew that it did work. Some argued that the Other Side sets the program, according to which a person develops. Others argued that, going up through the levels, it was the people themselves who had to pass to the next stage of development, because potential was inherent in everyone from the beginning.

But, regardless of all the speculation, the final result of transformation was well known: the energy reserve would increase, muscles became stronger and the passage of nerve impulses was accelerated. The latter allowed people to move faster, which Alex was particularly happy about as it meant he would now be able to flee that little bit faster from any monster he needed to.

All changes not related to the use of abilities that require energy would remain with a person even after returning to Earth. Because of this, people who'd been to the Other Side, even once, couldn't participate in professional sports. The difference between them and ordinary athletes would have been embarrassing.

Within five minutes, Alex's supply of powder had almost run out. There was only half a gram left. But the transformation was almost complete. Suddenly, Alex felt everything change again inside him and the flow of energy decreased sharply.

The sensations in his body changed. He seemed lighter, more mobile and stronger.

"Status!" Alex barked loudly, scarcely able to contain himself. Even his voice seemed different.

*[**Level**: 1*
***Energy:** 123/123 units.*
***Transformation:** Body: 0% / Structure: 0% /*
Brain: 0%

Signatures: *Simple: Walker (15%)*
Normal: *Night Filter (max), General Body Enhancement* (76%).*
Rare: *Space Barrier** (90%), Space Scanner** (93%), Pump** (89%), Space Scissors** (95%).*
Talents: *Touch of Death, Sense of Space]*

Finally! It had worked, he was officially a level one!

The long journey from a hospital bed to now seemed scarcely believable but now it seemed like he had a chance to move on with his life. True, his immediate future was still in doubt and he was a long way from home, but the first step towards a final recovery had been taken.

The main change, the one that would determine the outcome of many a future battle, was the growth of his energy reserve from thirty-five to one hundred and twenty-three units. Even if these units were just a conditional indicator, these numbers clearly demonstrated just how much his strength had increased. Now he didn't have to wait several minutes between using Scissors. He could also simultaneously maintain the Barrier while using the Scanner. All these things were game changers for the young prospector.

But what about the Pump. Here Alex froze… He had to check the Pump to see if he still had a trump card up his sleeve. If the Pump hadn't upgraded, then he was just a powerful prospector without proper energy support.

He quickly drained his reserve with several

blows of Scissors. He waited for a moment and breathed a sigh of relief when he saw the reserve fill rapidly.

"Yes, it worked!" He shouted in ecstasy.

He didn't want to admit it, but if any one of his abilities hadn't upgraded to the standard he'd hoped for, it would have seriously dented his confidence that he could get out of here. Luckily, that wasn't the case and the Pump was still on hand to fill his reserve quickly and efficiently.

He checked everything again quickly. Everything basically worked as it had before, just with a much higher capacity. But the Pump was a trump card he was glad to hold onto.

He didn't need to check General Body Enhancement. Of all his abilities, it was the most studied. Right now, at maximum expenditure, he calculated it would up about a third of his energy reserve per minute. He'd basically become three times stronger. His body had changed significantly.

And he hoped this was just the beginning. But even now, on only the first level, he was about six times more powerful than the average human on Earth. However, it was too early to celebrate. There were still plenty of monsters on the Other Side who would make light work of him in seconds.

Another bonus was that, after the transformation, his need for food and water decreased. The Other Side had recognized him, so now he could also, like the monsters here, take in the living matter contained in space. Of course, not as well as all the local creatures, but with each level he would get closer and closer to them. So even though his body had become stronger, he now needed less food. But that would only work like that on the Other Side. On returning to Earth, Alex would find himself needing to eat enough for two. On Earth, one could only get energy from food, rather than from the surrounding environment like on the Other Side.

The rest of the day Alex spent on adapting himself to these new skills. The readjustment was still ongoing and wouldn't be completed for a few days. If he'd been at a camp, he would have trained for a couple of days, while getting used to all the changes. Here he had no such luxury. He needed to pass back through the leeches' territory and, hopefully, make it back to camp. He'd managed to level up, but he just couldn't afford to relax yet.

CHAPTER 27

THE LIGHT AT THE END OF THE TUNNEL

The Other Side
Eva, level 2
20 km from Alex's camp

EVA STARED AT THE STREAM OF WATER in front of her. She'd been pretty exhausted over the last week, trying to think of ways to get out of here. She was beginning to think there was no way out, so she was starting to despair.

She was essentially stuck between a rock and a hard place. On one side, there were the ice leeches, from which she barely survived the first encounter and, on the other, was a lake full of unknown monsters and she was keen to keep it that way. She couldn't see them, but her abilities clearly showed that there were dangerous creatures dwelling there.

Ahead was an underground river that flowed into the main river and her camp was near the point where the two streams joined. At that moment, it felt like the only safe area, but that didn't help her any further than that.

Eva was an energetic, determined girl, but right now she was scared. Before this trip she'd heard that a lot of prospectors had been going missing. The rising numbers were quite alarming. Here, stuck in this cave, unsure where to go, she wondered whether she'd be joining this rising statistic. Eva was different from the majority of prospectors in that she wasn't gathering pollen or hunting monsters. She was here purely for research purposes.

She was no fool and she wasn't afraid of hardship. To survive on the Other Side, you had to have a certain amount of resilience, but even she felt a little unprepared for the situation she was in now. First of all, she had hardly anything with her. She'd been returning from a holiday on Earth and as she came out of the buffer zone, instead of arriving at the place she normally did, she'd ended up here. As a researcher, she knew about all the mysterious losses that had been recorded so she figured this was how people had been disappearing.

Even though she had level two, she was still up against it here. Like other researchers, Eva spent almost all her time at a secure base and many of her skills were related to research, not fighting. Of course, she'd been involved in a few skirmishes; no one could raise their level without doing that but she normally had a few experienced fighters around her when she ventured out of base. That had always been the way when it came to researchers and scientists. The government simply provided them with everything they needed from pollen to armed protection and they rarely wanted for anything.

So, in spite of everything, almost all of Eva's abilities were useless here. The only combat skill she had was telekinesis. It was what she'd used as her combat skill to level up. But an ability like that wasn't going to help her much here. Using her mind to throw stones at monsters wouldn't help her get out of here alive and, apart from that, she just had a small set of darts which would hardly penetrate the skin of some of these high-level creatures.

She looked sadly at the small rucksack with her personal belongings. She now wished she'd been sent with some special load to bring back. Anything would have been a help in that moment.

Her only hope was for some kind of rescue team but that seemed like a long shot.

* * *

The Other Side
Alex

Over here, the body needed about fifteen hours sleep to adapt to any radical changes. Once Alex had done that, he woke up feeling powerful. His body literally felt like it was filled with energy from top to bottom.

Everything felt like it had been completely transformed.

Today he had a long, hard journey ahead of him. But under the protection of the light Alex felt confident, even if he had to drag a cartload of rocks behind him.

The polyp zone stretched for some twenty miles, but the leeches' domain could have stretched a lot further than that. Alex had only explored a few miles of it and, as far as he saw, there was no obvious end in sight.

Alex reached the site of his last encounter with all the leeches. Like last time, the temperature had risen and the frost under his feet had disappeared. The glow of the rocks had reduced slightly but they were still very much in working order if Alex had needed them again.

With the new level, Alex started to enjoy himself a bit. He just felt stronger in every way. Even carrying rocks didn't wear down his skin like it had done before. As he was carrying these rocks, he found that the cold was about two miles away from where it had been. So the leeches still weren't far away.

He extended the fortifications so they went further into the cave, then he advanced into the darkness to draw out the leeches in a now familiar ritual.

Like clockwork, Alex made light work of the two hundred odd leeches that came slithering his way. It took him about five hours to deal with all of them, but the new level really did make his life easier.

Now he could use Scissors about three times more often, while still supporting all the other abilities just as much as he wanted.

It became almost boring. But that didn't bother Alex. He calmly dealt with all of them and he tried to see it as just light training.

Once he'd finished, he glanced at the Interface.

[Transformation: *Body: 1.5% / Structure: 1.9% / Brain: 1.5%]*

Not bad for one day!

But then he looked at the pile of rocks behind him and knew there was still plenty of work to do. There was no way round it. He just had to get on with it.

* * *

In the next eight days, Alex managed to walk twelve miles in the dark. Strangely enough, there seemed to be fewer leeches here than there'd been further back. But on the plus side, he made plenty of use of Scanner and Scissors and he felt like he was strengthening these abilities all the time.

The further he walked, the more the rocks dimmed. The moss was definitely not as luminous as he would have liked. He found himself having to ditch some of his supplies as he walked as they just slowed him down.

As he walked, he thought it might be time to move his camp to somewhere in the leeches' territory. But just as this thought came to him, he spotted a glint of light ahead in the distance. He was only able to see it with the help of the Night Filter, but that didn't matter. Alex didn't get too excited, but he knew full well that this source of light could be the way out he was looking for.

Unfortunately, there was a shallow pool of water up ahead which it looked like Alex was going to have to cross if he was to make it to the light. Right now, he didn't want to go anywhere near the water, fearing that any number of monsters could be lurking there. He felt a lot safer regarding it from a distance.

It looked like it was about knee deep but the main problem was the light here. Dark outlines of boulders protruded above the surface, showing that it was about knee-deep. It was passable, but the main problem was the lack of light. In water, the luminosity of the moss wouldn't last long. He looked at the small stretch of water and wondered the best way to cross it.

He decided it should probably be crossed in one swift movement. He had no doubt there would be something living in the water. Judging by the temperature it was probably ice leeches or some of their close relatives, but he was too far away to see anything.

However, once he got closer, nothing came out to meet him. He even went and dipped his hand in the water. But still, no signs of life. Alex didn't understand it. The lack of monsters here was worrying him slightly. He didn't like not being able to see his enemy.

Eventually, Alex returned to camp and did a quick count of everything he had. Only fifty rocks remained, most of which were barely glowing. That was all. If he wanted some new ones, he'd have to go all the way further up the shore. He knew that would require several days' work. He shuddered and told himself to get on with it. He assured himself that, if he was working, near the shore, there probably wouldn't be any large creatures waiting to attack him. If they were big, they probably wouldn't be in shallow water anyway.

Instead of building a fortification near the water, he decided to build a temporary point nearby so the moss might survive the battle. To do this, he moved fifteen boulders and built a small circle, more for some extra light than to distract the monsters. Then he approached the shore and slowly made his way towards the shallow water, periodically activating the Scanner.

When there were about a hundred feet to the water line, Alex suddenly sensed something. He froze and looked around. The surface of the water was as calm as he'd ever seen it, but there was definitely something out there. He took a few more steps and did a volumetric scan. He quickly saw there were five monsters hiding near the shore. But they didn't look like the leeches he'd seen before. Whatever these were, they were bigger and more powerful than that.

Everything was still. Alex didn't move. He waited, but the water remained calm and flat. Somewhere far away the river murmured barely audible sounds. The silence was roaring in his ears.

When all the energy was restored and Alex had reactivated the Barrier, he started screaming at the top of his voice:

"Aaaaah!!!"

As soon as he finished shouting, he turned around and ran the other way. The cry he emitted had filled the cave but, on looking back, he saw that the surface of the water remained as unchanged as ever.

He bent down to pick up a rock and hurled it at the spot where he thought these creatures were hiding. The stone fell noisily in the water, making a splash. But beyond that, nothing happened.

"Okay, let's try something else," he said threateningly and took out his pollen container.

He got within striking distance of the shoreline and hit out at the same spot with Scissors. As soon as Alex had unleashed this skill at the water, he promptly turned tail and fled. A second later, he heard a loud noise behind him as if something had just landed heavily on the shore. A familiar sound of pursuit swiftly followed and Alex guessed he was now being chased.

He stole a glance behind him as he ran and quickly saw a large leech like creature following him. He was glad it was only one. He scanned it as quick as he could.

[Ice Leech: Level 2]

The six-foot long monster was similar looking to the ones Alex had seen before. But they clearly behaved differently. Alex was convinced there had been several monsters lurking in the water but only one had come out to attack him. So maybe they weren't pack animals. As he ran it made a creepy squeaking sound which Alex was also hearing for the first time. All these new thoughts were running through his head, but the one key thought he had on his mind right then was the fact that it was catching up to him.

He ran as fast as he could, just looking straight ahead as he tried working out how he was going to defeat a monster like this if he couldn't outrun it. His brain was working fast and it needed to.

He knew he couldn't outrun it. He had to turn and fight. As a last resort he could always use the lighter or the moss back at camp. But he really wanted to defeat the creature in combat. In his mind, if he couldn't handle one single monster, how would he destroy the others?

The circle of dimly lit stones appeared ahead. By this time, Alex's energy reserve had refilled. He leapt over the line of stones which served as a small barrier. He landed, but quickly gathered himself together and, having grabbed his spear, turned to face the onrushing predator.

A black shadow darted towards him. It hesitated for a moment, but this creature wasn't like its level one brethren. It wasn't so bothered by the light. As it moved it leapt forward, somehow managing to spring off the ground and shot through the air like an arrow towards Alex's den.

He tried to attack it with Scissors while it flew through the air, but he missed. Everything was happening just that little bit too fast for him. It flew through the air moving at forty feet a second. Seeing that he was about to be hit in the chest, he turned slightly but, again, he wasn't quite fast enough as he felt the leech make connection with his body and hurl him to the ground.

The leech folded and fell on the rocks with a thud. Alex was dazed but, miraculously, he hadn't been seriously injured.

Despite the pain, he jumped up quickly. He felt dizzy, but he steadied himself and pointed his spear at the leech. It promptly started readying it-self for another attack.

"Get down, you bastard!" he yelled as he tried the Scissors again.

This time he didn't miss. The monster froze, halfway through gearing up for another attack. Without thinking, Alex jumped up and thrust his spear at it as hard as he could. He pressed on the weapon with the full force of his whole body, driving the weapon as deep as possible.

"I said stay down!"

The leech slightly came to its senses and began to wriggle. The spear was almost ripped out of his hands, but Alex desperately clutched at it and held on for all he was worth. The monster was strong, but Alex was stronger. The blow it took from the Scissors had seriously weakened it so Alex definitely had the upper hand here. The creature's torso looked like it had been cut to ribbons.

They continued to fight each other desperately, the monster wriggling frantically while Alex did everything he could to keep it pinned down with his spear. There was a lot at stake here and Alex didn't want to let his chance slip. He waited for his energy to build up and once the reserves were filled. Wham! He hit it again in exactly the same spot. A familiar, bright blue liquid flowed from the open wound and it fell back on the floor twitching lifelessly.

Breathing heavily, Alex assessed the situation. The energy background was rising. That was a bad sign, a really bad sign! He grabbed the leech by the tail and threw it as far away from the circle as possible. From far away he heard splashes of water and the scraping of dozens of bodies on the stone floor. The new monsters were definitely a lot lazier than their more primitive counterparts. A direct attack on a pack member didn't force them out of the water, but as soon as there was a whiff of free energy in the air, they decided to make an appearance.

"So this is how I should have lured them out! I could have just sprinkled some pollen around and they would have come running." Alex realized.

He didn't wait for them to appear. He turned around and ran to the intermediate camp he'd set up earlier on in the cave. There he froze and listened.

After about an hour, the noise had gone so he decided to return to the shallow water. The moss on the rocks had faded, but it was still holding out, but now Alex knew that this was useless against monsters of this level. Even if the moss had been in its original state, it was useless against an enemy that clearly wasn't afraid of it. Having level two made these creatures a lot braver.

Evening came and Alex returned to the main camp on the shore. He had an idea about what to do next, but he needed some time to execute it.

The next day he went back to the same place on the shoreline and just stood there waiting to see if the leeches would come out or not. As he'd predicted, they completely ignored him. But Alex didn't mind that. To make this plan of his work, he needed to work uninterrupted and it seemed that the nearby leeches had no plans to disturb him anytime soon.

The beach, like the rest of the cave, was strewn with a wide variety of rocks, from small cobbles to large boulders. Some of them were too big for Alex to move, even with his newfound strength. Of course, these new building materials didn't have any moss, but they could still be useful.

All day long, he hauled large stones to where he was going to need them. He chose the biggest ones he could carry or roll. The noise was deafening. He felt like he could be heard for miles but nothing seemed to care. All the creatures here seemed utterly indifferent to what was going on around them. Alex was glad of their indifference as he wiped away the sweat from his brow.

Alex continued to work throughout the day until an unexpected find stopped him in his tracks. It was a prospector's helmet. He was amazed he'd just come across it like that. He picked it up and looked at it for a long time. It didn't take a genius to guess what had happened. The poor guy had ended up here, just like Alex had. He'd probably been trapped and surrounded by hundreds of monsters and would never have stood a chance. Alex tried to picture all of this. He felt a shiver run down his spine as he imagined the last moments of this poor guy trapped so many miles from home with no idea where he was.

He stopped working for a bit as he tried to look around the area. He wanted to find something else if he could. Unfortunately, there was nothing else around. Eventually, Alex took the helmet to the river and slowly lowered it into the water. He let it float for a second, then he released it so it flowed gently down the river. He watched it float away into the darkness, then he silently returned to his work.

* * *

Once he'd finished, he stood back to admire his handiwork. He'd basically managed to fashion a small house out of stones which could only be climbed onto from one side. There wasn't much room inside, but Alex didn't need much.

The inner circle consisted of the largest and heaviest boulders. Flat stones with a wide base went on top. In addition to the first contour he'd added three more. He wanted the foundations to be as strong as possible.

All the gaps had been filled with smaller boulders and, on top of that, all the mossy stones. Although he knew they wouldn't drive away the larger creatures, he still put them there just out of force of habit.

Having made all the necessary preparations, he returned to the camp on the shore for one last time. The following morning he checked the whole structure again.

With difficulty, Alex climbed inside and barricaded the gap behind him. Finally, he was ready. All that was left was to bait the leeches. To do so, he took out a container and sprinkled some pollen nearby.

Soon he heard a familiar noise and he knew that the bait had worked.

A crowd of them came slithering towards the stone fort and a couple of them immediately climbed onto the roof, looking for any other spoils. Most of them just circled around the outside. The leeches were all testing the structure, but they still seemed relatively calm.

Once enough of them were there, Alex activated the Scanner, selected one of them who was circling around and immediately struck it with the Scissors. Alex wasn't sure if he'd killed it but he knew he'd done enough to spill some blood and that would be more than enough to attract more of them.

After waiting for a while, he scanned the battlefield again. As he'd thought, all of them had gathered in that one point and he could see there were more of them now. He didn't even need the Scanner to know that. It was enough just to hear them.

Alex struck twice with the Scissors at this new gathering. He thought he managed to kill at least one and a quick glance at the Interface confirmed his suspicions.

After this, the sounds outside intensified and Alex could feel the tension rising. The killing had infuriated them and they began to throw themselves at the rocks, but to no avail. They were going to need a lot more force than that to bring down this structure.

From his point of safety inside the fort, Alex continued to strike out at the leeches. He no longer wasted energy on the Scanner but simply struck all his blows at the same point where they were gathered.

The Interface showed Alex that things were moving slowly, but they were at least moving. Not every strike killed the enemy, but almost all of them reached their target. It was a strange fight. While the monsters were raging outside, he was calmly destroying them from the inside. In some ways this fight reminded him of when he'd been fighting the crawlers from the rock, only these opponents were much dumber and swarmed well within his reach.

Curiosity took over and he checked to see how many monsters were still left. The scan showed over a hundred of them.

They had to be all creatures from the shallows. *But they can all die today,* he promised to himself.

The next few hours passed in a similar fashion. He just used the Scissors and, occasionally, he activated the Scanner to check how it was all going. Alex knew that if the blades hit the same spot, two attacks would have sufficed to kill one leech, but he was striking blindly, so the fight dragged on.

Gradually the monsters all died, but, just as their numbers were dwindling, more started to arrive. Alex had hoped that he'd already lured all of them out, but he wasn't deterred. He continued doggedly with what he'd set out to do. The fight continued all day and continued into the next one. After about thirty hours, the stream of leeches finally ran out and Alex breathed a sigh of relief.

His body was stiff and he could barely haul himself out of the position he'd been in. He waited for about an hour and then, finally, made his way out of the fort.

He kicked a few stones out of the way and emerged out into the open. As he climbed out, he found himself to be covered in blood and he looked like a zombie as he emerged from his hiding place. But Alex didn't care. The main thing was that he'd managed to survive, unlike the poor guy whose helmet he'd found.

The mountain of corpses he saw and the silence all around him gave him a sense of satisfaction and a feeling of his own strength. A few hours ago, this place was bustling with life and now hundreds of monsters were dead. Perhaps the same fate awaited him, but not today! Today he was the winner.

All the moss on the rocks had finally gone out. He looked around and went back to the temporary camp, where the last glowing boulders still shone. Alex had done his job and with complete peace of mind he lay down and went to sleep.

*   *   *

He slept for a solid fifteen hours and, after waking up decided to return to the water. On the shore he gazed for a long time at the distant source of light he'd seen earlier, wondering what it was exactly. He put his hand into the water. It was distinctly warmer and Alex took that as a sure sign that the area had been cleared.

Alex was sure it was safe to cross, but first he needed to deal with two of his abilities.

Earlier on, he'd felt like the Scissors and General Body Enhancement had changed slightly, but he hadn't bothered checking them while he'd been busy slaughtering leeches.

"Status."

*[**Level:** 1*
__Energy:__ 123/123 units.
__Transformation:__ Body: 10.9% / Structure: 15.9% / Brain: 14.5%
__Signatures: Simple:__ Walker (15%)
*__Common:__ Night Filter (max), General Body Enhancement** (86%)*
*__Rare:__ Space Barrier** (90%), Space Scanner** (98%), Pump** (90%), Space Blades (0%).*
__Talents:__ Touch of Death, Sense of Space]

He decided to deal with General Body Enhancement first. Everything else could wait. On looking at the data, his calculations were confirmed.

At maximum energy expenditure it made him five times stronger than his former self. The addition of his new level amplified that even more.

But the main change worth noting was the Blades of Space, seemingly an evolution of the

Scissors which he already had. Alex guessed that the Scissors had reached a hundred percent and now the name had changed to reflect the evolution of the skill.

To test it, Alex looked at a small cobblestone not far away and then poured out all his energy just like he used to do when activating the Scissors. The small stone split in half.

"Yes!" Alex almost jumped for joy.

Now he could use his entire reserve for a single strike which, obviously, made him much stronger. Unfortunately, the shape of the blade didn't change, but he wasn't going to lose heart over that. He felt confident now, even though he knew there was plenty of room for improvement.

"Well, time to go," he exclaimed in a satisfied voice as he picked up his rucksack. There was nothing to keep him on the shore now.

Alex slowly waded through the shallow water, clutching his spear in one hand and the brightest of the remaining stones in the other. The depth was about knee-deep, occasionally coming up to his waist. No new surprises were waiting for him here and he reached the opposite shore with no trouble.

When he reached the dry rocks, he threw off his rucksack and went off to explore. After literally a hundred yards, the beach began to narrow until it was only a few paces wide. He stopped when he got here, but he could see ahead of him that the river continued in a straight line.

The opposite side of the river looked the same

as the one he was on. But there was a smaller river flowing into the main one which looked a little bit different. There was a glow coming from somewhere further down it. There was a slight wall in front of him preventing him from seeing any more of this source of light. He slowly approached it and cautiously peeked over the edge.

END OF BOOK ONE

Want to be the first to know about our latest LitRPG, sci fi and fantasy titles from your favorite authors?

Subscribe to our **New Releases** newsletter: http://eepurl.com/b7niIL

Thank you for reading *The Other Side!*

If you like what you've read, check out other sci-fi, fantasy and LitRPG novels published by Magic Dome Books:

NEW RELEASES!

The Selected
A LitRPG Action Adventure Series
by Vasily Mahanenko & Yuri Vinokuroff

The Afflicted
A LitRPG Apocalypse Adventure Series
by Konstantin Zubov

The Dark Summoner
A Portal Progression Fantasy Series
by Andrei Tkachev

The Banned
A LitRPG Adventure Series
by Michael Atamanov

How I Built a Magic Empire
A Portal Progression Fantasy Series
by Konstantin Zubov

The Order of Architects
A Portal Progression Fantasy Series
by Oleg Sapphire & Yuri Vinokuroff

The Hunter's Code
A Portal Progression Fantasy Series
by Oleg Sapphire & Yuri Vinokuroff

The One Who Changes the Future
A Dystopian Portal Progression Fantasy Series
by Boris Romanovsky

An Ideal World for a Sociopath
A LitRPG Apocalypse Adventure Series
by Oleg Sapphire

The Healer's Way
A Portal Progression Fantasy Series
by Oleg Sapphire & Alexey Kovtunov

The Last Portal Jumper
A LitRPG Progression Fantasy Series
by Konstantin Zubov

The Dark Healer
A Historical Progression Fantasy Series
by Alex Toxic & Nadya Lee

Lord of The System
A LitRPG Progression Fantasy Series
by Alex Toxic & Furious Miki

A Shelter in Spacetime
A LitRPG Apocalypse Series
by Dmitry Dornichev

The Coming of God of Death
A Portal Progression Fantasy Series
by Dmitry Dornichev

The Village
A LitRPG Progression Fantasy Series
by Dmitry Dornichev & Alexey Kovtunov

Condemned (Lord Valevsky: Last of the Line)
A Progression Fantasy LitRPG Series
by Vasily Mahanenko

Living Ice
A Portal Progression Fantasy Series
by Dmitry Sheleg

Ghost in the System
An Apocalypse LitRPG Series
by Alexey Kovtunov

Crossroads of Oblivion
A Portal Progression Fantasy Adventure Series
by Dem Mikhailov

The Goldenblood Heir
A Portal Progression Fantasy Series
by Boris Romanovsky

Law of the Jungle
A Wuxia Progression Fantasy Adventure Series
by Vasily Mahanenko

More books and series are coming out soon!

In order to have new books of the series translated faster, we need your help and support! Please consider leaving a review or spread the word by recommending *The Other Side* to your friends and posting the link on social media. The more people buy the book, the sooner we'll be able to make new translations available.

Thank you!

Till next time!

9 788807 022705